DRAKE'S STORY STONE

A NOVEL BY

T. F. PUMPHREY

To: Sarah Anne —
Always believe in yourself
because you are capable of
great things.

Pumphrey

TONS OF IMAGINATION, INK. LLC

Library of Congress Catalogue Number TXu 1-668-016

Cover design by SMBP

Tons of Imagination, Ink. LLC
www.DrakesStoryStone.com

ISBN: 1468183648
ISBN 13:   9781468183641

Library of Congress Control Number: 2012900591
CreateSpace, North Charleston, SC

For my girls...
Never be afraid to live your dreams!

"I respect your decision to leave us, as I know you will be back. Heroes always come back."

MADORI

DRAKE'S STORY STONE SERIES

CONTENTS

CHAPTER 1

The Stone

The bell sounded and he headed down the hall. With thumbs looped under the straps of his backpack, Drake aimed for the door. A grin spread across his lips at the anticipation of the rush of sunshine that would soon fill his face. He stopped at the large metal doors, unhooked his thumbs, and pushed his way out. Glancing around, he saw that Zack, Collin, and Shane were nowhere in sight, which was odd as these boys were always together. After meeting in the fourth grade, the foursome rarely separated. So where were they? *I guess they bolted early,* Drake thought while checking his watch. It was exactly 3:30 p.m.

School was out. Better yet, it was out for the summer. He was free for the next two and a half months.

Shrugging, Drake continued on his usual path home from school. The boys walked to school with all the local children; however, they took a shortcut through the woods to get home. Drake and his friends discovered a worn path about a year ago. It lay hidden just beyond a ridge of trees snaking its way into the woods. They had made a pact to keep it as secret as possible, but knew it was not hidden from everyone.

Drake thought that perhaps the guys were planning to ambush him on his way home. *I'll be ready for them*, he planned as he stepped toward the trees. A sudden wind blew. Leaves whipped and swirled about his feet. With shivers running up the back of Drake's neck, he stopped, now wary of entering the woods alone. Straining his eyes, he attempted to peer beyond the first few trees, but was unable to see anything through the dense foliage.

Unsure of why, Drake decided the woods loomed darker and more menacing today.

Come on, he said to himself, *you've grown up in these woods. Quit being such a wimp.* He pushed himself to walk forward once again.

"Drake?" came a voiced from behind.

Jolted, Drake spun around and found himself face to face with a girl who he had not spoken with for some time.

Reigan stumbled back a few steps to giggle at Drake's reaction. "Are you okay?"

"I'm fine. I just wasn't expecting anyone to be following me." Drake ran his fingers through his thick, brown hair, pushing it off his forehead. He stared at the ground and kicked at a partially exposed rock.

"I wasn't following you. I just saw that you were alone and thought I'd say hi."

Drake's gaze rose up to meet Reigan's bright blue eyes. "Oh...hi."

Drake and Reigan stood a couple of feet apart staring at one another. As children they'd been best friends, but when Drake turned ten, and it was no longer *cool* to have a "girlfriend," he'd severed all ties.

"Whatcha up to?" Reigan asked.

"Nothing. Hey, you haven't seen Zack and the guys around, have ya?" he asked. She told him that she hadn't. Drake looked toward the woods and took a deep breath. "I gotta be going now...gotta get home."

Reigan glanced in the same direction and asked, "Are you going on your 'secret path?'"

Drake's brown eyes narrowed.

"Can I come with?" asked Reigan.

He began to bite at the inside of his cheek while glancing upward. Drake then glared toward the trees and thought of his lonely walk home. The dark woods drove his friends, and the earlier ambush presumption, out of his mind. "Ah...sure."

Reigan peered toward the woods, then back to Drake with narrowed eyes. "Is everything okay?"

"Yeah. Everything's fine."

The two started through the woods, walking at a steady pace. Drake racked his brain, trying to think of something clever to say, as the awkward silence was making him nervous. After some consideration, he asked, "So, what are you doing this summer?"

"Not much. My dad has to go away on a few trips over the next couple of months, so I don't think we'll be doing a whole lot of traveling." Reigan responded, uninterested. "What about you?"

"I think my parents have a couple different trips planned to visit my uncles and their families. Other than that, I'm just hanging out with the guys."

"That sounds cool."

Silence enveloped them again as they walked on for another few anxious moments.

"Drake…remember when we were kids? We used to have a blast playing in these woods. I barely come out here anymore." Drake turned to stare at her. She smiled. "Those were some good times."

"Sure," Drake responded.

"How come things changed?"

Drake stared at the ground.

"Listen, I know your friends mean a lot to you. I think that's cool and all, but sometimes I just wish you—" Reigan abruptly stopped talking.

"What?"

"Did you hear that noise? I think it came from over there," she said, pointing to their left toward a clump of shriveled trees. Drake looked in the direction she pointed, staring at several gnarled trunks that were lying on the ground and looked as if they had been for quite a while.

Drake cut his eyes at her. "You're gonna turn all girly on me now, aren't you?"

"No, I really did hear something! It sounded like a muffled scream."

A shudder rushed through Drake's body, causing the hairs on his arms to stand on end. Reigan's eyes widened and her mouth dropped open as she continued to stare ahead.

"Where did you say it came from?"

Reigan pointed her shaking hand. "Over there. ᴵ'ᵐ scared. Something doesn't feel right."

He stepped forward a few paces. "I don't hear anything." Drake turned to face the chalked-faced girl and walked back toward her. Reigan's eyes met his as her lips began to tremble. Suddenly, it hit him. *What if the guys are behind this? I've gotta get rid of her.*

"I'm not sure what the noise was, but I think we need to get out of here. Run as fast as you can and don't look back. I'll be right behind you," Drake said in a rather low voice. Reigan took off running and she never looked back, just like he said. Drake wiped his brow and let out a heavy breath as he turned away from the fleeing girl.

He slowly edged toward the fallen trees, wondering if she had really heard something. As he inched along, Drake could make out a faint humming. At this point, he admitted to himself he was a little nervous. If his friends were behind this, they were doing a fantastic job.

With each step, the dry leaves crunched and crackled under his feet. Drake couldn't help but think of every horror movie he had ever watched. His heart beat irregularly. An ache crept into his stomach as a curious concern settled over him. He pushed himself forward, focusing his attention on the trees ahead.

A high-pitched whistle shot through the air, tearing his gaze from the trees. Drake gazed skyward and watched a fiery blast rocket toward the ground. The flaming object hit the earth with such force it shook the ground, sending blinding lights and thunder exploding through the air. Drake dove behind a cluster of trees and bumped his head on the rough bark as he landed on the ground. Leaves scattered as he pulled his body close to the trunk. Trembling, he waited. A hush settled over the woods. Desperate, Drake clung to the hope that somehow his friends were behind this.

"Hey Collin…Zack…Shane? Is that you guys?" Drake called. There was no answer. "Come on guys, I know it's you."

Drake waited for a response, but a muted atmosphere was all that surrounded him. He scrunched his body tightly to the tree. The coarse bark scraped his arms as he huddled close. He felt something trickle down his cheek and quickly wiped at it with his hand. Blood spread across his palm from a fresh cut just above his eye.

Without warning, a thunderous racket discharged all around him. He tucked his head to his knees. "Not again."

A light show soon followed like a huge fireworks display. Intense flashes of red, blue, yellow, and white lights were so brilliant that even as he closed his eyes a burning sensation remained. Behind closed eyelids, Drake could see the flashing continue to erupt. He placed his hands over his eyes and blocked out some of the intensity, but the heat radiating toward him made it feel like he might burst into flames at any moment.

Extreme, high-pitched screeches and screams emanated from the blasts. Drake pulled in tighter behind the trees and covered his ears.

"What's going on?"

At the sound of his voice, everything fell silent. Drake sat in his scrunched position unwilling to move a muscle. After several moments, he uncovered his ears. The absolute quiet was strangely calming, and he knew the chaos was over.

He emerged from his protection with unbelieving eyes. With all the pandemonium that had just occurred, he could not understand why there was not more devastation. Everything around him seemed to be intact, with the exception of the old fallen trees ahead. All that was left of the hollow, gnarled limbs was a smoldering patch of ash. Straining his eyes, he saw a pulsing light coming from under the cinders. His feet moved forward, without his control, pulling him to the site.

With great care, he kicked away the ash to reveal a shimmering stone. It was about the size of his palm and pulsed with a brilliant blue hue as it lay among the smoldering debris. Its smooth surface produced a blinding light. Drake squinted and looked away.

He quickly surveyed the area. Satisfied that no one was around, he shrugged off his backpack and began searching for something he could use to pick up the mysterious stone. Spying his gym tee shirt, Drake whipped it out of his pack.

He gazed back down at the glowing rock as it lay among the still smoking embers. The stone's light appeared to be growing dimmer. With each pulse a new color showed. Curiosity held his eyes to the treasure while strange emotions stirred within him. Taking a deep breath, he licked two of his fingers and lightly touched the stone. It sizzled from his damp touch, burning his skin. Whipping his fingers back, he held them inside his mouth, startled by the pain. With his gaze still fixed on the stone, Drake's eyes rolled back into his head. For a split second, an image soared through his mind. He saw an ocean-blue sky with clouds flashing past at lightning speed. A whipping sound erupted followed by a deafening roar. Then all was silent leaving Drake standing before the glowing stone in the still empty woods.

"What was that?" Drake asked aloud.

Pulling his fingers from his mouth, Drake touched the stone yet again. The same sizzling sound, followed by a burning pain, caused him to shake his hand wildly. Again, his eyes rolled back in his head. This time a new vision zoomed in close on a dark, dismal scene. He could make out a tree or two, but the blackness made it almost impossible to see anything else. An ear-splitting squeal, then a flurry of wings filled his sight. With a jerk of his head, Drake snapped back to reality. He gazed around him taking in his familiar woods.

"That's not right," he said shaking open his gym shirt.

However, before wrapping the stone tightly, Drake licked his fingers one last time. He cautiously touched the smooth gem, anticipating the sizzling followed by the burn, but it never came. It had finally cooled. He touched it again and again, waiting for a bizarre vision to spring before his eyes, but nothing happened.

Drake wrapped his shirt around the surprisingly light stone. He glared at the ashen trees wondering if he should take it home. With only a moment's hesitation, Drake delicately placed it into his backpack.

Not wasting any more time, Drake jumped back to his feet. He wobbled, stumbling backward, as a tingling sensation soared throughout his body. His knees grew weak, and he nearly fell over. Exhausted, he grabbed hold of a nearby tree, balancing himself for only a moment. He shook his head, and looped his right thumb under the strap on his shoulder. He pushed his weight off the tree with his free hand. Drake glanced around once more and set off for home.

Drake reached his house in no time and silently pushed open the door. He shrugged off his backpack and delicately removed the wrapped stone. Drake slipped it under the shirt he was wearing and dropped his backpack on the stairs. Taking two steps at a time, he dashed to his room, plopped into his multi-colored thinking-chair, and began rocking back and forth.

"That didn't just happen," Drake called out before he glanced down at his bulging shirt.

CHAPTER 2

Where Could She Have Gone?

At Drake's sudden outburst, his oversized sheltie, Jessie, got to her feet. She jumped onto Drake's bed and watched her master intently. Jessie adjusted herself then flopped down with a grunt. Watching Drake rock back and forth was proving to be hypnotic. Try as she might, she could not fight the drowsiness that hung in her eyes. The canine wanted to stay alert, but the comforting rhythm of Drake's rocking was too much. Her eyes drooped, reopened, and then finally closed for a short nap.

Drake partially revealed the stone from underneath his shirt. Jessie opened her eyes, suddenly wide-awake. She emitted a low whine while she watched her master observe the object. Drake paid her no mind, but continued to stare unblinkingly at his discovery. The curious canine tilted her head to one side, sniffing at the air. A troublesome aura grabbed hold of the dog's keen senses, and her whine grew in volume.

Drake looked at Jessie. "Shhhhh girl, what's the matter with you?"

Jessie immediately laid her head on her paws and issued one last disapproving whine.

Gazing back at the stone, Drake saw that it still pulsed, but not as brilliantly as it had in the woods. He turned the stone back and forth. It looked like an oversized gemstone. The surface was smooth as glass. As he rotated it, there were several times it almost slipped from his grasp. The stone's color reminded Drake of the deepest ocean, and when he maneuvered it just right, small flecks of silver seemed to catch the sun's light, making it sparkle.

Drake pivoted the gem completely around. A glare of sunshine bounced off it. Shiny specks flickered on the wall at the opposite end of his room. Still grasping the stone in his shirt, he turned it repeatedly.

"What are you?" he asked aloud, still rotating the stone.

The stone felt familiar in his hands, as if he'd always had it. Recalling his visions in the woods, Drake touched the stone with one finger. A spark of energy flickered through his hand, up his arm and throughout his whole body.

"That was weird."

He touched the stone again. The same spark of energy soared through him. His fingers, hands, and arms felt warm and tingly.

He flicked his free arm several times, but the sensation remained. Confused, Drake scanned his room and shook his head. He tried to come up with one reasonable clarification for all that was happening, but he could only surmise that the stone did not belong in his world.

Drake looked toward his door and decided that perhaps a break from his thoughts might not be so bad. He stood up and delicately placed the stone on his chair. Drake backed away from the gem while surveying his room. His heel hit his bookshelf and sent the case rocking back and forth. A book hit the floor. With squinted eyes, Drake read its title: *Luke of Kropite*. He reached down to retrieve it.

Bringing the book close, Drake smiled as the story's main character, Luke, sprang to the forefront of his mind. Luke had the ability to fly and talk to strange creatures that roamed Kropite, an alien world. He was the world's guardian and always seemed to be there to save the day. Drake's grin grew as he pictured Luke using his superhuman abilities to keep Kropite safe.

Drake ran his fingers over the book's raised title. A low hum pulled Drake's gaze to the stone lying unguarded upon his chair. Jessie abruptly sat up and stared at the stone. Drake's eyebrow slowly rose as he turned his ear to listen. Unable to hear anything, he moved toward the gem. The stone lay noiselessly upon the seat of his wooden rocker, pulsing different shades of blue.

"Weird."

Drake leaned so close that his ear practically touched the stone, but he still heard nothing. Shrugging, he stared back at his book. Opening *Luke of Kropite*, with its pages facing down, the boy tented it over the rock then headed for his door. Jessie immediately jumped off his bed.

The dog walked by the stone, sniffing the air suspiciously, gave another small whine, and then scurried toward her master. Drake glanced back at his chair just as a sliver of sunshine sliced into his room and slid across his book. Its silvery embossed letters sparkled one-by-one. Drake's eyebrow rose again then he moved into the hall.

Before making the stairs, he slipped into the hall bathroom. He reached up and ran his fingers over the cut above his eye as he looked in the mirror. There was a small amount of smeared, dried blood surrounding the cut. Drake wet his fingers with cool water. He dabbed at his injury, cleaning it as best he could. Drake patted his head with a hand towel, looked in the mirror, and smiled. His cut did not look nearly as bad as it had before. Rubbing at it one last time, he headed out of the bathroom.

Just before reaching the stairs, Drake peeked into Bailey's room. He sighed aloud when he saw she was busy playing superheroes with all of her stuffed animals. Drake smirked. He never could understand his little sister's preoccupation with superheroes. She was always pretending she was one or needed to be saved by one. He might have thought it was cool when he was younger, but that stuff was for babies now. Being thirteen meant no more pretending.

Even with the afternoon Drake had, he whistled happily as he walked down the stairs into the kitchen. His mother was fixing dinner and humming.

"Hi Drake! How was your day, sweetie?"

"Pretty good. How about yours?" Drake poured himself a glass of milk.

"Fine dear, thanks for asking."

"Have you seen the guys at all today?"

"No, why?"

"No reason." Drake shook his head and made a grab for the cookie jar.

"Only one dear, or you'll spoil your—" his mom stopped mid-sentence as she pulled his chin closer to her. "Drake Hanson, how did you get that cut?"

Drake pulled away from his mother. "It's nothing. I tripped in the woods on the way home." Then he immediately shoved the entire cookie into his mouth.

"My graceful little boy."

Drake gave her a sideways grin, took a huge gulp of milk, and headed back upstairs with Jessie hot on his heels. After shutting the bedroom door, he put his glass down on his desk and glanced over at his chair. His mouth gaped as he stared at his now empty rocker. Diving toward the chair, he rummaged on the floor searching frantically through clothes and papers for the stone. He darted back to his door, flinging it open. He stormed in Bailey's room. It was vacant.

Where is she? If she loses that rock, I'll kill her!

Drake's thoughts strangely shifted to the fact that Bailey could be in danger. After all, how much did he really know about that stone? He had no idea where it came from, or why it glowed and pulsed.

Jessie began pacing back and forth. Drake ran back to his room, almost tripping over the anxious dog. "Not now girl, I've got to find out what's going on. Go!" he instructed her.

Jessie slumped to the ground, refusing to leave his side. As Drake turned his attention back to his task, he spied Bailey's favorite ring lying right next to his chair. This was no ordinary ring. It was very special to Bailey. Her best friend, who had to move away last year, had given it to her. Bailey never took this ring off her finger, not even for a bath. Drake held his stomach as he bent over to pick it up. As soon as he touched it he smelled something burnt, like the way the trees smelled after they'd been blasted in the woods.

Where could she have gone? Without her ring? And where's my book? Drake rubbed his head and stumbled over to his chair. He squeezed his temples as he leaned back to rock. The expected flow of his rocker never came. Instead, an intense numbness filled his insides while his body whirled around in all directions, like he was falling down a tunnel. There was no control. With flailing arms and legs thrashing about, his chest whipped back and forth. The speed at which he was traveling made breathing hard as he choked and gasped for breath. He tried to grab at the walls, but couldn't grab anything.

His head began to pulsate with pain. It was like millions of tiny explosions were erupting inside his brain. The ache was unbearable. Drake closed his eyes as tightly as he could in hopes that the misery would soon subside, but the spinning only made it worse.

Drake pulled his legs toward his stomach, and wrapped his arms around his bent knees. The position eased the pain a bit. A high-pitched screaming made his eyes pop open. Strange images whirled all around making him question whether he was dead or just dreaming. Dragons, winged horses, massive snakes, and many other creatures whirled around him.

What's happening to me?

Drake closed his eyes and his body spun out of control. Pulling with all his might, he was able to lift his hands to clutch his head. The spinning grew faster. Drake was sure he was going to blackout.

The same shrill screams he had heard moments ago exploded all around him. He cupped his hands over his ears as tightly as he could, stiffened his body, and yelled, "Stop!" As if frozen in time, the entire world halted its motions. Drake's body struck a hard surface. All of the air whooshed from his lungs. Drake pulled himself to his knees as he spluttered and coughed for breath. With eyes closed, he gripped his head. When Drake finally regained his breath, he opened his eyes. He inhaled warm, clean air, and peered around him

Tall, wispy grasses engulfed his entire body. He was lying in a sprawling field. Drake brushed at the weeds as they swept across his skin, irritating it. He scrunched his eyes to take in his surroundings. Far in the distance, he could make out what looked like a large forest occupying most of the area to the left of the field, and huge mountains lay off to the right. A slight breeze sailed through the air carrying with it a strange, yet familiar aroma. The scent of lavender and popcorn drifted on the breeze.

"Where am I?" Drake asked aloud.

Alarmed by a strange whirring coming from behind him, Drake spun around on his knees. Sprawled out before him, suspended in mid-air, was a gyrating mass at least six-feet-wide and six feet tall. Inside it a pinwheel of colors swirled around, reminding him of something he had seen in a science fiction movie. Drake reached out to the strange mass, but it vanished.

Sitting back down, he put his hands over his face and shook his head. He groaned as he rubbed his eyes. A low chuckle suddenly caught his attention, stopping him mid-rub.

A flurry of air buzzed past his ear. Drake jerked his head but could see nothing. He glanced around only to have another flurried frenzy whiz past his face, swoop around his head, and sail behind him, whipping his hair as it zipped by.

"What are you?" Drake called out.

"I've been waiting for you," a voice sang from behind followed by a giggle.

Drake jerked his neck. Nothing.

After several more flybys, a creature slowly descended in front of him and hovered before his face.

"Congratulations, young Master. I am so delighted you could finally join us! I welcome you to Kazoocal Field."

Drake leaned in to get a better view of the extraordinary creature. It was just over a foot tall, with large wistful eyes, and a grin filled its whole face. The creature hung in midair pulling Drake's attention to its wings that flapped with such speed they were a blur. It's body shifted from blue to green depending on how the sunlight hit it.

Drake reached up to touch the creature with one finger. "You feel so real, but this can't be…What did you call me?"

"Young Master. I'm sorry, would you prefer Drake?

"How do you know my name?"

"Good question. I will explain it to you eventually. For now we need to get going."

"Get going? I don't even know who you are? Better yet, where am I?" Drake gazed around scratching his head. "I could have sworn I was just in my bedroom. I must have fallen out of my chair and hit my head. Is this some kind of concussion?"

The bug cocked its head to one side. In a very serious tone it said, "Well, Master, if you're done trying to figure things out on your own, I could possibly be of some help to you. Unless, of course, you could get more help from this Mr. *Concussion* you speak of." Drake stared blankly back. "Okay, I will help you out. My name is Sponke and I am your humble guide. I can tell you almost anything you want to know about Kropite."

"Kropite!" exclaimed Drake. His mind exploded with vivid images of the setting found *only* in his favorite book. He glanced past the bug to gaze at his surroundings. "What are you saying?"

Agitated, the bug glared while shaking its head. "This might be harder than I thought." Glancing over his shoulder, Sponke yelled for Groger. A large, hairy, simple-looking beast bumbled from the tall grasses.

Groger was a giant, nine-feet-tall, with large, pointed ears jutting out on either side of his head. His eyes were sea-foam green, accentuated by a pair of bushy black eyebrows. A tangled mass of thick, black hair covered his enormous head and hung down past his shoulders. Dressed in a tattered yellow shirt and brown pants, the giant stumbled forward.

Drake stepped backward with his opened hands positioned in front of him. "Whoa! What's that?"

"That, my boy, is Groger. No need to be afraid."

"No need to be afraid? Are you kidding?"

"You're a jumpy, young thing. Stop moving away. He's completely harmless."

Drake stopped, but held up his hands. Groger tilted his head and looked at Drake. "You are not needing to be ascared of me," Groger said with tear-filled eyes.

Drake's fear left as quickly as it had come. "I'm sorry. You're kinda big and—"

"I know, I know. I are sorta scary looking, huh?"

"No, not really. I just wasn't expecting you is all."

Groger looked toward Sponke. "Who's are we having here, Sponkie?"

"This is Drake. He is here for, you know…the thing."

Groger cocked his head again and scrunched his eyes. Sponke immediately flew close to the giant and proceeded to whisper in his ear. Groger's confusion soon turned into a beaming smile.

Drake frowned at the secret meeting. "What are you two talking about?"

Sponke looked down at Drake. "Oh nothing. My big friend here gets a bit confused sometimes. Everything is fine."

Drake held his head and took a seat on a nearby boulder. "I'm sorry, but I'm really confused. Maybe you could explain a little more about what's going on."

Sponke flew in front of Drake and hovered just inches from his face. "You, sir, are in Kropite, and I have information regarding two things that might interest you. The first being the Story Stone! The second is, well, Bailey."

"Bailey!" exclaimed Drake jumping to his feet. "What do you know about my sister? Is she okay? Where is she?"

"Drake, please," Sponke tried to interject.

"Do you know where she is? Will this Story Stone help me find her?"

Sponke rested a hand on Drake's shoulder. "Calm down, *now*."

"What is a Story Stone? Are you talking about the stone I found in the woods?"

"I will answer all of your questions as soon as we find Luke."

Hearing Luke's name was almost too much, as Drake could not believe his ears. "Luke? Luke of Kropite?"

"Why yes! Luke lives here in Kropite, and he will be able to clarify things for you. Do you know our Luke?"

"I know of him, but that's beside the point. What does Luke have to do with my sister?"

"There you go asking questions again. I told you, I *will* explain things once we reach our destination. Didn't I already say this?" Sponke looked from Groger back to Drake.

"You did, but I need more. You can't expect me to just pick up and follow you when I have no idea what's going on! I don't know how I got here, and my sister is missing!"

"Your sister is missing? I didn't say that."

"But you said you had information about her."

"Did I?"

Drake narrowed his eyes. "Yes. Are you *trying* to confuse me?"

"I'm sorry, but that is not my intention. I was hoping you would come with Groger and me, and maybe we could share a few things on our way."

"So you'll tell me more if I go with you?" Drake asked while glancing at Groger.

Sponke looked at Drake for several moments without saying a word before he nodded.

Drake considered the fluttering bug before him. "So, what you're saying is, if I come along with you, you'll help me find my sister because that *is* why I'm here. Right?"

"We might be able to discover Bailey's whereabouts as we travel, and if we're lucky, we'll discover a few other things along the way. If you must believe that you are here for Bailey, so be it."

"I'm sorry, I don't mean to be so stubborn, but I'm obviously not from around here." Drake gazed past the bug, scanning his strange surroundings once again, then he looked back at Sponke. "Where I come from, we don't have talking bugs or giants."

Sponke looked away, offended. "I can understand this. This is all new to you, and maybe a little adventure in your life wouldn't be so *bad*."

"A little adventure? Are we going on an adventure?"

"You *could* say that."

"You just did say that. Your exact words were *a little adventure wouldn't be so bad.* Why do you talk in circles? You *are* trying to confuse me."

"No. I am not meaning to confuse you, Master. I just want you to travel with Groger and me, and maybe we can help each other."

Drake began to pace back and forth. Sponke looked to Groger for help, but the giant just shrugged his squared shoulders.

"All right, let me get this straight. I have no idea how I got here, but I'm here, and for some reason you already know me. I have no clue who you are, but you want me to follow you to your friend, Luke, and he will be the one that can help me find my sister. Does that sound about right?"

Groger and Sponke nodded their heads in unison.

"What other choice do I have? I guess this is all happening for a reason."

Drake stared at the ground and rubbed his head. *This is all a dream. I hit my head. It's a dream, it won't hurt to go with them. Maybe I'll wake soon, and everything will be back to normal.*

"Lovely, Drake. May I ride on your shoulder? We have quite a lengthy journey ahead of us." Drake agreed with narrowed eyes and Sponke settled himself on the boy's left shoulder. Groger pulled a ragged, brown satchel and canteen from the tall grass and slung them around his neck.

CHAPTER 3

Mt. Creesious

The giant ambled forward through the grassy field. The dry, wispy weeds swished against Drake's legs and scratched his skin. The boy looked ahead at Groger and tried to reassure himself that Sponke and the giant were merely figments of his imagination. *Did I read about these two in the book? Maybe I saw them in a cartoon?*

Soon into their journey, the threesome came to the base of a small hill. "Up we be going!" Groger yelled out as he began to climb. Drake stopped for a moment then continued after him. Sponke sat silent on Drake's shoulder. Drake could feel Sponke's eyes on him. It made his heart speed up a little and his breathing feel a bit unnatural.

"So, what do you think of Kropite?" Drake jerked his head to look at Sponke. "Did I startle you?"

Looking around, Drake said, "No...no. I think it's nice."

"Nice?"

"I really haven't been here that long. I don't know much about it," Drake said thinking back to his book *Luke of Kropite*. In reality, he did know some things about this fabricated world. It had not been that long ago he was leafing through the pages of his favorite book. Mesmerized by its detail and imagery, the book's play on words had captivated him. The story wound its way into his mind pickling it with colorful descriptions of a world in which he was somehow now standing.

"I hope you find Kropite as *wonderful* as I do." Sponke gazed ahead. "It is a grand world full of amazing inhabitants."

Drake chewed at the inside of his cheek as his book's words continued to dance in his brain. He glanced around and recalled reading that Kropite was a world set apart from all others. This was a land filled with untouched terrain and extraordinary creatures, cohabitating together but protected by one individual.

"Luke," Drake whispered.

"What did you say, Master Drake?"

Drake shook his head. "What? I didn't say anything." Drake's mind continued to reel. Luke was Kropite's ageless protector. Even though he looked seventeen, the guardian was well over two-hundred-years-old. Drake shook his head and marched on.

They continued their hike for what seemed like miles when Drake began to feel its effects. The sun blazed overhead, beating down on the travelers as they hiked along. Beads of sweat formed at Drake's hairline and gradually slid down his cheeks. He wiped at his forehead to remove some of the salty moisture that had begun streaming into his eyes. "It sure is hot out here."

Sponke nodded his head but said not a word.

A strangled dryness crawled into Drake's throat. He rubbed his neck. Swallowing a couple of times helped, but it never lasted. Before long, the parched and scratchy feeling resurfaced. Gazing upward, Drake was unable to view the top of the hill because a haze hung in the air, hiding its peak. At the onset of their journey, he had thought the hill was small, but now it looked to be never-ending. He questioned whether they would ever reach the top.

Drake pulled at his throat once more. "Do you guys have anything to drink?"

"Groger, how about letting Drake have a bit of your jagga." Drake peered at Groger. "Don't worry, it is a tasty liquid that will instantly quench your thirst, my friend," Sponke explained. Groger retrieved the canteen he had slung around his neck. He handed it to Drake, who unscrewed the cap and began gulping down the jagga right away. As the cool, clear liquid rolled down his scratched throat, relief filled his body. It tasted like water, but with a hint of sweet grape.

Drake licked his lips and smiled. "Thank you, Groger."

"Not any problems. I be having plenty of jagga to share."

Drake handed Groger his canteen. "How much farther until we find Luke?"

Sponke flew off the boy's shoulder and continued up the hill.

"Wait, Sponke."

Groger grinned at the boy and turned his gaze toward the retreating bug. "Drakie, don't you be worry your head about distances. You be in Kropite a wondrous world full of…" Groger trailed off as he stared wide-eyes up the hill.

Drake followed the giant's gaze up the hill only to find Sponke zooming straight at him yelling, "Rock benders!" Drake, taken off guard, had no time to think. Groger grabbed Drake and threw his hefty body over him. The giant crouched over both Drake and Sponke, shielding them with his bulkiness. Groger's enormous mass easily covered them, but Drake stubbornly squeezed out to see.

Up the hill he observed gigantic boulders barreling toward them. Drake quickly ducked back under Groger, bracing himself for the impact. The boulders crashed down the hillside rolling right over Groger's back. Groger groaned. The thudding and pounding made Drake cringe at the pain Groger must be experiencing.

After the commotion ceased, the giant rose slowly. He nodded his big head and released Drake and Sponke from his protection. Drake got to his feet and watched as the boulders continued their descent. Once they reached the base of the hill, a turbulent crunching and cracking split the air. Drake watched as the rocks became beings that stood upright and began to walk.

"Wow! That was completely insane. Did you guys see that?" Drake asked. Sponke, busy dusting off the dirt, took no notice of Drake's anxiousness.

Drake, now trembling with excitement, tried again to ask Sponke and Groger what had just happened. "What are they?"

Sponke cleared his throat and hovered near the boy's ear. "Those, Master, are rock benders. They are relatively harmless, unless you happen to be in their path as they are crashing down the mountain." Sponke scratched his head. "Although, come to think of it, I've never spoken to one. I know Luke has mingled with a few rock benders in his time, and I'm pretty sure *he* said they are harmless."

"That's good to know," responded Drake. He looked at Groger, who appeared a little wobbly. "Are you okay, buddy? That had to hurt."

Groger shook his head a couple of times. "Nah, I is okey dokey, Drakie. I has just a few bumpies and scrapies, not a thing major."

"Okay. If you're sure...because that was *awesome!*" Drake said as he looked back at the retreating rock benders.

Sponke buzzed next to Drake as he perched back onto his shoulder. "Let's get going."

He pushed on, following the stumbling giant ahead. Sweat continued to trickle down his face and back. He pulled at his shirt as irritation began to bubble inside of him. Before Drake could voice his complaint again, a breeze wafted by, brushed across his forehead, and rustled his hair. Drake raised his head to suck in as much of the cool air as he could. The light wind carried a scent past his nose, lingering for only a moment before it disappeared down the hillside. Drake tried to place the scent but had trouble deciphering what it was. When he had arrived at Kazoocal Field, he remembered smelling a fragrance of lavender and popcorn, but this one was altogether different. Sniffing the air, Drake hoped the breeze would soon return, but it was gone.

Sponke tapped the boy on the head. "What are you doing?"

Drake shrugged, causing Sponke to wobble, then picked up his pace to catch up with Groger.

After a while, the travelers reached the top of the hill. Drake stopped for a short rest. He wiped the sweat from his face.

"Finally! I thought we'd never make it to the top of this hill," Drake stated as he watched Groger meander on down the other side.

"Oh my, you are mistaken! This is no hill, Master Drake. We have just scaled Mt. Theazus." Sponke smiled.

Drake turned to look down the mountainside. He shook his head. "This can't be real."

Traveling downhill was a relief, and Drake's tired legs welcomed the reprieve. As they neared the bottom of the mountain, a dirt path began to snake its way along the land. Sponke urged the travelers onward, telling them to pick up the pace. Drake began to jog behind Groger, and they reached the bottom in no time at all.

"Can we stop for a rest? My feet are killing me," Drake grumbled.

"We can rest, but only for a short while. We need to climb Mt. Creesious and reach its base before sundown," Sponke said.

"Mt. Creesious?" Drake ran his hand through his hair and repeated the mountains name again in his head. It sounded oddly familiar. "We have to go up another mountain?" Drake asked.

"Yes. It's the only way."

"Why do we have to get to the bottom before sundown?"

"There is a dangerous creature who resides in a cave set into the mountainside. By day we are safe, but by nightfall he will surface. We must hide at the base of the mountain among the trees. We will set up camp...after Mt. Creesious," Sponke said.

Groger flopped to the ground with a grunt. Unscrewing the top from his canteen, he gulped back the cool jagga. Drake's mind raced as he tried to recollect where he had heard of

Mt. Creesious. Just then, a behemoth of a monster, seeming to be a mixture of ogre, gargoyle, and giant, popped into his memory.

"The zatherosod!" Drake nearly yelled as it came to him.

"What did you say?" Sponke asked with concern.

Drake was unsure exactly how to respond, as this dream was beginning to get carried away. He really did not know its limits. "I didn't say anything," Drake responded. Sponke shrugged.

Drake walked over to sit next to Groger as *Luke of Kropite's* description of the zatherosod replayed through his mind. The giant pushed his canteen toward Drake, which he gladly accepted. He guzzled the refreshing liquid. After returning the giant's canteen, Drake asked him if he had anything to eat. Groger rooted around inside his satchel. Drake's stomach grumbled at the prospect of food.

"Here ya go, Drakie boy," Groger said holding out what looked like a lump of dough.

"Thanks." Drake took the snack and sniffed at it suspiciously.

"It be okey dokey. It be merlump. My mum used to be making it. It is not being as good as hers, but I is always trying."

Drake smiled as he took a tiny nibble of the merlump. It reminded Drake of a doughy honey bread.

"Not bad, Groger."

As Drake finished his small snack, Sponke flew over to move the crew along. "We need to get going now," Sponke said, peering at the sun.

Drake and Groger grunted as they got to their feet and began trudging along the trail. Sponke situated himself upon Drake's shoulder and pointed them toward a mountain that lay ahead. Drake grumbled at the thought of scaling another mountain.

"See it there? Mt. Creesious!" Sponke shouted. "Let's pick up the pace a bit. Just thinking about the zatherosod makes me nervous."

"I thought it only came out at night," Drake said.

"Yes, but I certainly don't want to take a chance. I can happily say I have traveled up this mountain three times *never* having laid eyes on the creature."

"Are you sure it's even there?" Drake asked.

"Oh yes! The zatherosod lives. So many brave creatures have tried to battle him in hopes of getting at its secret." Sponke drew close to Drake and began to whisper. "Apparently, several swords and shields lay at the entrance of its cave, left by the brave ones who have sought the zatherosod's treasure. The discarded weapons serve as a reminder for anyone who approaches."

"What is the secret within the cave?"

"Legend says that deep inside the zatherosod's home lies a great treasure. No one knows what it is, but most are drawn purely out of curiosity."

"Then what's the point of going after it? I wouldn't."

"It has been said that the treasure is something so powerful that with it one could do great, great things."

Drake's mind drifted once again to his book. He recalled Luke battling the zatherosod, but not to get to its secret. He fought the monster to save a friend the zatherosod held captive in its cave. Luke was successful, but there was never any mention of a treasure.

"Does the monster eat anyone it catches?"

"I don't know. I've always heard that it drags its prey deep inside its cave, never to be heard from again."

A shutter went through Drake. He reassured himself it was all a dream.

Once they reached the base of Mt. Creesious, Drake's gaze soared to its peak. He furrowed his brow while staring upward. The mountain's steepness reminded him of a black-diamond slope at a small ski resort he went to on vacation, minus the snow.

"This mountain doesn't look stable. It's crumbly," Drake said as he kicked at a few loose rocks. His action caused a small rock-slide to rumble over his foot. "Groger's a big guy. Are you sure it's safe to climb?"

Sponke nodded his head while flying off Drake's shoulder to take the lead. Groger took a few steps up the slope sending several more rocks tumbling downward. He glanced back at Drake. "What's ya waitin for? We need to be getting up there."

Mt. Creesious was much steeper than the last mountain. It was void of grass or vegetation of any kind, comprised only of rock. Various-sized chunks of brownish-red rocks with thin cracks jetting in all directions covered the mountain. With each step, the rocky terrain cracked and crunched beneath their feet. It seemed no matter how soft he walked, loose rocks still rumbled toward the base of the mountain. Drake stopped every now and again and looked downhill, watching as the rock debris gathered on the ground below. Sponke stopped to look back at Drake.

"What is it, Master Drake?"

"Nothing. I just can't believe how brittle this mountain is."

"Not to worry. Just keep moving," Sponke said resuming his lead.

Drake's eyes met the wobbly giant ahead of him. With each of Groger's massive strides, larger chucks of the mountain rolled downward. Several times Drake had to jump out of the way of the toppling rocks. Farther up the mountain, a thumping sound caused all three travelers to stop their climb.

"What was that?" Drake asked.

"Not sure." Sponke looked around. "We better keep moving."

Groger's mouth dropped as he pointed toward the top of the hill.

"Run!" Sponke yelled at the dusty, crumbling mass bearing down on them. "Run!"

Tiny bits of rock began pelting Drake in the head and shoulders. Drake spun around and sprinted as fast as he could. The terrain was too loose, causing him to lose his footing. He crashed to his rear, sliding toward the bottom. Dust filled the air as rock bits and boulders bounced behind Drake. The roaring rock-fall muffled any yells or screams. Drake careened toward the bottom with boulders pushing at his back. Once his legs met the ground at the base of the mountain he tried scrambling to his feet, but the cascading rocks were too close and bowled over him.

Drake lay in pain under the pieces of rocks. After several minutes, the thundering noises ceased and Drake pushed his way out of the wreckage. He brushed himself off and looked around. He saw no signs of his friends.

Cupping his hands around his mouth, he yelled, "Groger! Sponke! Where are you?" His voice echoed back at him. He tried calling again and again. Drake looked at the crumbled hillside, resigned. He continued to call his friends as he hiked. Drake trudged on. "I hope they're alright." Knowing Groger's strength put his mind a little at ease. He took a deep breath as he gazed toward the top of the mountain. "This can't be happening!"

A slight breeze blew past him, bringing with it the same, strange scent he had smelled back on Mt. Theazus. This time the smell lingered—pine needles. Drake searched around confused. There was not a tree in sight.

Off in the distance, a thunderous boom grasped his attention.

"Groger! Is that you?" Drake yelled scrambling around the side of the mountain. The resounding thunder stopped. Drake found himself at the entrance to an expansive cavern sliced into side of the hill.

The cave was pitch black and reeked of rotten meat. Drake shuttered as he observed a pile of bones, several swords, and two battered shields to the left of the cave entrance. *This isn't real*, he thought as he moved cautiously over to one of the swords. The weapon was cold and heavy. Drake struggled to hold it in one hand. Interlocking his fingers around the handle, he swished the blade through the air while voicing swooshing sounds. Slicing upward and downward, Drake pretended to fight a massive opponent. He spun around, bringing the sword in front of him. Drake laughed at his own actions.

Intrigued by its appearance, he pulled the weapon close to his face to inspect the tiny etched nicks that riddled the blade. All along the sword, Drake noticed a splatter of dark red spots. His stomach churned.

Drake turned the blade and its shiny, surface caught the sun's light, sending a blinding beam slicing into the cavern. The ground began to shake. One ferocious growl after another resonated from inside the cave. Drake dropped the sword. He stood at the mouth of the cave unprotected, unable to move a muscle. The commotion inside grew louder and louder, telling Drake he should run for his life, but fear rooted him to his spot.

"This is only a dream! This is only a dream!" he yelled over and over while staring into the dark cave, waiting for the creature to surface.

Something in his brain clicked. *I'm a sitting duck!* He reached down and picked up the sword again, along with a shield.

"What am I doing? Drake said aloud. "I know, I'll just stand here. Once this thing comes out, I'll scream. My screaming will wake me up. Yeah, I will scream myself awake."

The thudding continued to shake the ground for several more seconds before it ceased. Drake waited with his sword and shield at the ready. Beginning to feel foolish, he lowered his weapon, moving slowly toward the cave's entrance. As soon as his foot crossed into the cave's darkness, a tremendous, hairy hand shot out, grabbed hold of his leg, and dragged him inside. A monster towed Drake's body down a long, winding tunnel. His body bounced along the ground.

"Why-y am I f-feeling this? I sh-shouldn't b-be feeling-g this," Drake stammered.

He could only see the creature from behind as it pulled him along, but there was no doubt it had to be the zatherosod. It was huge and bulky, nearly hitting its head on the tunnel's ceiling. Jagged horns—curving upward on either side of its head—scraped along the rocky roof, like nails on a chalkboard. Drake winced at the god-awful noise. A resounding roar, mingled with heavy grunts, echoed from the monster.

A sour, moldy stench permeated the cavern walls causing Drake to gag. Drake gazed downward, relieved to see he had managed to hang onto the sword while being pulled deep inside the cave. Without giving it a second thought, he hoisted the bulky sword up and swung it with all of his might. It was a direct hit. A gooey, blue substance shot upward as Drake's body came to a complete stop. He stared wide-eyed at the monster's severed and bleeding hand, still gripping his leg.

"Blue blood?" Drake screamed and flailed his legs. The hand's grip loosened and it flew upward, striking the wall, tumbling to the floor with a thump. The hand lay on the floor twitching while its last ounce of life faded away. Drake jumped to his feet, holding his sword out. An unexplained power surged throughout his body. He felt prepared for battle. The creature turned, peering down at its severed hand. The zatherosod stood motionless, it's eyes bulged and it's bottom lip jutted out.

Drool hung from the beast's oversized mouth and strands of stringy, thin hair draped over its face and into its eyes. Drake glared at the stunned creature taking in its large, flat nose and beady red eyes. "That's right. I did that! You overgrown dimwit!" Drake yelled.

The zatherosod's eyes rose from its severed hand and settled on Drake. A blazing red glare bore into Drake as the beast shook with anger. Throwing back its head, it bellowed its displeasure. The thunder coming from the monster shook the ground. It charged at Drake, swinging wildly at him, but Drake was able to duck in time. The zatherosod crashed into the wall and stumbled backward. He tried to move away from the enraged creature by skirting around it, but its body was too thick. The zatherosod blocked Drake's only escape.

The monster shook its head and roared. Thick, black goo surged from its mouth, spewing all over Drake's face, and into his gaping mouth. The beast's spit hung on the taste buds at the back of Drake tongue. He spluttered and hacked, trying to relieve himself of the awful taste of vomit and overcooked broccoli. Drake whipped his hand up and wiped at his tongue.

In a matter of seconds, the zatherosod assailed again. Drake's newfound confidence vanished as he cowered close to the ground, closed his eyes, and wrapped his arms around his head. While cocooning himself, he kept his sword aloft.

The giant charged toward Drake, bumbling over the rocky ground. A boulder, off to the side, rolled directly into its path.

Drake opened his eyes as the monster tripped on the large rock, pitched upward, and careened, spread-eagle, toward him. The zatherosod fell directly onto Drake's erect sword.

Drake was pinned to the ground with the monster's arm strewn across his chest and its lifeless body stretched alongside him. A dark blue fluid oozed from under the creature spreading across the ground. The thick liquid wound its way toward Drake. He pushed the limp arm off him and scrambled to his feet. Drake stared down at the gruesome scene. He scrunched his face as he watched the blood flow across the cave and pool against the cavern wall.

Wiping his bloody hands on his shirt, Drake looked around, surveying the cave. He could not block out his sudden desire to find the treasure—the deep, dark secret that would allow him to do great things.

Drake left the lifeless monster and jogged deeper into its home. "Where is it?" he asked as he ran. He stopped to listen. A hum vibrated against the cavern walls. He touched the cold, hard surface and felt a tremor. Cautiously, he walked farther into the darkness. A faint light blinked at the end of a passage. As Drake drew closer the buzzing grew louder. Once he reached the passage's end, he saw a small cloth bag lying upon the ground. A glowing object quivered inside the bag. Drake squatted to the floor to retrieve the small pouch. He shook it and the buzzing stopped. He carefully opened the bag, anticipating his great find. A shot of air and a flurry of wings sailed past his face. Drake spun to watch a strange, flying insect speed down the passage and out of sight.

"A lightning bug! All that for a lightning bug!" Drake threw up his hands, dropped the bag, and headed back toward the cave entrance. He passed the dead zatherosod lying on the ground in a pool of its own blood. A shiver soared through Drake as he leaped over the beast's large arm. A stench filled his nostrils. Drake pinched his nose as he scurried forward, toward the light at the mouth of the tunnel.

CHAPTER 4

Dream Within a Dream

Drake emerged into the welcome sunlight and shielded his eyes. He stopped just at the cave's mouth. Drake grinned at his dusty friends standing before him. "What happened to you guys?"

"What happened to us? What about you? Is this the home of the...the zatherosod?" Sponke asked.

Drake looked back at the cave. "Yes."

Sponke flew up to inspect Drake. "What is this all over you?"

"I kind...I kind of killed the zatherosod."

"*You* killed the *zatherosod?*"

"It was by accident really. I was looking for you guys. I was checking out the swords and shields, and next thing I knew, he dragged me inside."

Sponke and Groger took in every detail.

"It was really sick. The thing had blue blood," Drake said, pointing to his shirt and legs.

"Did you find the beast's treasure?" Sponke asked.

"I found his treasure. He sure had you all duped. It was a lightning bug stuck in a bag."

"A what?" Sponke scrunched up his tiny face.

"A lightning bug. You know a flying bug that has a light on its butt. It flies around, lighting up at night."

Sponke stood shaking his head. "No! Do you still have the bug?"

"As soon as I opened the bag, it took off."

Sponke began to look around. "Did you see which way it went?"

"No...why does it matter?"

Groger began to chuckle. "Drakie. Yous has lots to be learning about our world."

"What are you guys talking about?"

"The creature you speak of is called a *morolark*. It secretes a serum from its *lighted-butt*, as you call it. With only one drop of this serum, you will have the ability to live forever," Sponke explained.

"Forever?"

"Yes. A gift *anyone* would want."

"Are there more morolarks around?" Drake said glancing behind him.

"No. Only one that I have heard of and you, my *friend*, let it get away."

"If it's the only one, how did the zatherosod get it?"

Sponke shook his head. "I don't know. No one knew he had it until now. He must have been keeping it for something, but now we'll never know."

"So killing that monster was a bad thing?" Drake said pointing back at the cave.

Sponke put his hand on Drake's shoulder and smiled. "No, no. It was an *impossible* thing."

"If he had the morolark, why isn't he still alive? I mean, wouldn't he stay alive even after he fell on the sword?"

"*Obviously* he hadn't used the serum. Maybe he didn't know how, or maybe he was saving it for something else."

Drake narrowed his eyes. "Saving it?"

Sponke glanced upward toward the retreating sun, and then cleared his throat. "We need to get going."

"Wait. Where have you two been?" Drake asked. He looked at Sponke with speculation.

Sponke wiped some lingering dust from his shoulder. "Buried alive. It took us forever to dig out from under the rubble."

The threesome trudged on without words. Sponke flew up to continue his lead. As they walked, Drake kept telling himself he was dreaming, even though his head was killing him. They reached the top of the mountain and made their decent before the sun began to fade.

"Hey guys, why don't we stop for the night? I'm beat," Drake called out as he ran alongside Groger.

Groger nodded his weary head in agreement. Pointing to the bottom of the mountain in a clearing near the woods, Groger said, "That be the best spot for tonight." They reached the bottom of Mt. Creesious and began to build camp near the trees.

Groger set about collecting sticks while Sponke cleared a suitable spot for the giant to build his fire.

"Can I help?"

"No, no, Master Drake. You take a seat, and we'll have this fire going in no time. I think your encounter with the zatherosod was quite enough activity for you for one day."

Drake plopped to the ground with a grunt and watched the others scurrying about. Groger produced a roaring fire in a matter of minutes. The giant took a seat next to Drake and offered him some more of his doughy snack. Drake gladly accepted, stuffing an entire piece of merlump into his mouth. After washing it down with an enormous swig of jagga, Drake sat back to enjoy the heat of the fire.

"Sponke, have you lived here your whole life?"

Sponke fluttered next to the boy and settled himself onto a branch hanging near Drake's face. "Why, yes. I have.

"How old are you?"

Sponke adjusted himself on his perch. "That is not a very polite question. Have you *no* manners at *all*?"

Groger let out a laugh as he slapped Drake on the back. The boy lurched forward, catching himself with his hands before toppling onto his face. "You funny boy, Drakie. Sponkie be sensitive about his age."

"I am not sensitive. I just don't think he should be asking me how old I am is all."

Drake pushed himself up and sat back down next to Groger. "Jeez. Sorry for asking." He turned his attention to the giant. "What's your story, Groger?"

Groger grinned. "I be a rare breed of sadcad. Sadcads not from Kropite, we from Cooplaroo! It be beautiful and peaceful there...until new king came. King Moezar full of hate and ugliness. He sent all of us, sadcads, away. We sadcads, we come to Kropite. Well..." he paused and stared into the fire, his big hands scratched at the dirt around his feet. "Well, many of my families got separated. I be the only one here right now, but I sure they be coming sometime. Luke say he will help me find them, my families." Groger began to weep. He wiped at his eyes and snorted a few times.

"I be alone here until I meet Sponkie. I sat under the Great Arenok Tree, sad to be lonesome, when here comes along Sponkie. He talk to me, and I knew right then, we be bestest friends."

Drake shook his head, hoping Sponke and Groger's stories would eventually sound familiar to him, but there was no way that these two creatures were in his book.

Groger glanced down at Drake. "Where are you coming from, Drakie?"

Drake snapped out of his thoughts. "Oh, me? I live in a place called Annapolis, Maryland, in Cape Coast."

Sponke tilted his head. "So you call your world Cape Coast, or is it Annap—"

"No, no. My world is called Earth," Drake interrupted.

"Oh, I've heard of that," Sponke said with a nod. "Keep going with your story, Master Drake."

Drake chuckled. "It's a pretty big neighborhood that's been around for a long time. My dad and grandparents grew up there."

"What do you do at home?" Sponke inquired.

"Oh man, there is so much to do there. My neighborhood is right on the mouth of the Magothy River, which dumps into the Chesapeake Bay. I have a fifteen-foot Boston Whaler. You know, a boat." Drake said. Groger and Sponke just nodded.

"Anyway, my dad helped me fix it up. My friends and I are out in it practically every day of the summer. We love to wakeboard back in the small creeks off the Magothy or behind this really cool island called Dobbins." Drake grinned. "But man, there is nothing better than launching my Whaler off the waves of a huge cruiser!"

"Cruiser?"

"It's just another type of boat, only really big." Groger tilted his head while Sponke's grin seemed to grow. Drake snickered at Sponke's obnoxious smile and shrugged his shoulders. "When we aren't in the Whaler, we spend a lot of time at the community beach. We ride our bikes there and spend hours horsing around in the water. "

"Fascinating," responded Sponke. Drake realized he was speaking a foreign language to his new friends, but talking about home made him feel good. Drake stretched his arms into the air and yawned. Groger followed suit.

"I think it's time for a bit of shut eye." Sponke nodded as he spoke.

Drake yawned again and scrunched himself into a ball upon the ground. He was so exhausted from the day's adventure that he fell asleep almost immediately.

A hazy numbness cascades over his mind. He walks alone through a dense, dark forest. The dismal trees tower over him, making everything pitch-black. His hand is indistinguishable, even as he holds it directly in front of his face. Shrieks and wails erupt all around him, sending him crouching behind a wide-girthed tree. Off in the distance, a grunting and thumping draws closer and closer. He covers his ears hoping to dispel the maddening clatter as it approaches him, but to no avail. The exasperating racket only grows in volume. Just as it descends upon him, he finds himself floating out of the forest.

As he peers upward, he is unable to identify what is towing him. Whatever it is, launches him out of the trees and propels him into the midnight sky. Sharp, dagger-like teeth dig into his arm while his body dangles below like a ragdoll. They soar higher and higher away from the dark forest.

The night air is cool. It rushes past him causing a shiver. His eyes gaze upward fixing on the millions of stars suspended in the black sky. Stars are familiar to him. Focusing on them relaxes the tension in his joints. Stinging pain shoots through his arm, but he finds it bearable. Without any notion, Drake raises his hand over his head. He can feel warmth flowing in and out of the massive nose of his flying predator. Its breathing is constant and hot, ruffling the hair on the back of his neck. His hand brushes upward along a furry muzzle and with a jerk, the staggering jaws release him. He looks down. He's heading toward a clear lake.

Drake crashes into the lake. He glides toward the watery floor. In his descent, an image of his sister flashes in front of him. He reaches for her. Just as Bailey melts away, a deep growling jolts him awake.

Roused from his sleep, he was relieved to see that the growling was only Groger's snoring. Drake sat up and rubbed at his eyes. He did not even want to rationalize how he had just had a dream within a dream.

Drake silently got to his feet. He spied Groger's discarded satchel lying next to a rock. He rummaged inside the sack for more merlump then walked several yards from the campsite. A short distance away, he found a small stream glistening in the morning sun. Drake popped the lump of dough into his mouth and strangled it down his dry throat. He gazed longingly at the clear, cool water.

Drake knelt at the water's edge. He leaned over for a refreshing drink when his reflection startled him. He dipped his hand in the water and ran it through his tangled hair, pushing it over to one side. Once the stream stopped rippling, he stared back down at his image. His reflection showed a ragged boy with cuts and scrapes etched across his face. He reached up, running his fingers over his wounds. *Why are they here?* His mind wavered through the cringing encounter he had with the zatherosod. *Was that real?*

He cupped his hands together and dipped them into the stream. Brimming with water, he pulled them close and slurped it into his mouth. The fresh, sparkling liquid ran down his parched throat. He was wide-awake now. Drake jumped onto a large rock perched beside the stream. Standing tall, he looked far into the distance and saw rolling hills for miles. Everything was green and clear.

A slight breeze wafted by, moving his messy, damp hair back across his forehead. As if alive, the breeze circled around him, blowing past his ear, bringing with it a faint cry. Drake turned his head, trying to decipher the sound, but it was gone, carried away into the distant mountains. Staring straight ahead, Drake sifted through his memories to try and place the noise. Turing his head to the left the same cry floated past once more.

"Bailey!" he called out.

Her face appeared in his memory vividly. He bent over again, gazing back at his beat-up reflection. The zatherosod, his scraped face, the dream, his sister—the startling realization rushed over him like a waterfall. This was all real!

Drake bent down and thrust his hand into the creek. He pushed forward with great force and whipped water into the air.

"How's this possible?" Drake looked out across the land then back at his still sleeping friends.

A loud squawk sounded, pulling the boy's eyes skyward. Drake craned his neck just before a hefty force struck him from behind and pushed him forward. Pain shot through his body. Before Drake could turn to view his assailant, a ripping ache pierced his shoulder blades and the squawking returned. Drake screamed as his body jutted forward, then began to rise into the sky.

"Sponke! Groger! Help!" Drake screamed as he scrambled to grab hold of the creature's legs protruding just behind his head.

Sponke bolted upright and began flapping ferociously around the campsite. "Drake! Drake! Where are you?"

"Sponke! Look up! Help!"

The bug stopped his frenzied motions and gazed upward. "Groger! Wake up! A flaming foradore has Drake! We have to try and follow it." Groger ambled to his feet, yelling for his little friend. Drake could see Sponke and Groger clambering about below, unable to find their direction.

Drake pumped his legs and twisted his body. With every movement, the razor talons dug deeper into his skin. Gazing upward, he tried to get a better look at his attacker but was unable to see anything through the monster's thick plumage. He rocked back and forth hoping to loosen the monster's grasp. Although the pain was almost unbearable, Drake fought throughout his entire air journey. The giant bird flew on, mile after mile.

Unwilling to give up, Drake continued his jerking movements and yells. The creature began to make its decent, enabling Drake to see what lay below him now. A dry, rocky terrain sprawled out before him. Swinging his legs upward, Drake kicked at his carrier's underside. The bird released a squeal and unlatched one of its feet from the boy's shoulders. All the while, the creature drew closer to the ground. Drake dangled below, barely in the monster's grasp. Seeing his chance, Drake reached up, latched onto one of the its legs, and swung violently back and forth. He pulled his legs up, and with several heaving kicks, the bird released him. Drake struck the ground, bounced several feet, than lay sprawled upon the dirt. Dust billowed around him, leaving him coughing and spluttering for breath.

CHAPTER 5

Irick

Drake stared into the sky searching for his giant attacker. He groaned then rolled onto his stomach. His body ached, his head pulsated, and he could barely see for the cloud of dust that surrounded him. Slowly, he pulled himself to his feet. Parched earth spread in all directions. He rubbed his head, then spun around to look behind him. There was nothing.

He gazed at his torn shirt and shorts. Reaching back, Drake lightly caressed his shoulder blades. They ached and his shirt was moist. Pulling back his hand, he recoiled at the sight of his own blood. Drake held his side and groaned. He glanced into the sky for one more look. He rubbed his head again then cupped his hands around his mouth shouting, "Sponke! Groger!" His voice echoed though the wasteland.

A screech sounded overhead. Drake began sprinting in no particular direction. He ran on until the shrieking disappeared. He held his chest as he slowed his pace. Drake noticed a warn path etched into the hard-packed earth. Unsure of his destination, he stumbled along the trail.

The dirt lane was dry and cracked, scorched by the boiling sun. The blistering heat beat down upon him, bringing with it an itchy sweat that trickled down his back. Squinting his eyes, Drake could make out cascading mountains far in the distance. He longed to reach those hills, imagining them to be much cooler.

"Why is it so hot here?" he yelled out. His voice echoed into the air then disappeared into the clouds.

He scratched at his neck and chest. His shirt felt heavy and his hair dripped with sweat. Drake groaned as perspiration trickled into the wounds on his back. He pulled at his shirt once more as it stuck to his cuts.

Drake clutched his head and grunted. "This is all real. I should have known. But how?" Throwing back his head, Drake yelled, "Where am I?"

He stumbled over a rock lying in the middle of his path and sent it spiraling ahead. A few more minutes along, Drake stopped and glanced around. The vastness surrounding him was empty. He sighed heavily, wiped at the sweat steadily trickling down his face, and advanced.

Not long after he resumed his course, a faint clatter sounded behind him. He quickly turned his head, but saw nothing except an empty trail. Drake moved on. Within seconds, the clattering was back. It seemed to be moving along behind him. Drake stopped, turning his whole body around to investigate. Nothing.

This time Drake focused on his own movements. Maybe the noises were footsteps. Drake stopped once again to turn his head. He saw nothing out of the ordinary. He kept up this monotonous pattern of stopping and starting, and each time the noises stopped and started with him. *Am I just being paranoid?* he thought as he turned again to see if anything was following him. Of course, there was nothing. He was about to move on when he noticed a gigantic boulder on the side of the trail. *That's odd, I don't remember passing that.*

Turning away from the rock, he trudged onward. Just as before, the clumping noise returned. Drake tried to block it out, because he knew that when he turned there would only be an empty path. Without regard, he kept up his momentum.

Before long, Drake noticed the sun fading, then growing bright again. He looked upward, expecting to see a bulky cloud sailing across the sky, which would have been a welcome reprieve from the heat. To his bewilderment, there was not a cloud in the sky. Confused, he looked down at the ground where he witnessed a monstrous shadow looming over him. The hairs on the back of Drake's neck stood on end as he assumed his bird attacker had returned. Slowly he pivoted, but this time he held up clenched fists. Relieved, he found nothing except a boulder. The same boulder.

Glaring at the huge rock, Drake said, "Are you following me?" Drake meandered over and lightly touched its hard, grey surface. Walking around the giant boulder, and not exactly sure what he was hoping to find, he placed both hands on it and pushed with all his might. He was unable to budge it.

Pulling his hands away, he clapped them together and sent a smoky dust cloud though the air. Drake sneezed and coughed as the dry particles made their way up his nose and down his throat. He kicked at the bottom of the rock, sending dust billowing out and around his feet.

"All right, how are you moving? Something strange is going on here."

Drake still looked around. He looked back at the rock and decided if nothing else it might be a nice place for a short rest.

Drake gazed toward the top of the boulder, searching for a way to climb onto it. Spying a few deep grooves gouged into the rock, Drake reached up with both hands and inserted his fingertips. With one heavy grunt, the boy scaled the boulder and pulled himself up.

Just as he was getting comfortable, a turbulent rumbling startled him. A cloud of thick powder stirred from the commotion, blinding him. Slowly, he found himself rising upward. Not able to jump off in time, Drake grabbed onto the sides of the huge rock. He felt himself rising higher and higher off the ground.

"What's going on?" Drake yelled as he clung to the stone.

Dangling about twenty feet above the ground, he was unable to make out what was beneath him. It was on the move.

"Wait! Stop! I'm sorry! Please let me down!" Drake yelled.

A booming voice echoed from below. "You are very small, and I very big. How you like I sit on you?"

"I'm sorry, I didn't know! I thought you were just a rock."

"Just a rock! No, I not just a rock, I a rock bender!"

Drake's mind reeled. Groger had shielded him from the rock benders barreling down the mountainside at Mt. Theazus.

"I'm sorry. I'm not from Kropite! I don't know these things. I live in Cape Coast."

"Cape Coast?"

"Yeah, Cape Coast. It's, well, nothing like Kropite, and we don't have rock benders where I come from."

The rock bender reached up with his long bulky arms, pulled Drake off its head, and held him aloft. With a bewildering gaze, he studied Drake for several seconds.

"You look a little like Master Luke." Drake's eyes narrowed. The rock bender continued to stare at Drake. "Yes, you look like him. You seem like nice fellow," he said with a soft smile.

Drake was unable to study the rock benders before as they tumbled down the mountainside, but now he was only a few inches away from this huge creature's face.

The creature's body was humanoid, only giant. He was made entirely of grey rock and the sheer size of his limbs reminded Drake of tree trunks. Drake's gaze fixed on the giant's head. The most prominent feature was his huge mouth. His sizable lips were hard, riveted stone, and they bumbled up and down, smacking one another as he talked. His teeth were granite grey, the exact same color as his body. The giant's forehead protruded over his eyes, making them look sunken and black. Although his eyes were dark, there was gentleness within his gaze that warmed Drake from the inside out.

Even though the rock bender was huge and made up of cold stone, his huge grin and child-like speech allowed the tension to drain from Drake's muscles. Drake could not explain it, but he found himself drawn to this beast. He knew he meant him no harm.

After several moments, the rock bender settled Drake on his shoulder and continued walking. He sat upon his rocky perch, not exactly sure what to say next. The giant clomped along for a few minutes then jerked his head toward Drake.

"You have some place to go? *I* take you to that place."

Drake chuckled. "I wish I knew where I was going. Unfortunately, I'm lost in a place that I can't leave."

"Why you can't leave?"

"Because I'm searching for someone. Without her, I'm stuck here."

"You not like it here Mr...what your name?

"My name is Drake Hanson. And don't get me wrong, Kropite is a neat place. I don't want to offend you, but this place is *not* normal. I mean, only people talk in my world, not animals and rocks."

"I not rock! I rock bender, Drake Hanson!"

"I'm sorry, I'm really sorry! I just can't win. I'm saying all the wrong things, and I feel like I'm getting nowhere here." His shoulders slumped.

"My name Irick, and I sad that you sad, Drake Hanson. Please tell me your story. I good listener." The rock bender sounded so sincere that Drake could not deny him.

Drake told Irick everything, starting with the stone he found in the woods, and ending with the flying creature that almost had him for lunch. Irick listened intently. As Drake finished his story, the rock bender tilted his head.

"You a remarkable creature. I understand about half of what you is telling me. I think you are neat little guy, and I help you."

"That's great, Irick, but I don't know where I'm going or how you can help me," Drake responded.

"I is big and know Kropite like back of hand. I can take you anywhere you need to be going."

"Like I said before, I really don't know where that is."

Irick clomped along with a simple smile plastered across his craggy face. Drake wondered if maybe the rock bender knew something that he did not. The giant began to hum as he trekked along. Drake tried to make himself comfortable and figured if anything, at least the rock bender was good company. Maybe Irick *could* help him. Traveling alone was not nearly as entertaining as being with friends, so Drake decided he would stay with him.

As they walked along, Irick revealed a bit of rock bender history. Drake grinned as he soaked up all that the giant had to say. He learned that Irick's race was at war with each other because several hundred rock benders had chosen to rebel against their king.

"My king, King Boukapong, is wonderful leader and full of *kind* heart. Some of my people don't like a kind heart and think war is more fun. They are outcasts and bad company. Hopefully we not meet them."

"I hope not either," Drake said looking around them. "What about you, Irick?"

"Me? I love my king. He is helpful, loyal, and fair. He is good guy, but not dumb. He knows outcasts wage war often, so we train for fight. Irick is *skilled* warrior."

"That sounds awesome."

"Yes. But I choose to fight *only* if no other choice. Irick has patience and tolerance. I fight only if have to. I am defender of what is right, Drake Hanson."

Irick covered several miles before a sonorous crack echoed in the distance. The giant stopped his trek, peered behind him, and snorted. He stretched his neck as high as it would go and sniffed at the air.

"What is it?"

"Irick hears strange booming."

"What could it be?"

"Don't know. We keep moving."

Based on the bumping and clumping of his ride, Drake could tell that Irick had picked up his pace. He wondered why the rock bender's face had become stern and serious. Clutching onto Irick's shoulder, Drake adjusted himself several times.

"How often do you come across these outcast rock benders?"

The giant grinned. "Oh, they pop up every now and again. We in their territory."

"They live near here?" Drake said glancing around, a bit nervous.

"They could be anywhere, except in rock bender village. They are forbidden inside village."

"Like…what are the chances we could meet them?"

"You want to meet outcasts?"

"No!"

Irick chuckled. "You fine, Drake Hanson. You with me. I keep you *safe.*"

Stomping over the dry, rocky terrain, Irick kept up his steady pace. Drake watched Irick shuffle along. Every now and again, he would jerk his head to glance behind them, make a deep-throated grumble, and mumble something just under his breath.

"Where are we going?"

"We go to my village. You will be safe there and my king help you out."

"Are you sure that's a good idea? I mean, you can drop me off here, and I'll be on my way."

"Drake Hanson, we in *dangerous* area. I like to remove you from this part of Kropite. There many disasters for small being like you to fumble into. Understand?" Irick asked as he continued to look behind him.

Drake jerked his head following Irick's gaze. A hollow thunder sounded again. "What is that booming noise?" Drake asked.

Irick moved forward several paces before a resounding roar reverberated directly overhead. One crack after another filled the still atmosphere, reminding Drake of the echoing pop produced by a firework just after its light show.

Irick flung back his head and released an ear-piercing wail that soared through the empty sky.

Drake covered his ears. "Irick?"

The rock bender held up his hand and snorted. Within seconds massive boulders bounded from the sky. One mammoth rock after another thudded to the ground landing in a perfect circular formation around Irick and Drake.

Uncovering his ears, Drake called out, "Irick! I don't like this!"

"Not to be worrying. You must be doing what I tell you to. Do you understand, Drake Hanson?"

"I think so."

A tumultuous crunching and thwacking filled the air as each boulder transformed into a gigantic rock-shaped person. Drake's mouth hung open as he observed eight hulking rock benders standing before them with snarling mouths and glaring eyes. Each giant appeared much larger than Drake's big friend, but none looked as if they possessed Irick's kind nature.

Irick spoke to Drake in a whisper. "I will be getting us through two giants just behind us. Once I through, I send you forward. You run. Do you hear me, Drake Hanson?"

Drake stared down at Irick, watching his chest heave in and out. "Yes, Irick. But what about you?"

The rock bender chuckled. "No need to be worrying about Irick. Remember, I warrior. Maybe it is *them* who should do worrying." Irick chuckled again. "Besides, I summoned help. My people will come."

Before Drake could say anymore, a huge, husky rock bender growled and spit toward Irick.

"Hey, senseless grunge. You and your mini-rider in *our* territory. No king's crony allowed out this far."

The beasts tightened their circle making any escape appear impossible. Drake clutched hold of Irick's shoulder.

"We leave your area. Move to let us pass, and we be on our way," Irick bellowed.

The outcasts all began to laugh. "You nothing. We bigger and stronger. You small and *weak*. We say what you do. Any of us take on tiny grunge like you," the leader of the crew roared as he gazed around at his small army.

Irick stood before the giants with eyes closed. A slight growl surfaced as he clenched and unclenched his hands. A dusty powder billowed from Irick's fists causing Drake to choke.

"You and your king soon answer to me. Foolish King Boukapong will learn it not pay to be kind. This not way of this world. You soon call me king. King Horzik!"

This last remark sent ripples through Irick's body, leaving Drake struggling to hold on.

"King Boukapong is king, not *you*. I *die* before I ever call you king."

A rock bender standing to the right of the leader snarled at Irick. Horzik put his hand on the raging giant. "Wait, Zoriff. You get a chance soon."

Irick reached up, grabbed Drake off his shoulder, and placed him gently on the ground. Drake could not take his eyes off the enraged Zoriff, his nostrils flaring and chest heaving. He hoped his friend had a good plan. Irick stepped back a few paces as the leader laughed at him.

"You run, twit. Run away. Cry to your king. Maybe after we smash you around, we pay visit to your shabby village. We take your king and smash him around, too."

Irick glared at Horzik. "Irick not run. Irick has no other choice, I choose to fight." With this, Zoriff and Irick leapt at one another. They met in the air with a deafening crash. Irick pulled his arms up over his head and smashed down upon Zoriff's shoulders, sending him hurling toward the ground. Drake's mouth dropped open as a dazed Zoriff landed in a heap right next to him. Irick quickly landed behind Drake and scooped him up onto his shoulder. Drake gasped for breath as he hung onto the fast moving giant.

"Grab tight, Drake Hanson. Remember what I is telling you!" Irick yelled as he spun around and charged at the two rock benders directly behind him. Drake speedily maneuvered himself over Irick's shoulder, so he was lying across it. He clutched to the rock bender's back, holding on for dear life. Irick bellowed a war cry as he flew into the two giants. He ripped through the burly rock benders as if they were nothing. He plowed his body forward, leaving dust in his wake. Drake clung to his ride and watched the two outcasts explode into rubble. The other outcasts stared in disbelief at their fallen members.

Irick charged ahead while gently pulling Drake from his shoulder. He flipped the boy forward and lowered him to the ground. He leaned in close to whisper one last message. "We will meet again, Drake Hanson." Irick sent Drake sliding ahead with blinding speed. Rocks and dry dirt wafted upward and filled the air. The rock bender stopped his momentum and spun around to face the outcasts once more.

Irick held his head high, hollered his war cry, and plunged back into battle. Drake finally came to a stop. He lay in his cloud of dust coughing, sputtering, and badly bruised. Sitting up quickly, Drake waved away the dust as best he could. He listened for his burly friend. Yells, cracks, and snaps issued all around. Drake jumped to his feet. With squinted eyes, he could see a powdery cloud rising from the battle he knew Irick was fighting. Limping, Drake pushed himself back toward the combatting rock benders. Irick's orders were gone from his mind.

A clatter off to his right caught Drake's attention. He scrunched his eyes once more to get a better look. A wide line of rock benders, led by a king, marched straight toward Irick and the battle. Drake looked back to the fight. In the distance, he could see Irick lifting opponents twice his size and hurling them away. "I guess Irick was right. No need to worry about him." Drake smiled as he witnessed most of the outcasts quickly retreating.

CHAPTER 6

Forest of Bleet

Drake resumed his journey, limping away from the battling giants. He stared down at his aching left thigh. His cargo shorts were torn. Pulling at the fabric, Drake ran his fingers over scrapes set inside a swollen yellow and purple bruise. Pushing his pain to the back of his mind, he urged himself onward.

Without a path to follow, Drake ambled along aimlessly, alone again. He stared at the ground concentrating on each of his long strides. Sometimes he shortened his steps just for a change in momentum, but he never stopped moving. Tired of watching his footsteps, Drake looked ahead of him. Nothing. This vast empty space caused him to shake his head and groan.

Drake gazed upward and noticed the sun was much lower in the sky than he had anticipated. He shivered as a slight chill woke his senses. He breathed in and stopped. The aroma of fresh pine needles, mixed with sodden leaves, shocked him. The scent reminded Drake of the aroma he had noticed on Mt. Creesious. Drake put his head down and trudged on mile after mile, refusing to look up or ahead. The crisp air and pungent fragrances drove Drake forward until a barrier of towering trees halted his trek.

The mammoth trunks along the outskirts of this vast forest were enormous, easily dwarfing the simple trees he would find in Cape Coast. Drake stopped at the edge and tried to peer inside. He swayed back and forth while scrunching his eyes, hoping to see what lay beyond the first stand of trees. He saw nothing but pitch-black.

Unable to pull his gaze from the trees, Drake tilted his head. "I know this place," Drake said aloud.

At the sound of Drake's voice, a flapping of wings burst within the woods, followed by short squeals. Then all fell silent. He moved his head forward, trying to see inside, but did not dare move his feet any closer. Drake rubbed his forehead. If only he could remember...

"The Forest of Bleet!" Drake said aloud.

His brain burst into action as he tried to recollect all he could about Luke's adventure in the Forest of Bleet. Images of strange creatures, some bad and some *horrible* came to mind. He also recalled Luke's ability to speak to the forest creatures, which was certainly a great advantage. Debating whether to enter the forest, Drake found his thoughts wandering back to Sponke and Groger. He missed them more than he thought he would. He could really use their guidance here.

"Wait a minute. If I can speak to them, and to Irick, maybe I can speak to whatever it is that lives in—" Drake's voice froze as a crunch emanated from beyond the trees. Small droplets of sweat formed at Drake's hairline and his heart thumped irregularly. The crunching soon changed to a gurgling. Drake took several steps backward.

Wiping the sweat from his head, and gnawing at the inside of his cheek, the boy turned to examine the parched, empty landscape sprawled out behind him. Several moments elapsed as he looked back and forth between the foreboding, dark woods and the vast, barren land. Sweat continued to bead then trickle down his temples. Wiping his hand over his face again, Drake listened. All was quiet with the exception of his haphazard heartbeat pounding in his ears. His breathing grew heavy. He sucked in air, and then slowly released it.

A sudden din from above filled his atmosphere. Drake gazed upward only to see his earlier attacker gliding open-winged across the sky. The foradore issued several short-blasted squawks as it barreled toward the ground. Landing with a sonorous thud, the bird advanced while squealing its threats.

Drake backed away from the angry bird, but it advanced toward him forcing his body against a tree trunk. Its razor sharp beak darted at Drake's feet. He swung his fists at the beast's moving head. The predator drew back and began to sway from side-to-side, still issuing its high-pitched squawks. Drake darted into the intimidating foliage. The aggravated creature remained at the forest's outskirts, shrieking and jutting its head in all directions.

Drake moved past several trees, trying to stay within the thin beams of sunlight seeping through the tightly packed trunks. The foradore followed, sidestepping along just outside the forest.

Drake pushed himself from tree to tree faster and faster, but the bird easily stayed with him. Stopping, Drake let out a groan and took a step into the sunshine. With blinding speed, the foradore charged forward slamming its beak into the ground right next to Drake's foot. Drake quickly withdrew and stood with his chest heaving.

"Let me out of here!" he yelled.

The beast squawked and squealed, then thrust its head toward the boy. Drake let out a yelp and jumped backward. Taking a deep breath, he cautiously turned to face the darkness of the forest. Shadows moved within the black lair, sending an icy-cold chill dashing up Drake's spine. He took several strides into the woods and stopped. It was incredibly dark. Drake glanced behind him once more only to see the foradore standing guard. He grumbled through clenched teeth, pounded his fist on a nearby tree, and then urged his feet forward.

As if crossing an invisible threshold, a strong gust roared past the trees, almost knocking him off his feet. Drake's heart took on its frenzied pounding once more as a lump rose in his throat. With doubt about to overtake him, he closed his eyes and reached back to rub his still aching shoulder. The thought of facing the giant bird, stalking him just beyond the trees, made him wince. Drake opened his eyes and took another slow deep breath.

"I have to do this," Drake told himself. He rubbed his chest, trying to swallow when an image of his sister sprung into his thoughts. "Bailey needs me." He lowered his head and clenched his fists, taking another step into the great, looming trees. Purpose filled his heart acting as a guide, dragging him deeper into the woods. Each stride fueled his confidence. Thinking of only his sister now, he shoved his fears aside, stared forward into the darkness, and pressed onward.

Drake glimpsed small shadows scurrying about the forest floor. He tried to put the creatures out of his mind by keeping his head up and focusing on each step. However, tiny feet crawled around and across his shoes making them difficult to ignore. He rose up on tiptoe trying to lighten his weight.

Try as he might, his careful movements were not enough. An unpleasant squishing beneath his feet slowed his momentum. As if carpeted with millions of jellyfish, the ground changed from hard, solid dirt, to a thick, gushy consistency. Drake cringed at the thought of trampling on top of the tiny inhabitants, but he pushed himself onward. Horrid little yelps and cries sprang up from below. He did not dare look down.

The wailing creatures, his inability to see anything, and the damp, gloominess of the woods beat on his brain like a drum. His face grew hot. The heat from his head began to flow down and throughout his body. Irritated, Drake pulled at his shirt trying to fan himself. His frustration rapidly turned to anger. An overpowering urge to scream surged through him. Unexplained heat bubbled just behind his eyes as the maddening effects of the forest fueled an unwarranted wrath. Even with his fury, he managed to trek farther and farther into the woods. Drake gritted his teeth and closed his eyes, hoping to will away the festering rage, wanting to suppress it in hopes that the heat building up inside of him would recede.

His burning eyes brought him to a sudden halt and dropped him to his knees. Drake buried his head into his lap. He rocked back and forth.

"Be strong. It's only the forest. Remember the book," he told himself. His head ached with searing pain. He thought it might explode. "What do I do? What did *Luke* do?" he repeated over and over to himself. Then it came to him in a blinding flash. The answer was above him the whole time. "The sun! Find the sun. The sun is the path out of the wickedness. In Kropite, the sun is the answer to happiness when trapped in darkness."

He had to get the sun into his view fast. Even though the fire in his eyes had nearly blinded him, he managed to jump to his feet, gazing skyward.

"No sun? There are too many trees!" Drake yelled, clutching the sides of his head.

This realization hit him so suddenly he felt flames burst from his eyes. One tree exploded, then another. Everywhere his glare settled a tree exploded, leaving splintered remains smoldering all around him. Drake stood among them utterly terrified at what had just occurred. After several seconds, his blinding gaze soared upwards. There it was…the sun! He had broken through the deep, dark forest.

The burning in his eyes left as rapidly as it came. The sun's warmth wrapped him in a blanket of light. An illuminated path appeared. Drake instinctively followed it. The lighted trail only lasted a few yards before dimming, then vanishing. Drake stood in the dreary, solitary darkness yet again. The trees consumed him, trapping him in a murky prison. There were no more fiery blasts exploding from his eyes. Fear enveloped him once more. Drake spun around with arms outstretched, hoping the answer would fall from the treetops.

"I don't like the dark!" he screamed. His voice bounced off the trees. A swishing of leaves exploded with his voice, disturbing the quiet that once surrounded him.

Something smashed into him. It crashed into his side, his legs, and then his head. Drake fell to the ground. Shaking his head, he tried to gather himself as he got back to his feet. A buzzing and whirring whirled around him, sending him diving back to the ground, covering his head with his arms.

He knew he had reached the heart of Bleet. He remembered reading about the black despair that waited in the heart of the forest. He lifted himself to his knees and called out, "Light! I need light!"

The buzzing ceased. An outbreak of light surrounded him. His request for light was a mistake of the worst kind. A ghastly scene appeared before his eyes. Hideous bug-creatures hovered so close he could feel the heat radiating off their bodies. The only comparison that came to mind was a mutated combination of an oversized fly, a lightning bug, and a wolf spider all squished together. Bulging eyes, hairy legs, huge pointed fangs, and distorted bodies were all Drake could see. Their wings were grotesque and torn, as though they had been tattered and beaten in a tangle of wars. Drake knew he had to win them over in order to survive.

The boy took a deep breath. "My name is Drake, and I come in peace." His mind fumbled for the right words as an image of Sponke pervaded his thoughts. "I know Sponke and he…he is my friend." Drake didn't know why he thought that knowing Sponke might help, but it was all he had. He closed his eyes then reopened them. "I have lost my way. I need your guidance out of the heart of this forest."

Drake's speech seemed to be working as the illuminated insects stopped crashing into him. One of the larger bugs flew to a branch hanging down in front of Drake's face. He responded in a voice that was deep and echoing.

"You are not a threat to us and we know this. We have great difficulty trusting outsiders, but I sense…something…in you.

Normally, we would have ripped you to shreds by now." The large bug grinned, baring his jagged teeth. "However, at the mention of Sponke's name, we will let you pass. I am sorry to be the bearer of bad news, but you are not yet in the heart of this wicked forest." The bug laughed. "You would only be so lucky if *we* were the most dangerous creatures you will encounter. There are far worse than us to meet. We will take you through the heart of these woods to ensure that you survive. However, the rest of the journey is up to you."

"Thank you. Thank you so much…I'm sorry, I don't know your name." Drake tried not to sound too relieved.

"My name is Kreeper. We are the kreetons. I will loan you two of my clan members."

He summoned two kreetons who were much smaller than he was. The eerie leader spoke to them in a language Drake could not understand. The creatures nodded and immediately flew to either side of Drake. They perched upon his shoulders.

Each kreeton had talon-like claws that dug into Drake's skin. He winced at the pain, but kept a straight face. Drake desperately thought back to *Luke of Kropite*. Like Groger, Sponke, and Irick, Drake could not recall reading about Kreeper, or his followers.

Maybe the book is some kind of guide, but how?

A sickening clammy-warmth issued from the bugs' skins, making Drake queasy. A constant whirring emanated from them, shaking Drake from his shoulders down to his toes. Quite possibly the worst part of his situation was the burdening weight of each creature. They had him struggling just to keep upright. He *had* to appear strong. With as much confidence as he could muster, he stood erect.

Kreeper began to speak again, but this time there was less of an echo in his voice. "Jaden is on your left shoulder, and Jude is on your right. They will lead you through the heart of the forest, making sure you get to its outskirts safely. You will travel approximately three miles from the heart before you are out of Bleet. You must use Jaden's light first. When his light is gone, you will use Jude's light. Do you understand?"

"I think...how do I use them?" Drake asked.

Kreeper smirked. "Jude will instruct you as you make your way. Listen to him and he will not steer you wrong." The leader flew directly up to Drake, practically touching noses with him. "Good luck, and *don't give up*," he whispered. Just then, he dropped five black stones into Drake's hand and nodded him farewell. Drake, without question, placed the stones in his pocket and returned Kreeper's nod.

Drake walked away from Kreeper, moving deeper into the forest. He was unsure of what to say to either of his new companions. The light from Jaden's body grew brighter. He soon moved off the boy's shoulder and flew a little ahead of Jude and Drake to create a well-lit path for them to follow. With his lightened load, Drake's pace quickened. They traveled for at least half a mile in absolute silence, with the exception of Jaden's whirring.

Finally, Jude spoke. "Master Drake, why do you come all this way?"

Drake took a deep breath to gather his thoughts and spoke in a whisper. "I'm looking for my sister. She's missing and I'm pretty sure she's here in Kropite."

"Why do you think she is in Kropite?"

"It's kind of a long story."

"We do have some time. This forest is quite large, and we have a little while before we reach its depths where we must be silent."

69

A nauseous ache flitted in Drake's stomach, but he decided to tell Jude some of the things he had been through so far.

"You are a marvel, aren't you? To come all this way to look for a mere sibling is very impressive."

"Wouldn't you look for your sibling if something happened to them?" asked Drake.

"Absolutely not! My siblings are my enemies. I would rejoice."

Drake's eyebrows narrowed as he drew back his head.

"Our kind has to fend for themselves from the very beginning. After hatching, we need to take flight immediately and hide from one another. Our goal is to escape before an adult makes a meal of us." Jude grinned. "If a sibling is close, we often use them as a decoy in order to escape. If we are successful, we live in hiding for several days. When we feel it is safe, we seek out a clan. If we're lucky, a family-clan is established and it starts over again."

Drake's eyes, nose, and mouth scrunched inward. "You mean…you would eat your own child?"

"Oh, yes indeed! What a tasty treat a young kreeton makes!" Jude drooled a little.

"That is *so* wrong."

Jude looked confused. "Why is this so wrong? Is this not how you do things?"

"No way. My parents take care of me, love me, and help me whenever they can."

"Are they able to help you now?"

"Well…no, not now. They don't even know I'm here."

"Would they help you if they could?"

Drake did not respond right away as his mind drifted to thoughts of his parents. He thought back to all of the times his father would let him help while he worked on his boats and cars in the garage. His dad owned a local marina, and Drake loved to hang out there whenever he could. He remembered going to funny movies with his family. His dad would laugh so hard and loud that people would turn around and stare. Drake would get so embarrassed, but what he would not give to hear his dad's crazy laugh right now.

His mother was fun, strong, and determined. She used to be a fourth grade teacher at Cape Coast Elementary School. However, two years ago, she became an author. His mother created imaginative picture books for children about local legends and historical events that took place in Cape Coast. She had so many stories about their neighborhood. He used to think that she made most of them up, but he didn't care if she did.

Drake knew his parents would be right here by his side if they could.

"Yes. Absolutely. My parents would be here, and they would help me find Bailey."

Jude knew he struck a nerve in Drake. "Then why did you come alone?"

"I don't know. I just ended up here. I met Sponke and Groger when I first got to Kropite, but some crazy, giant bird picked me up and dropped me in the middle of nowhere. Then the same stinking bird came back and forced me into Bleet."

Jude tilted his head. "A crazy bird?"

"Yeah. I think it wanted to eat me." Not knowing how far they had traveled, Drake turned to Jude. "Hey, how close are we to the heart of Bleet?"

"Ah, we are close, but not quite there yet," Jude responded.

Drake felt as though they had been walking for miles. Just as he was about to continue probing Jude for more information, three unbelievably terrifying things took place: a resounding roar erupted, Jaden's light went out, and an incredible force crashed into Drake from behind.

Every ounce of breath rushed from Drake's lungs as he crashed to the forest floor. He rummaged around on the ground frantically searching for something with which to defend himself. Panic consumed him, making it all that much harder to breathe. He needed to clear his mind. He forced himself to sit perfectly still, and breathe.

Drake sat motionless for several moments before he realized the roaring had stopped. He dared not move or make a sound, though his heart beat hard against his chest. Sweat beaded on his forehead. A steady hissing circled the boy, telling him something large was very close. The leaves scuffed across the ground as the creature pushed itself along. These sounds were not the same skittering of tiny feet he had heard at the beginning of Bleet. This creature slid across the dirt and leaves.

A whisper of hot breath caressed his ear. "Be still, Master Drake. Do not speak." Jude remained quiet for several moments. "We are in the presence of a terrifying evil. This is not something you want to see, so it is fortunate that Jaden's light ran out." He rested a hand on Drake's shoulder. "The creature is not aware of us just yet. *Please*, calm yourself, or the beast will be able to hear your pounding heart." Jude drew closer to Drake's ear. "Slowly stand up."

Placing his hands on the ground, Drake pushed himself to his feet. As he unfolded his body, every muscle throbbed, but he dared not make a sound. Drake closed his eyes and tried to imagine himself anywhere but in these dark woods. He concentrated on slow, methodical, noiseless breaths. He pictured himself at home, in his room, rocking in his chair. Drake stood motionless. A scaly, slithering body bumped into Drake's shin. He caught his breath, refusing to release it. The creature's skin continued to brush Drake's shin as it slid on and on, pulling its body deeper into Bleet. Images of the world's largest anaconda passed through his mind. Drake remained unflinching until the creature had disappeared.

CHAPTER 7

Mezork

Jude drew close to Drake's ear once again. "I think it's gone. We have to move now. I'm not going to use my light just yet, but if you will reach into your pocket and grab one of the stones that Kreeper gave you, that would be most helpful."

He retrieved one of the stones and tried to hand it to Jude. "No, you must do it."

"What do I do?" whispered Drake, afraid the snake-monster might come back.

"You must hold the stone tightly in your hand while picturing in your mind what you need most right now," responded Jude.

Drake held the smooth, polished stone and pictured Jaden's light. Within seconds the stone emitted a dim glow. It was just enough for the travelers to make out a path. Jude situated himself back onto Drake's shoulder as they moved down the poorly lit lane.

Low squawks and shrill squeals pulled Drake's gaze in every direction. Large shadows loomed ahead, darting in and out of the trees.

"Where's Jaden?" Drake whispered.

"We are done with him. He flew home to renew his light."

Drake nodded then turned his head to look at Jude. "What was that thing back there?"

Jude touched Drake's forehead with a gnarled finger. "That was a hide-a-bind. We are quite lucky we heard him before he heard us. They usually slink among the trees, slithering under leaves waiting for their prey. When they sense something is close, they move quietly and wrap themselves around it. Their prey can't even feel them until it's too late. They work their way to your head, swallowing you whole while you are still alive. It's a most appalling death."

"Why didn't it find me? I mean it even *crashed* into me—"

"Shhhhh," Jude whispered. "No more talking. We are in the heart of the forest."

Slowly, the light from the tiny stone grew dimmer. The darkness was closing in on him again. He couldn't think straight as fear gripped his heart, disturbing its natural rhythm. Distress poured over him as uncontrollable shaking seized his body. The simple task of breathing became difficult. With shaking hands, Drake held the stone, watching its light melt away. Within seconds, darkness blinded him.

Drake stopped in his tracks, unable to feel his feet. He tried to move to no avail. No longer feeling the weight of Jude on his shoulder, he realized he was alone again. Waving his arms in front of him, he could feel nothing. It was an endless world of darkness that Drake hated with his whole being. *When I get home, I will never turn out my light again,* he silently vowed.

Drake wanted to scream, but could not find his voice. He had never felt more alone in all his life. It was a world of nothingness. Determined to speak, he reached way down deep, summoning what little voice he had.

He whispered, "Jude? Jude, where are you?"

Jude did not reply. Drake whispered out repeatedly, but Jude was unresponsive. Reaching out with both hands, Drake felt around him. He advanced, keeping his arms outstretched. Blindfolded in darkness, his eyes refused to adjust to his light-less environment. A low rumble reverberated above him, traveling through his body and into the ground. The rumble shook the forest floor. A stillness soon followed, halting Drake's efforts. He stood clenching his teeth to stop them from chattering.

"Who's...there?"

Drake's response came quickly. Behind him, a flurry of wind lashed up followed by a thud. He knew something had dropped from the trees, but he refused to turn around. The creature grunted in the shadows. The rumbling returned. Without a moment's hesitation, Drake leapt forward trying to escape. Powerful swooshes of air swirled around him. With one mighty thrust, he was struck from behind. The force sent Drake's flailing body soaring through the air.

Several yards away, Drake crashed to the ground, then rolled into a tree. He came to a rest with his legs in the air against the base of the tree. He lay where he landed for several moments, moaning and groaning. Soon that familiar warm breath wisped past his ear once again.

"Drake, don't move," Jude breathed.

"I wasn't planning on it. I don't think I could, even if I wanted to."

"Are you okay?" inquired Jude.

"Sure, after just being kicked about a *hundred* yards and smashing into this tree, I'm cool," Drake whispered.

"Okay. Good. I don't think it saw you. I'm fairly certain it has moved on."

"What is it now? Another hide-a-bind?"

"No, definitely not. It could only have been one of two things. It was either a zeekier, or a mezork. I would believe the latter of the two, because zeekiers travel in packs. This beast was alone."

"I don't know what these things are!" Drake nearly shouted.

"Calm down now, Drake. You must talk quietly." Drake took a deep breath and Jude touched his shoulder. "Let's see…zeekiers are a cross between…let me see…in your world, from what I know of it, I guess you could say it is closely related to a…goat."

"A goat? What's so scary about a goat?"

"Imagine, if you will, a goat that is five feet tall, seven feet long, with huge, sharp teeth."

"That doesn't sound so good," Drake responded.

"No, it's not. They are *extremely* irritable and, like I said, they travel in packs which can make the encounter much worse." Jude took a moment to ponder. "A mezork, on the other hand, is a solitary animal and a bit fiercer. It is a cross between a, what is it you call them, a jungle cat and a dragon."

"A jungle cat? Like a lion or a tiger?"

"Which one is white and has the stripes?"

"A white tiger?" Drake shouted.

"Shhhhh! That one then."

"Okay, so if it *was* a mezork, what is it capable of?"

"They are powerful, swift, agile beyond anything else, and—"

"Let me guess, they breathe fire," Drake interrupted.

"Yes, Drake, you are really catching on to our world now." Jude closed in tight next to Drake's ear. "Legend has it, the mezork is tamable. So I've heard anyway."

"Tamable, huh?" Drake's mind raced back to the rescuer from his dream.

"What are you thinking, Master Drake?"

"I was just thinking that if a mezork is tamable, maybe *I* could tame it. Then it can fly us out of here."

"Oh, wow, what a fantastic idea!" Jude smacked Drake's head. "Tame it? You idiot. *You* cannot tame it! A mere boy. There is no way you can tame a mezork."

"Why not?"

"Because you have no idea how to!"

"No, but you probably do. Right?"

"It is only a legend. I have never heard of *anyone* actually *taming* a mezork."

Drake clenched his teeth and grumbled as he bent his arm back to reach into his pocket. Pulling out another of Kreeper's stones, Drake rubbed it between his fingers.

"This stone gave me light back there. Can it heal me? I mean, can it make me be able to move again without this pain?"

"Yes, you just have to do the same as you did before, only think about healing."

A grin spread over Drake's face. "I'm gonna do this!"

Drake held the smooth stone tightly in his fist. Thoughts of being able to walk again ran through his mind. In a matter of minutes, his body began to heal. He slowly got to his feet. "I need your light, buddy."

"No! I won't do it, I will not watch you kill yourself!" Jude yelled.

"I'm doing this with or without you. It's our only way out." Drake cut his eyes. "I can't take this forest any more, or the vicious creatures that live here. I'm scared out of my mind. Please help me."

Jude stared at him for several seconds then nodded his head. "Okay, but Kreeper is going to banish me for this." After looking at Drake a few moments longer, he made a soft groan. Jude closed his eyes and within seconds, a brilliant glow filled his hovering body.

Instead of riding on Drake's shoulder, Jude flew up ahead of him. Drake looked in the direction where he had encountered what he thought was a mezork. He saw a large shadowy figure and reluctantly inched toward it. Drake's steady breathing allowed him to focus on moving forward. He was surprised at how calm he felt.

Drake and Jude walked about a hundred feet before Drake realized they had company. Crunching and crackling of sticks sounded behind him. Warm, exhaled-air ruffled his hair, sending goose bumps down his back. Drake felt sure the creature following him had to be a mezork.

He turned his head slightly, focusing on the creature's thudding, booming steps. Even when Irick had been following him, his treads were nothing compared to what was behind him now. Thump. Slide. Thump. Over and over.

Jude, oblivious to what was happening, flew ahead while Drake continued his slow systematic steps. The boy sucked in a mouth full of air and let it gradually seep from his lungs. Closing his eyes as tightly as he could, he tried to envision anything besides being in Bleet Forest. He stopped walking. He focused on his steady breaths.

Drake turned around to meet his follower. Wide-eyed and gaping, Drake found himself face-to-face with a hybrid no one could have prepared him for. Although it was dark, Drake could see the beast well, as if it were producing its own light.

The mezork was tall, and had to strain its neck downward just to be on level with Drake. The size of the creature reminded him of a semi tractor-trailer. It appeared to be at least 30 feet long, head to tail. It had a white tiger's face with enormous frost-blue eyes, a huge, pearly-pink nose, and long, stiff whiskers twitching on either side of its muzzle. Great, gleaming-white canines hung over its lip. Its body glowed with velvety snow-white fur, and intermittent midnight black stripes crossed along its back. Despite the creature's frightening beauty, it was the enormous black dragon wings that captured Drake's eye.

The mezork gently pressed its nose against Drake. The boy stood, unblinking. A low rumbling sounded deep within the creature's belly. It rattled the forest. Continuing its low growl, it pulled its head several feet away from Drake's face. He could see its nose twitching. It was taking in his scent. Jude had gone on a few more feet before realizing Drake was no longer with him. He spun around in time to see the stare-down between Drake and the mezork. The kreeton gaped wide-eyed, floated to the ground, and tried to choke out a warning to his friend.

The low rumbling stopped abruptly. The mezork tilted its head. Slowly, it raised one of its immense paws and placed it against Drake's chest, which sent him stumbling backward. At Drake's movement, the mezork pulled back and let out a low hiss. It displayed its dagger-like teeth. Now doubting his plan, Drake scooted his body backward along the ground. He slid over the hard dirt using his hands and heels. The mezork watched as Drake got back to his feet, turned, and slowly moved away. Jude held up his hand trying to speak, but was still incapable of words. The kreeton hung his head and turned. He felt as though Drake had sealed his fate and couldn't bear to watch the large beast consume his defenseless friend. Jude dashed for home.

Drake pushed forward. He could see nothing in front of him. Holding his hands out, Drake made his way by pushing himself from tree to tree. A resounding growl sounded behind him, accompanied by the mezork's thumping footsteps. He moved farther into the woods.

The big cat's movements suddenly died away. Drake stopped his forward momentum. He grabbed hold of a nearby tree and pulled himself behind it. Pressing his back against the trunk, he tried to slow his rapid breathing. His chest heaved erratically. Flattened against the tree, he held his position for several minutes before relaxing his body, but he didn't dare move from his hiding spot.

An eerie quietness settled over the forest. Still smashed close to the bark, he turned around to face the trunk. Drake latched both hands onto the tree while moving just his head to the side. His face collided with thick, soft fur. The mezork stayed, unflinching, as Drake drew his head back to witness its bulky body directly in his path. He forced his gaze upward. The beast peered down at him.

The mezork lifted its head and yawned. As its jaws reconnected, the winged beast licked its lips and lowered itself to the ground. On eye level, it pushed its cold nose into his stomach. Drake bit at the inside of his cheek as he considered the wild beast. After only a moment's hesitation, he reached up to brush his hand along its muzzle. The fur was short and stubby near its mouth. Drake's hand skirted the mezork's eye causing it to blink. He brushed downward grazing its mouth. The mezork pulled its lips back, exposing its pointy canines. Drake jerked his hand away. Its blue eyes pierced Drake's as it tilted its head. The creature pushed at his hand with its nose as a house cat might.

Drake smiled as he stroked the giant feline again. At Drake's touch, a deep, grumbling purr rattled from the beast. Drake stared into its eyes. He felt more sure of these actions than he ever had about anything.

"It's okay. I'm a friend. You sure are beautiful."

The mezork's ears perked and twisted back and forth. Suddenly, an enormous, red, coarse tongue overtook Drake. The boy's eyebrows narrowed as he wondered, *Does it like me, or is it tasting me?*

The great beast continued its humming purr as Drake gently stroked its face. The mezork's hypnotizing eyes held the boy's gaze. There was comfort here, comfort like Drake had never known.

The winged-cat slowly pulled its head away from Drake, giving it a jerk.

"Can I? Can I really ride on you?"

Keeping his hand on the giant, he slid it along its neck talking to it all the while.

"I'm not afraid of you, not now anyway. I've never seen anything that even compares to you." The mezork laid its head upon its paws and continued its sedative purr. "Are you really going to let me do this?" he asked.

The big cat's ears continued to perk and twist as if taking in every word the boy uttered. It was as if it understood exactly what Drake was saying. Drake's hand slid through the cat's dense fur as he moved slowly toward the animal's wings. "I've never seen anything like you before." Drake glanced around. "I can't believe you actually live in this dark forest. Can you take me out of here? Can you leave this place?" Not expecting an answer, Drake continued his rambling, trying to convince himself that what he was doing was going to be okay.

He was tempting fate, but felt as though he had earned this creature's trust. Besides, the cat was his only ticket out. He positioned his foot on the edge of one of the mezork's wings, hoisting himself onto its back. It swiftly got to its feet and bellowed a most ferocious roar that echoed deep within the forest. The mezork's eyes glowed as Drake sat atop its back. The creature pawed at the ground, anxious to take flight, as if she could *sense* Drake's fear of the forest.

He smiled while calling to Jude, "Jude, come here! We've found a friend. I need you to come with me, to help me find my sister. Jude! Jude where are you?" Jude never answered. "Where could he have gone?" Drake looked around. Knowing Bleet was the kreeton's home, he hoped the bug was okay. With one last look around, Drake gave the mezork a gentle nudge with his heels. It spread its leathery wings. The winged-cat pumped them, sending dirt and debris swirling around Drake's head. Stunned by it all, he forgot to grab hold of the cat as it lurched forward and sprang into the air. Drake toppled head over heels and rolled from the mezork's back. He landed on the dirt in a twisted heap. Shaking his head, he watched his only release from the forest flap its way into the sky.

"Wait! Come back! Don't leave me!" he screamed into the black.

Drake felt his hope fly away with the mezork. There was a low thud to his right. He turned in the direction of the noise even though he couldn't see. The thudding grew louder and the ground beneath his rear shook. Drake jumped to his feet and reached to grab onto a tree. However, nothing was there. There was no trunk to seek refuge from whatever was hurriedly approaching him.

"Who's there?" he called out, his voice cracking.

The forest fell silent. He stood, unguarded, waiting. His heart thumped in his ears. Darkness surrounded him, leaving him unprotected from the monster that stood only inches from his face.

Hot breath smelling of rotten flesh wafted forward. Drake grimaced and pulled his head back. A roar shortly followed, sending saliva spurting into his eyes. He held deathly still while the beast drew so close that its dripping, wet nose touched Drake's cheek. Slime slithered onto his shoulder. Drake stood as stiff as a statue. A low, rumbling growl surfaced from deep inside the predator as it circled him. Its nose prodded him, taking in his scent. Stopping in front of Drake, the beast raised its head and howled into the dark abyss. Instinctively, Drake jerked his arm up as a shield. An unexpected gust of wind whipped above him. His attacker squealed in pain. A sudden ache shot through his arm as he glided up and out of the forest.

Drake knew exactly what to expect. With squinted eyes, he looked upward and there it was, his mezork, pulling him to safety. The mighty beast gently clamped Drake's arm in its mouth and, just as he had dreamed, the pain did not bother him. It carried him outside of the forest and delicately placed him upon the ground. He rubbed at his arm. Drake glanced at his sleeve observing trickles of blood soaking through his shirt, a scrape, really. Then it hit him. The darkness was gone. He could see!

The mezork lowered itself to the ground and Drake happily climbed onto its back. "Let's get out of here!" he yelled as he clung to its fur.

The mezork hurled itself into the air. It reached a great height in no time, rising higher and higher toward the clouds. As if riding in an elevator, Drake's stomach lurched. He clutched tighter to the mezork. With heaving gusts, its giant wings pushed them into the clouds. Thick mist hung in the air, making it impossible to see anything, but Drake didn't care. He was out of Bleet. This blindness was a welcome reprieve. The mezork dipped just below the clouds and Drake sucked in a mouth full of crisp air. He closed his eyes, relishing in the freedom he felt. Wind whipped across his face and through his hair.

Soft shrills and a delicate humming caused Drake to open his eyes. Impulsively, he ducked behind the mezork's bulky noggin, hoping to hide from the creatures that glided just yards away. He thought of the huge bird that had abducted him and forced him into Bleet. He shuddered and rubbed his shoulder. The soreness had long since passed, but the memory festered.

Drake peeked over his carrier's head and watched the creatures acrobatically swoosh through the air. A full spectrum of colors covered massive wings that stretched at least fifteen feet across. Some had sharp, pointed heads with beaks to match, while others had smooth, rounded heads with beaks much too large for their faces. These majestic birds made the most incredible noises—something between a whistle and a hum. They glided through the sky, flying in circles around Drake. The mezork was completely unfazed by them as they flew within inches of it.

The cat-dragon flapped on, leaving the birds to continue their dance above Bleet. Drake glanced back and grinned then turned back to the mezork. He ran his fingers through its silky fur and soon became completely absorbed in the motions of the creature's head gently pitching back and forth with each pull of its wings. Reaching forward, Drake ran his hand through the fur on the beast's neck. Without question, Drake knew that nothing in Kropite could ever hurt him as long as his winged-savior was near.

"What should I call you? I don't even know if you're a girl or a boy." The mezork's ears twitched back and forth as Drake spoke. "You seem very gentle, especially since you didn't eat me back in the forest." Drake laughed a little. "You gave me a chance when you let me climb onto your back. A male cat would probably be too territorial." He rubbed the cat's fur. "You're a girl, aren't ya?"

A deep rumble echoed throughout the mezork's body. He was right. This creature was no doubt a girl, and she understood him.

"We need to give you a name, girl. How about Tigra? Or Fira? No...Sky Bird! Hey, how about Sky Tiger? No, no. It's got to be special, not lame." The mezork flew on with perked ears.

Unsure of why, his mind wandered to a report he had done in school last year. His class was studying Native American tribes of Eastern North America. After several weeks on the unit, Drake's teacher assigned them a research project on Native American tribes of the mid and western regions of North America. Drake had chosen the Chippewa Nation, because he hadn't heard much about them.

He discovered the Chippewa warriors were brave and determined, yet friendly. These traits forged a connection with Drake, making him want to learn more and more about this tribe. Drake grinned as he recalled the unique names he encountered in his research. His mind whirled with one name after another until finally the perfect name surfaced.

"I'll call you Migisi. It means *eagle*. I think that's a perfect name for you! What do you think, Migisi?"

With the new name in place, Migisi let out an ear-piercing roar of approval. She headed upward, flying just above the clouds. The sudden change in altitude left Drake clutching his mid-section. Migisi seemed to sense Drake's queasiness and descended just under the clouds.

"We need to fly a bit lower, girl. I need to figure out where we can land," Drake said as he rubbed his grumbling stomach.

He looked toward the ground, but they were still too high to make out the landscape below.

"Migisi, could you fly lower?"

Migisi immediately made her descent closer to the land. She glided just far enough above the ground to allow Drake to soak in the landscapes. The terrain was clean and pure. There were no houses or buildings, just wide-open fields leading into large forests. There was a small, crystal-clear lake ahead, with animals that Drake had never seen before drinking from it. He squinted his eyes taking in the peculiar creatures. Some appeared to be a mixture of buffalo and deer while others looked like a cross between a kangaroo and a monkey. Sitting up straight, Drake smiled then gazed below once again at the surreal paradise.

CHAPTER 8

Dragon Raiders

They continued flying close to the ground, but Drake was unable to decide where to land. "Migisi, I just don't know where to go."

With Drake's pleas, Migisi swung her head upward, pulling them higher into the sky. The cat-dragon's behavior drove Drake to assume that Migisi knew where she was going. He tried not to think about the queasiness that wriggled in the pit of his stomach as they soared higher into the air. Drake thought if he concentrated on the world around him, maybe he could dispel the motion sickness that seemed to demand his attention. He scanned the sky, but saw nothing except white clouds.

He instead focused on the details of Migisi's wings. He studied the leathery-skin stretched tightly over her large bones. Veins, thin as thread, crossed over one another and scattered in all directions. Closest to him were two sharp, spear-like points on both wings, jutting away from her body. Long bones split each wing into seven sections. The sectioned portions ended with six identical spearing points facing downward. Her wings gracefully flapped in unison.

He wondered if Migisi had spent her whole life in the darkness of Bleet Forest. Drake had always heard that the white and black of a white-tiger was camouflage. When he had made contact with her, she appeared to glow. This did not seem like effective camouflage. *On the other hand, does she really need camouflage? What could possibly be stupid enough to hunt such a powerful animal? So maybe Bleet isn't really her home. However, if it is, why does such a beautiful animal hide from everyone?* he thought. *I wonder where the other mezorks live. Do they call Bleet their home as well?*

Drake ran his fingers through Migisi's soft, dense fur, watching the black stripes blend into her gleaming white pelt. He had always longed to pet one of the white tigers at the zoo, and now, here he was sitting atop the largest tiger anyone from his world could ever imagine. Not only that, this tiger had *wings*!

Thinking like this relaxed the tension that filled his body. He smiled and sat back. They flew for quite a few miles before Drake asked, "Where are you going, Migisi?" She answered with a growl that stirred deep inside her. Drake dug his heels into her side as the mezork's whole body vibrated.

"What's going on, girl?"

He looked ahead. An enormous mass seemed to be barreling across the sky toward them. Drake strained his neck forward with squinted eyes. The low, unsettling growl continued. He grasped a tighter hold of Migisi's fur.

Within seconds, Drake identified five dragons beating their wings ferociously toward them. The scaled monsters were ashy-green in color with large emerald-colored wings. Individually, the dragons did not compare to Migisi in size, but reminded Drake of oversized flying horses. Nonetheless, he still felt outnumbered.

"Shouldn't we leave?" Drake yelled.

She tossed her head and let out an ear-splitting roar. Migisi stopped flying forward. She lightly whipped her wings, keeping her huge body hovering in the air. *She's waiting for them*, Drake thought to himself.

The dragons pulled to a stop several feet in front of them. Drake was able to observe the creatures clearly now. Each dragon had a rider—half-wolf, half-man. They wore protective gun-metal-gray armor and displayed magnificent swords strapped to their sides. The wolf-men snarled, gnashing their teeth. They pulled at their dragons' harnesses, demonstrating their dominance.

The wolf-riders circled around Migisi, trapping her on all sides. Her malicious, low growl resurfaced from her belly. One of the riders yelled out, "Why are you in our skies, intruder?"

"*Your* skies! I wasn't aware that anyone owned the sky," Drake retorted, shocked by his own bravery.

"You are wrong, youngling. We *own* these skies and you need permission to fly through," one wolf insisted. Another wolf joined the conversation.

"Who are you? What is this creature you are on?"

"My name is Drake, and this is Migisi."

"Migisi? What kind of ridiculous name is Migisi?" a snarling wolf asked, laughing. The remaining wolves laughed as well.

With narrowed brows, Drake responded, "If you will please just let us pass, we can get out of your way."

A snorting dragon steered by its wolf drew close to the mezork. "We are Dragon Raiders, and we say you *may not pass*. We *control* the skies. You and your flying friend need to go back to wherever it is you came from."

As the wolf spoke, the other four Raiders closed in tighter around Migisi. Without warning, the mezork raised one of her huge paws and swiped a Raider clean out of the sky. Both the Raider and his dragon bulleted downward then smashed into the ground.

The dragons roared and spit fire toward Migisi. Accepting their challenge, she reared her head back and let loose an enormous burst of fire, engulfing two more of the Raiders and their dragons. Their ashes fell to the ground as the last two watched, speechless.

One of the remaining Raiders pulled out a long, thin, fluted object and puffed into it. Drake covered his ears to protect them from the high-pitched sound it emitted. As he looked up, he saw many more Dragon Raiders approaching from the distance, heading straight for them. Drake pointed in the army's direction. Migisi reared up and roared. Grasping her fur tightly, he bent his body low, remaining close to the cat's back.

The Dragon Raiders reached Drake and Migisi, whizzing past them at blinding speeds, chanting and hollering. Once all of the soldiers had arrived, they crowded around them, continuing their random yelling. Some of them wielded their swords while others jutted spears up and down.

Suddenly, the shouting ceased. Drake sat up tall. The Raiders separated into two masses in the middle of the sky. They methodically created a clear, open path. A drum echoed from deep within the crowd of Dragon Raiders. From far back in the throng, a single black dragon made its way down the open passage. Perched upon the midnight dragon was a menacing creature, looking as though he arose right out of the Forest of Bleet. The grim Raider wore a dark helmet, so Drake was unable to see his face. Sidling up to them, the Raider removed his helmet.

Drake gaped in disbelief at a she-wolf sitting atop her dark dragon. The Raider's dark hair untwisted from the confines of the helmet, flowing down her back with the gentle breeze.

"I am Mallainy, and I am the *ruler* of the Dragon Raiders. You seem to be lost, youngling." Her voice calmed Drake.

Smiling at her, he said, "As a matter of fact, I am lost. I'm searching for my sister."

Mallainy gazed at Drake with piercing, yellow eyes, which caused Migisi to pull back a few feet. The fierce feline snarled at the dark leader. The black dragon whipped its wings forward to put a bit more distance between itself and the winged-cat. Mallainy glared.

"You need to keep your beast in check, youngling." Her words were so harsh Drake snapped out of his trance, seeing her for what she truly was.

"What? My friend doesn't seem to like you much, and I trust her instincts. Please let us pass and no harm will come to anyone else."

Mallainy leaned her head back and laughed at him. "I think the only harm will be to you and your friend. No matter how big your beast is you are undoubtedly outnumbered."

Drake looked around at all the Dragon Raiders. Several Raiders hurled their spears at Migisi. Instinctively, Drake ducked to avoid the sharp weapons. The pointed rods pelted Migisi, but bounced off her skin as if she were bulletproof. A few spears grazed Migisi's ear, causing a trickle of blood to run down her cheek. The mezork did not acknowledge the wounds. After the Raiders finished their assault, Migisi scanned her attackers. She pulled back her jowls revealing her thick, pearly teeth. A threatening hiss emitted from her wet mouth, spraying out her challenge. Drake could see the Raiders' awe, and their fear.

Unhappy with the results, Migisi stretched one of her huge paws, to expose her deadly claws. As she swatted at the air, several dragons flew backward, dodging the mezork's blows. She raised her head and exhaled her fiery-breath skyward in warning.

Unfortunately, the Raiders did not take heed of Migisi's signals. Instead, they held their ground, pumping their weapons into the air. *These guys are dumb*, Drake thought. He could feel the mezork's muscles rippling beneath him. Her body grew stiff and ridged as the hackles rose on her back. "This is gonna be awesome," Drake said under his breath. He tightened his body, holding on with all his strength, preparing for his friend's brutal attack.

Migisi swung her massive head through the air, knocking several Raiders off their dragons. They screamed while they fell to the ground. She swiped her paws through the air at several others, sending them to their deaths as well. The mezork began jerking her body while churning her wings up and down, creating huge gusts of deadly wind. Scores of Raiders plummeted. She exhaled her burning breath upon the others, creating her own path through the chaos. The fire continued to bellow from Migisi as she lunged ahead. The army was no match for her.

Raiders fled to escape a fiery death. In their departure, Drake glanced back to see Mallainy commanding her wolf-men to attack. Most of the remaining Raiders disobeyed her, fleeing for their lives. The skies cleared, leaving the leader only five men to order her offense on Drake and Migisi.

The odds are getting much better, Drake thought with a proud smile.

"Migisi, you have five more Raiders on your tail!"

She swung her head to confirm Drake's warning. The mezork let out her deep-throated growl while moving into a speed Drake had not yet experienced. Racing ahead, she left the Dragon Raiders far behind. Migisi did not slow her pace until she felt sure she had enough distance between herself and the sky-soldiers.

Drake exhaled loudly and released his tight hold of Migisi's fur. He slumped close to her back, relaxing his muscles. Without looking, Drake reached forward to caress the back of her head. Her fur felt moist. Drake pulled back his hand to find it wet and red. Pulling himself closer, he saw droplets of blood trickling from a gash in her ear.

Drake sat up straight. "Migisi, I think we need to land."

She made her descent toward a large sprawling field below. They landed next to a creek, cutting through the middle of the field. Drake slid from Migisi's back and led her to the water. She slumped to the ground then proceeded to lap up the clean liquid. Drake examined her wounds. He pulled off his shirt and dipped it into the water. He gently dabbed at her gashes, but the cat nosed him away, only to lick at them herself.

"Fine, be that way," Drake said, smiling. He snapped his shirt in the air then pulled it back on. Drake wandered a few feet away, collapsing to the ground with a grunt. Sitting back against a large rock, he watched his huge friend clean herself. Just as a house cat might, she licked at her soft, bulky paws then rubbed them over the nicks and scrapes on her ears and head. She continued her systematic doctoring for several minutes, then pulled herself to her feet. She dipped her coarse, red tongue back into the water.

Drake watched her, mesmerized by her slow steady movements. With the retreating sun, his eyelids grew heavy, but he sat upright, shaking his head, wanting to interrupt the drowsiness. His stomach rumbled with hunger. He gazed around wondering what he could eat. Just then, a fishy odor wafted from the creek. Migisi was catching an evening meal.

Drake watched as she pulled fish after fish from the cool water. Instinctively, he searched for a bare patch of ground. Upon finding an adequate spot, he dug down an inch or two with his hands. Next, he gathered some rocks lying nearby and encircled his shallow hole with them. After collecting small branches and twigs, he arranged them into a neat pile inside the circle of rocks. Grinning at his creation, he waited for Migisi to finish fishing.

He slumped back to the ground and proceeded to sharpen a few extra sticks on a large rock. Drake smiled and nodded his head while spinning the small spears in his fingers. Glancing up, he noticed Migisi was no longer fishing, so he jumped to his feet and scurried to the creek's edge.

Gazing at her, he said, "Hey girl, can I have some of your fish?"

Migisi eyed the fish then Drake. She lowered her head, pushing some of her catch toward him with her nose. Drake gathered them into his arms and carried them over to his makeshift fire pit.

After Migisi had eaten her fill, she padded over to where Drake was sitting. He pointed at the woodpile. Migisi obliged, breathing out a spark of fire, igniting the wood. Drake skewered several fish with his handmade spears and held them over the flames to cook. Remaining close to the fire's warmth, he ate until his stomach could hold no more.

Migisi stayed close, watching Drake feast, appearing quite pleased with her role as provider. Soon it began to grow dark, and Drake could no longer fight his drowsiness. He promised himself and Migisi they could continue exploring Kropite later.

"Let's try and get some sleep, girl. We can figure out where to go in the morning." Drake curled up close to his furry friend.

The confrontation with the army of Dragon Raiders had proven exhausting, even though Migisi had done all the work. His mind floated into an abyss of serenity and relaxation.

Drake's body hovers unaided just above the ground. He floats along a dirt road. As if on a conveyor belt, moving to parts unknown and against his will, the road leads him to a small dwelling almost completely concealed by vines and brush. A white cottage sits just off the road, nestled between two huge, ragged oak trees. The trees loom over the house like guardians. Massive outstretched limbs snake over the roof, wrapping around either side of the cottage. Drake cannot fight an overwhelming feeling that the trees are looking directly at him, daring him to enter.

Trying to move his feet, he makes a feeble attempt to turn around and run. He desperately wants to rush in the opposite direction to get as much distance between himself and the sinister house as he can. But his body is still out of his control.

"Why am I here?" Drake wonders as he continues sliding toward the front door. Trying to dig his heels into the ground, he makes a last attempt to stop himself, but fails.

"No. Wait!" he shouts, watching his hand rise on its own to turn the knob. The door swings open, shedding a profound light that meets Drake head-on. The high-powered spotlight penetrates his eyes to their very core. Shielding his face, he floats over the threshold. The intensity of the light makes it impossible to see anything in front of him.

"Why am I going in here? Where am I?" he questions while trying to grab onto something, wanting to stop himself from moving farther into the house.

"No!" he finally shouts. The electricity to the whole world disconnects, leaving Drake motionless and in absolute darkness. He waves his arms, hoping to connect with a piece of furniture or something to grab hold. There is nothing. The room is completely void of anything. Drake stops his search dropping his arms to his side. He stands feeling helpless.

"Why am I here?"

"You need to stop, Drake. Stop trying so hard," a voice echoes from the darkness. Fear prevents Drake from deciphering whether it is a man or woman speaking to him. "Who are you?"

"It doesn't matter who I am. It matters who **you** are. You need to stop trying so hard."

"Trying so hard? I don't know what you mean. What am I trying to do?"

"I cannot tell you that. You have to **listen** to me."

"I'm trying, but I don't understand."

"Drake, you have a purpose here, and you will soon find out what that purpose is. I need you to trust me. Let go. Let go of your fears. They're holding you back. If you cannot let go, then you will never accomplish what you need to. Believe, Drake. You have to **believe!**"

"Believe in what? Are you talking about Bailey? Do you know where my sister is?"

"Drake, there is so much more to you than you'll ever know. Bailey is…" the voice trails off into nothingness.

"What? Bailey is what? Tell me, please. I don't understand!"

Drake falls to the floor. He is no longer hovering and has regained control of his body. Slowly, he pulls himself onto his knees then forces himself to stand. Urging his feet to move, he struggles to feel his way back to the door.

"I need to get out of here!" Drake inches through the house in what he thinks is the direction of the door. The room is still pitch-black, yet he is able to move through relatively easily with nothing obstructing his path.

Drake reaches to feel in front of him. His hands meet a stark, clear wall. Drake slides his fingers along the wall, hoping it will lead him to an exit. After stumbling past a viewless window, he finally makes his way to a door. Drake grasps the knob forcefully and jerks it open. A cool breeze and trillions of stars greets him as he shuffles out of the house.

The brisk night air meets his skin sending a burst of energy rushing through him. He sprints back to the dirt road. Once on the road, he turns and peers back toward the cottage. The trees that once stood gnarled and stationary begin to move. At first, he believes it might be the wind setting the branches in motion. However, he soon sees that the slight breeze in the air is not strong enough to move the massive limbs. He watches as one of the tree's large branches, acting as an arm, wraps around the little house. It gathers it as a mother might do to her child, cradling it, rocking it back and forth.

Drake spins around and dashes down the dirt road. He runs on and on until he feels a safe distance from the twisted scene he has just witnessed.

*Slowing his pace, he begins talking to himself. "Why can't anyone help me? I just want to find my sister, and get **out** of here."*

"Drake!" a voice screams, interrupting him.

Drake's heart races.

"Don't be scared, it's me, Sponke."

"Where are you? I can't see you."

"I'm not far. You have to find me..." Sponke's voice trails off.

Drake woke. Sitting up, he rubbed his eyes. "Oh man, what a dream."

CHAPTER 9

I'm No Hero

Drake got to his feet and looked for Migisi. He spotted her, perfectly poised like a statue, down by the creek. He strode over, stopping within feet of the large cat. She slowly bent her head to look down at the boy. Her blue eyes glistened in the morning sun. She blinked once, and then yawned, baring her gleaming teeth and floppy tongue. Drake grinned as he walked closer to her. The mezork lowered herself to the ground and placed her head upon her bulky paws. Still grinning, Drake ran his hand along her neck. Drawing his face close, he gently tugged at her ear. Migisi turned her head, allowing the boy to examine her wounds.

"Nothing more than a few nicks. You're one tough girl, Migisi."

The mezork leaned her head into his hand then brushed her cheek across his body. Drake stumbled back and chuckled. Moving close again, he continued to stroke her bulky head while the dragon-cat closed her eyes and released her sedative purr.

"I don't know about you, old girl, but I sure am hungry."

Migisi pulled herself to her feet and instantly dipped her face into the creek. Within seconds she surfaced with a wriggling fish caught between her teeth. The mezork laid the fish at Drake's feet. The boy smiled, picked up the fish, and carried it back to the fire-pit he had constructed the night before.

After breakfast, Drake rubbed his stomach and sighed. He got to his feet and stretched. "Maybe we need to explore a bit more. I've got a feeling we're close to my friend, Sponke. Are you up for some more flying, Migisi?"

The mezork swung her head, purring her response. Drake took this as a definitive yes and placed his foot delicately upon the base of her wing. He issued a small grunt as he hoisted himself onto her back. She rose to her feet, sending a ripple through her body. This sudden motion sent Drake scrambling to hold on as his legs flopped over her side. He swung his legs back into place and tried to make himself comfortable. Once securely settled, Drake gave her a nudge with his heels.

Migisi loped along, gathering momentum with each stride. In seconds, the mezork was running at top speed with long bounding paces that induced the muscles under her shoulder blades to jerk back and forth. Her motions were so fluid and light that he could barely feel when her feet touched the ground.

Migisi ran on and on without slowing. Drake swore they had traveled several miles before she finally stretched her wings. She pumped them in beat with her strides. Gusts of cool air encircled Drake, creating a wind tunnel effect. He settled in close, grasping her fur, pressing his knees into her body, and hunkering close to her neck. The queasy sensation in the pit of his stomach resurfaced at the anticipation of the thrust that would launch Migisi's body into the air. The force pulled Drake's body back, making him grasp hold of her fur as firmly as he could. Visions of sliding off the mezork, just as he had in Bleet, caused him to pull in even closer.

With wings steadily pumping, Migisi sprang into the sky. A sense of giddiness spread through Drake causing him to laugh. Surprised by his response, he gathered himself and smiled. He looked around and observed Migisi's graceful movements and the pristine landscape below. The sky was clear this morning without a cloud in sight. He soaked in every moment.

They flew on and on, faster and faster. Trickles of moisture ran down his cheeks as the wind whipped into his face. It stung his eyes. He squinted and crouched just behind her head to block the wind enough for him to see.

"Hey girl, we need to fly a bit lower. I need to figure out where it is we're going."

He felt foolish for saying this, as he had no idea where he was, let alone where he was going. Migisi followed his orders though, making her descent. They flew close to the ground for several miles while Drake scanned the land below. He was not sure what he expected to find, but hopes of spotting his friends consumed him.

A clear lake opened before them and Migisi swept low, skimming so close that her dangling paws dipped into the water.

Startled by the swishing, Drake peered over her side. He grinned as he watched her large, bulky feet slice the lake. She pulled her paws up, climbing just high enough to clear some trees up ahead. He reached out, wanting to touch the treetops but stopped himself. *My luck, I'd get caught on a branch and fall*, he thought.

On the other side of the small forest, the winged-cat dipped low and flew close to the ground once again.

"I don't know where they could be, Migisi." Drake hung his head. A low growl rumbled from Migisi causing Drake to look up. "What is it, girl?" he asked with squinted eyes. Drake stared ahead. He spotted something large and moving clumsily.

"I think it's Groger! Look, Migisi, it's my friend down there!" Drake pointed in Groger's direction. Migisi took Drake's cue, aiming right toward him. "I can't believe you found them," Drake said with narrowed brows. "It's like you knew where to go all along!"

Groger, as usual, was oblivious to his surroundings. Sponke, however, was the first to look up and notice the descending mezork.

"Look out Groger, we're under attack!" Sponke screamed as he dove under Groger's shirt.

"Huh? What is you talkin' 'bout, Sponkie?" Confused, Groger glanced upward.

"Oh my goodness!"

He sank to the ground and covered his head with his arms. A muffled squeal rose from the terrified giant. He trembled as Sponke shimmied even further into his shirt.

Migisi swooped to the ground and landed with a powerful thud. Her feet pounded the dirt as she steadied her body. The mezork stopped directly in front of the giant, folding her wings to her sides.

Drake's brow rose slightly as he sat atop the large cat with his eyes glued on the cowering giant. "Let me down, girl."

Migisi lowered herself to the ground. Drake slid from her back. He stumbled as he tried to find his footing. Drake reached back and patted Migisi. He walked over to Groger and knelt down beside him. "Hey, it's me, Drake. It's okay. She's not going to hurt you." As Drake spoke, he gently placed his hand on Groger's back.

"Huh?" was all Groger could say. He slowly emerged from hiding beneath his arms.

"Master Drake...it's really you?" spluttered Sponke. The distressed bug flew out from under Groger's shirt and hovered.

"Yeah. Where have you guys been?"

"Where have *we* been? Where have *we been?* Sponke repeated. "We've been searching for *you!* Ever since that flaming foradore plucked you from our camp, we have been beside ourselves with worry." Sponke abruptly stopped talking, gazed past Drake, and shivered. Drake glanced back at the mezork as well.

"She's awesome, isn't she?"

"A monster. You've brought a monster with you?"

"She's not a monster. She's as gentle as a kitten." Drake smiled at her. "Her name is Migisi."

At the mention of her name, Migisi swished her tail and angled her head.

Sponke buzzed close to Drake's ear and perched on his shoulder. The bug scrutinized the big cat. The mezork stared back at Sponke, and then opened her mouth in a massive yawn. "Migisi? What's a Migisi?" Sponke responded, his head cocked to one side.

"Oh she's not *a* Migisi, she's a mezork...you know, half-dragon, and half-white tiger. I just named her Migisi because it means—"

"*This* is a mezork?" Sponke interrupted. "I've never seen one, in *all* my days. I've only heard legends of them. They are very fierce creatures, only tamable by—" Sponke stopped mid-sentence. His eyes grew large.

"What's wrong, Sponke? Finish what you were going to say."

Sponke flew from the boy's shoulder and hovered silently before Drake. After several moments he said, "Drake, where did you find this creature?"

"She kind of found me. I was walking through Bleet with a kreeton named Jude, and there we were—"

"Wait—" Sponke interrupted again, "—you were in Bleet? I can't believe you'd survive." Groger said nothing, but continued to gawk at the mezork.

"I'm lucky to be alive. I owe a lot of my success to Jude. Hey, do you know a kreeton named Jude?" Drake asked.

"Jude? Yes, he's an old family friend. If you traveled with Jude, you must have spoken to Kreeper as well."

"Yeah. He was a pretty cool guy. Creepy, but still cool. He lent me two of his people—Jaden and Jude—but he only really spoke to me after I mentioned your name."

"You, Master Drake, are a very lucky boy. Do you know what lives in Bleet?"

"I kind of found that out the hard way. That bird, what did you call it?"

"A foradore?"

"Yeah, the foradore pushed me into Bleet and wouldn't let me back out."

"You say the foradore *pushed* you inside of Bleet? Why didn't it just carry you away as before?" Sponke asked while scratching his head.

"I have no idea. The thing kept pecking at my feet, like it was forcing me inside the woods. I really didn't feel like being eaten, so I went further into Bleet. If I had known that everything in the forest wanted to eat me too, I might have turned back to face the bird."

"The foradore pushed you in?" Sponke repeated.

"Why do you keep saying that? Look, I faced *way* worse monsters than the foradore in there." Drake held up his pointer finger. "First off, I was attacked by kreetons." Drake proceeded to raise his second finger. "Then a hide-a-bind nearly ate me!" The boy smirked while holding up a third finger. "Finally, my big furry partner here could have easily swallowed me in one gulp. I guess making friends with two out of the three isn't bad, right?" Drake said, reaching back to pet Migisi.

He told Sponke about his adventure with the rock benders and Migisi's small war with the Dragon Raiders. Sponke and Groger stood mute, listening with their mouths hung wide open.

"Hey, you were going to say something a minute ago. What was it?" Drake asked.

"Remember at the start of our journey when I stated that I would tell you everything you wanted to know?" Sponke said.

Drake nodded his head.

"I wanted to believe you were who I hoped you were, but my heart would just not let me *truly* believe."

"What are you talking about?"

Sponke put his head down, shaking it back and forth slowly. "I was worried about the safety of you and your sister. I thought it might just be a mistake, or maybe even a *coincidence,* that you happened to come to Kropite. I tried not to let it affect me too much, because if I did, I would be fraught with worry. I didn't really know you at all, yet I felt like I had known you *all* of my life. I was concerned about you and what would become of you if it were true."

"If what were true?" Drake asked.

"If you truly are the *one*. The one who is meant to help Kropite," Sponke finally said. "I had always heard from my parents that a hero would turn up when we desperately needed one." Sponke placed his small hand on Drake's shoulder. "Kropite really needs a hero, and here you are."

"A hero? Why am *I* a hero?" Drake glanced up to meet Sponke's gaze. "Why does Kropite need help? What's wrong with it?"

"Believe me, Drake, I want to tell you. I want to tell you *everything.*"

"What's stopping you?" Sponke refused to look him in the eyes. "I don't understand what's going on. Why am I supposed to help Kropite? I'm here to find Bailey."

"Yes, that's it!" Sponke squealed. "That's the answer! Something brought *Bailey* here knowing *you must follow.* You would have never come alone. That's why Bailey came first."

Drake tilted his head. "You've totally lost me."

"Okay, Drake. Don't get angry, but I have to make you wait a tad bit longer for all of your answers. We need to travel to the See-All-Lake, then I promise I will show you everything." Sponke looked behind him. "The lake is a great distance from here. It's not going to be an easy journey on foot."

"Not an easy journey? Has any of this been an easy journey? No! No, it hasn't! I'll wait for my answers, because it seems to me that all we have is time." Drake shook his head and raised his palms in the air. "I feel like I've been here for a week. My parents must be going insane with Bailey and me missing!"

"Oh, don't worry about that. Time works differently here."

"What do you mean, *differently?*"

"It is hard to explain. All I can tell you, based on what Luke has told me, is that time in Kropite is not like time in Cape Coast. Things move along on their own accord. Life travels forward and that is it. Don't think too much about it, Drake. I can assure you that your parents have no idea you're gone. No need to fret."

"So, Luke knows about Cape Coast?"

Sponke stared blankly at Drake unsure of how to respond. "You can ask Luke yourself when we find him."

Drake pointed at the fluttering bug. "You said that our journey wouldn't be easy on foot. Why are we going on foot when we have Migisi? She should have no problem carrying us to where we need to go, but you might have to show her the way."

"If what I have heard is true, this creature has very good navigational skills. I think finding the lake will not be at all difficult." Sponke smiled and patted Drake on the shoulder.

Drake turned toward the mezork and rubbed under her chin. "I guess we need to do some more flying. We need to find some lake." Drake continued to talk to the mezork as he ran his hand along her neck. He gently placed his foot onto the base of her wing and hoisted himself onto her back. Sponke and Groger both gaped at Drake's actions. "Let's go, Groger. You're next."

Groger shook his head and stepped backward. Sponke's eyes narrowed as he said, "Groger. Drake trusts her, and so do I. It's our quickest way to the lake."

Groger dropped his head and shuffled his feet toward the mezork. He stopped and peered back at the bug.

"Go ahead," Sponke instructed

Drake began to feel sorry for the giant and held out his hand. "Groger, it's okay."

Groger continued to shake his head as he carefully placed his foot on the base of the mezork's wing. With a heaving grunt, he hoisted himself atop the big cat. Drake reached back to pat the trembling giant on the arm and Sponke flew up to join them.

Sponke leaned in close to Drake's ear. "Groger is a bit of a baby at times. He just needs some reassurance."

"Hey Groger, you can trust me. Migisi likes me and she knows you're my friend. I promise, she won't hurt you."

"Okey dokey, Drakie. If you is saying so, but I am really not liking to fly. Specially on monsters. I try to be staying on the ground as much as it is possible."

Drake laughed and the threesome settled in for their flight. Sponke yelled, "To See-All-Lake, Migisi," The mezork raised her head offering her resounding roar. In no time, she was in the air soaring over Kropite with infinite ease. Drake grinned as he thought about his mysterious, flying friend. Depending on her mood, and whether she wanted to stretch her legs, she would run for miles before launching her body into the air. Other times she just leapt into flight from a standing position. Drake didn't question her actions because he was ecstatic just to be allowed on her back.

CHAPTER 10

See-All-Lake

Drake was glad to be back with his friends. He felt confident he was going to find Bailey now, especially with Sponke, Groger, *and* Migisi's help. He was amazed at how easily Migisi was able to fly with the load she was carrying. They piloted above the clouds for most of the journey, so Drake was unaware what lay below them. He hoped Migisi knew where she was going.

The mezork flew on, mile after mile, gracefully navigating the skies. She never appeared lost or misguided. She just seemed to sense her way. Eventually, Drake turned his head to look back at Groger. He chuckled as he observed his huge friend cowering with eyes clenched tightly. Sponke clutched onto Drake's shoulder, drawing near to the boy's ear.

"It is a *mighty* creature you have here, Drake."

Drake smiled. "She's amazing." Turning his head to face the bug Drake raised his voice so Sponke could hear him over the whipping wind. "Sponke, what did you call the creature that took me from camp?"

Sponke leaned in close. "A flaming foradore."

"Why did it take me?"

Sponke snickered. "My first guess would be…to eat you."

Drake gazed ahead, suddenly feeling a bit nauseous.

On and on Migisi churned her wings, pushing her hefty body through the crisp air. Sponke had long since nestled himself between Groger and Drake to take refuge from the gusty winds screaming past. Drake reached back every now and again to pat Groger on the arm. The giant would open his eyes for only a second, and then clench them shut again. Suddenly, Migisi dipped just under the clouds. Sponke drew close to Drake's ear and shouted for him to look down. He leaned out to peer around Migisi's bulky body. Like a mirror-ball, a vast lake sparkled below them, glistening and shimmering as if filled with billions of tiny pieces of glass. Its reflection was near blinding.

"Wow!" Drake mouthed.

Lush, thick grass surrounded the lake. There were various-sized boulders protruding out from the ground around it. Farther off to the right was a forest. Drake could sense this forest was not like Bleet. These woods were open and brighter, evoking a settling calm that made them inviting. Everything about this lake and its surroundings felt welcoming.

"That be it! Lookie, See-All-Lake!" shouted Groger who finally decided to keep his eyes open.

"How do you get this thing to land?" Sponke shouted.

Drake leaned close to Migisi's ear and softly asked her to land anywhere near the lake. She obliged instantly. After alighting with a jolt, her riders slid from her back. Drake smiled as he watched Migisi pad over close to the forest to curl up for a nap.

Sponke and Groger immediately started a debate on whether Migisi was more cat or dragon. Groger argued she was definitely more dragon, considering her wings and knowing the fire she was able to produce. Sponke, on the other hand, thought she was more cat, because of her body, and the sheer size of her claws and teeth. Drake found the dispute completely ludicrous because she was equally both in his mind.

Drake had experienced the power of her wings when they churned the air, knocking Dragon Raiders from the sky. He had witnessed her fiery breath as she blazed through an army to clear a path for their great escape. Drake had seen the gruesome devastation her powerful claws had unleashed on dragons and their riders. She was the most dominant species of any animal in the world, and one of a kind in his eyes.

Tired of his friends' bantering, Drake left them to their squabble. He walked over to the lake. The water shimmered in the sun. He looked out over the lake, captivated at how it sparkled. Growing up on the bay, he was around the water at all hours of the day. Never in his life had he seen water sparkle as this lake did. Its beauty was mesmerizing. Its waters lapped at the bank, whispering in his ear. The lake was calling to him. It pulled him closer. He knelt at the water's edge. Just as he was about to touch it, Sponke yelled at him.

"Please don't just stick your hand in there! You have no idea what could happen."

"Sorry. I couldn't help myself. It's just so perfect."

"I understand completely, but you have to be cautious in our world. Things are not always what they seem here. There is a special process we have to go through to make this work."

"Make what work?" Drake asked as he got back to his feet.

"To get the lake to show us what we need."

Drake rolled his eyes. "Oh, right." He looked back at the water. "Can the lake *really* show us everything?"

"Yes and no. It will show you bits and pieces, but you have to *think* and *say* the right things."

"Like with the stones Kreeper gave me?"

"Stones? What stones?" Sponke asked.

"Back in Bleet, Kreeper dropped five stones in my hand before Jaden, Jude, and I left. I've already used two of them. They really come in handy when you need something."

Sponke flew straight up, did three back flips, and landed upright on Drake's shoulder. "Do you realize how much *simpler* you have made our lives? I know about these stones. They are small but powerful. I feel they *will* be able to help us." Sponke grinned. "Now all we have to do is solve the Riddle of the Lake."

"What riddle?" Drake asked.

"The riddle should be around here somewhere," Sponke said while scanning the area.

"There!" shouted Groger as he scrambled toward a huge rock, much larger than all the others. *It looks like a tombstone*, Drake thought as he walked toward it.

Sponke was the first to reach the large stone. "Here it is, the Riddle of the Lake!" Groger arrived just behind Sponke with

Drake bringing up the rear. Drake leaned over the huge stone, rubbing his fingers along the scrolling words etched into it.

"Who put this here?" Drake asked.

"No one knows. It is a phenomenal thing though, isn't it?" Sponke replied.

"What do we do?"

"For starters, you can try reading it."

"That's a good idea," Drake said as he leaned over.

The lake will let you see all that you desire.
First you must solve these riddles in hopes that it will inspire:

It is small and delicate, but huge in power.
You may touch it, but beware, it's as fragile as a flower.

It is smart and cunning, yet not at first glance.
It's not very intelligent 'til its inner-light is enhanced.

Some don't believe, unless they can see
(Not a good idea unless you have the key).
You can see with your heart if only you try,
Open your mind and surely you'll spy.

It's all about imagination in the end,
Without this you're truly not able to fend
Off the evil that lurks all around,
Believe in yourself, or you will surely drown.

"We have to figure out a four-part riddle before we can even see anything in this lake?" Drake nearly shouted at Sponke and Groger.

They walked a few yards away from the riddle rock, and Sponke began explaining as best he could. "Not exactly. I think you have to answer the riddle bit-by-bit. With every portion that you answer correctly, it will show you different things. I've heard it's not a bad idea to offer the lake a gift with each answer."

"A gift?"

"Yes. Not an elaborate gift, something small and meaningful."

"Does everyone see the same thing?"

"No. When you answer each piece of the riddle, the lake's response will only be visible to you. I could be standing right next to you, and the lake would still appear perfectly clear to me. I believe this is just in case you have spies lurking about. It ensures there is no way for unwanted eyes to get a look into your thoughts."

"I guess I don't understand what it's going to *show* me," Drake said, now a bit calmer.

"I'm not sure what it will show you either," said Sponke. "I think it shows you what you want, or more importantly, *need* to see. For instance, if you asked the lake why you came to Kropite, it should reveal the answer to this question in some way or another. I truly think your question for the lake needs to be in your mind as you answer each portion of the riddle. I suspect it unveils more and more as you proceed."

"I need to be seeing that riddle again," Groger said as he meandered back over to the rock.

Drake watched Groger for a moment then said, "Is this riddle only meant for me?"

Sponke cocked his head. "What do you mean?"

"Is the riddle the same for everyone, or does it change for whoever needs information from it?"

"*This* riddle is only for you." Sponke nodded.

"That is so cool. So, all we need to do is ask the lake where my sister is."

"You have the right idea, Drake. But there is more to this."

"Of course. Nothing here is easy," Drake said. "Do you have to speak your questions out loud as you go?"

"No. They just have to be in your thoughts."

"What if my answer to the riddle is wrong?"

"I suppose if you answered it incorrectly, the lake would reveal nothing. My guess is you would have to keep trying."

"All right, let's get started then," Drake said, walking back toward the riddle rock.

"Hold on. First, we have to decide what it is you need to know, so you will be ready after each part of the riddle. I don't know how much time you have for thinking as you solve it," Sponke explained.

Drake nodded his head. "I want to see where Bailey is."

"I believe we need to start off a little simpler, like why the stone brought you here," Sponke interjected.

"That doesn't seem any simpler than my question. I came here because of Bailey."

Sponke let out a heavy sigh while shaking his head. "Let me explain a few things to you." Drake sat down on a nearby rock gazing at the bug. "Your world and our world are in danger. I have been trying to tell you that Kropite needs you. There is something going on that links your world to mine, and although I'm not sure what it is, I do know that Bailey is involved some-how." Sponke touched Drake's cheek. "I want to help you find your sister, and I will help you find her, even if it is the last thing I do." The bug shook his head. "I know it is hard for you to understand why I call you Kropite's hero. Honestly, I have had a hard time with this as well. A hero usually *wants* to help, but you don't seem to be a willing participant."

Drake looked away offended. "I want to help you, but you think I'm something I'm not. I'm just an ordinary guy, no hero. I am only a *kid* for crying out loud! I just want to find Bailey and go home."

"I know you do, Drake. That will happen, but we need your help along the way. You see, our world had a protector—"

"Luke is Kropite's guardian. What do you mean *had?*"

Sponke glared at Drake. "Yes. Luke. Someone has taken him from us. Groger and I have been searching for him ever since."

Drake sat quietly for several minutes. The words from his book, once again, poured through his thoughts. Originally from a world known as Zebenon, Luke and his people were called Helpers. Their leaders would assign them to places that were in danger of perishing. That is how Luke came to reside in Kropite. Initially sent as a child, Luke grew to prove to everyone that he was a warrior beyond warriors and the only one possessing the secret key to keeping this world safe. *Luke of Kropite* only spoke of a key, but never gave detail as to what the key was.

Eventually, Drake stood up and paced back and forth. He finally stopped and tried to speak, but he had no voice. With every passing moment, Drake's heart rate pulsed faster and faster. He attempted to calm himself by breathing slow, concentrated breaths. Sponke's wings beat furiously against the air, holding his body in front of the aggravated boy. He tilted his head and narrowed his eyes.

"Master Drake, *what* is *wrong?*"

Drake glared back. "Luke is missing? I thought in the beginning of all this mess, you were going to take me *to* Luke."

"Yes, we were hoping initially we might be able to locate Luke *through* you. You two are so alike."

"You're using *me* to find Luke? Just because I look like him, you thought this would help you find him?" Drake asked.

"I know it sounds bizarre, but it was all we had. You don't understand, because things are just different here." Sponke rubbed his head. "We think Luke and Bailey are together. A while ago, before you came here, a terrible explosion shook all of Kropite. Luke told us he needed to find out what caused the eruption and instructed us to wait for him." Sponke's face sunk. "We haven't seen him since."

Drake tilted his head to the side. "What caused the explosion?"

"Bailey."

"Bailey? How could it have been Bailey? She hasn't been missing for *that* long." Drake abruptly stopped when the realization of Kropite time hit him like a ton of bricks. "Oh, you mean it *has* been that long here on Kropite since Bailey came. How long after Bailey did I get here?"

"Remember, time is different here."

"That means Bailey has been missing for a lot longer than I thought. If anyone has hurt her, I swear—"

"Calm down, Drake. You see why we need to do this cautiously. There is a *lot* at stake."

Drake's hands trembled. "You really think Luke and Bailey are together?"

"It has to be more than just a coincidence that right after Bailey arrived, Luke disappeared," said Sponke. "Luke is vital to Kropite. Because of him, this is a safe and peaceful place."

Drake understood exactly what Sponke was describing; however, he could not recollect ever reading about Luke's disappearance.

"I just don't get it. I read the *whole* book and Luke never went missing. I don't remember reading about you and Groger either."

"Drake, you speak of a book. I don't know what you are referring to."

"I have a book about Luke and Kropite."

Sponke's eyes narrowed. "I'm confused."

"I am too. I just don't get it. The book is what I traveled through. It brought me here."

Sponke stared back at the boy with raised hands.

Drake groaned. "I was walking home from school, and I found a strange stone in the woods near my house. I took the stone home and put it under my book, *Luke of Kropite*. Then Bailey disappeared. One moment I was in my room and the next thing I knew, I was sailing through some crazy...wormhole thing, and found myself here."

"*Luke of Kropite*? My world isn't a book, boy. My world is a *real place*—" Sponke retorted, but stopped suddenly as his mind began to race. "Did you say you found a strange stone? I knew it! The stone *is* trying to help us, but why?" Sponke scratched the top of his head. "Okay, let me get this straight. You found a stone, set a book about *my* world on top of it, and this is how you came to be in Kropite?"

Drake nodded then summarized the book, *Luke of Kropite*. As he talked, Sponke's eyes grew wider and wider. Drake seemed to know Luke better than he did. But how? Drake had never even met Luke, yet he knew of his powers and all the exciting adventures he had experienced.

Drake went on to describe his encounter with the stone in the woods. He told him how he took it home and tried to hide it from Bailey, but she had obviously found it anyway. All through

Drake's account, Sponke's wings fluttered at such a speed the bug's whole body began to shake.

After Drake finished his story, Sponke said, "Drake, I have never heard a more foolish tale. However, there just might be something to this whole thing." Just then, Groger meandered back over and began clearing his throat. Sponke glared at the giant then back at Drake. "Give me some time, so I may think." He immediately flew over to the riddle rock and sat next to it rubbing his head.

CHAPTER 11

The Story Stone

Groger began to chuckle as he watched the retreating bug. He leaned over so only Drake was able to hear him. "Drake, I believe in you. I think you are what we have needed all along."

Drake jerked his head to gaze at the giant. "Groger, why are you talking like that?" he asked.

"I'm not as dumb as everyone thinks. It's more of an act than anything."

"Does Sponke know?"

Groger gazed at Sponke who was waving his small arms through the air and talking to himself. "No! He cannot know!

I feel it best if he believes he is the more capable one. He needs to feel as though he is responsible for making all the decisions."

"But why would—"

"Drake, please trust me. I have been listening to you both for a while, and I feel I might know how we can go about finding both Bailey *and* Luke. I have concluded there is an evil presence coming from *outside* of Kropite, but I don't think it is here to stay. I'm guessing its main objective was to take Luke from us and Bailey from you."

"Why?" asked Drake.

"I haven't figured that out yet," said Groger.

Drake shook his head. "This is all *too* much."

"What?" Groger asked with narrowed eyes.

"I come here and, at first, I think I'm dreaming. Then, this turns out to be some kind of *insane* reality. I find myself doing things that, just a short time ago, I had only read about in a book. I'm traveling around, battling creatures I thought were fictional. I meet you, Sponke, and Migisi." Drake turned toward the woods to check on his friend, still curled up and napping. "I have Sponke telling me I'm supposed to be some kind of *hero*, when I really don't feel very heroic. Groger, I think you guys might have this all wrong." Drake's right eyebrow rose. "Sponke's argument sounds good, but I just can't bring myself to believe it. I'm Drake, a boy from Cape Coast. Nothing more. I hate to disappoint you guys." He shook his head. "I don't want anything to happen to Kropite, but I just don't feel like I'm strong enough. I don't even know if I can save my little sister."

Groger chuckled. "I know this is a lot to absorb, but I think that over time you will begin to understand. There is so much more to you than you are *willing* to accept."

Drake furrowed his eyebrows and shook his head. "I hope you're right." He looked into the giant's eyes. "Maybe some of your confidence will rub off on me, and this will all turn out to be an awesome adventure after all. Don't get me wrong, it's been pretty cool up until this point." Drake gazed out across the lake. "And, if I'm supposed to become this great hero, well, that wouldn't be so bad, huh?"

"Not so bad at all. I think you should accept the challenge and face it head on. If you *are* in fact the chosen one, which I truly believe you are, you *do* have a sensational adventure headed your way." Groger smiled. "Never forget, you're not in this alone. We're here to help you."

"Thanks, Groger. That's a very good thing."

Groger smiled and patted Drake on the back.

"Can I ask you something?"

"Always."

"You don't have to tell me if it's too difficult…but what was your family like?"

Groger looked away and wiped at his eyes.

Drake bit at the inside of his cheek. "I'm sorry, you don't have to tell me. I was just missing my family and…I don't know."

"No, no, I'll tell you. It's just, I have only told my family stories to one other."

"Luke?"

"Yes."

"What about Sponke?"

"He really wouldn't understand, considering insects have so many family members. Family isn't the same for him as it is for you and me."

"Oh," Drake said peering at the ground.

Groger glanced back at Sponke still huddled close to the riddle rock. The giant shook his head. "Like I told you before, I grew up in a place called Cooplaroo. It was magnificent. We didn't have evil forests and monsters running about making trouble. It was a peaceful place to grow up." Groger looked down and began to kick at the dirt. Drake did not dare speak. "It was a safe place up until the worst day of my life. I was the oldest of five children in my family. My parents were wonderful and hardworking. When I was younger, they put a lot of trust in me because they worked so much and were rarely home. They both worked in the mines. Most adult sadcads worked in the mines, you see."

"What were they mining?" Drake asked as he watched the giant sadcad think.

"Mostly gems. The mines there are full of them. Cooplaroo was famous for its exquisite gems. I was fifteen at the time. My sister Kera was fourteen and my sister Mera was thirteen. I also had twin brothers, Sage and Bo, who were four." Groger chuckled. "The twins followed me everywhere."

"I know the feeling," Drake said, thinking of Bailey.

"They were so special to me. I loved being a big brother." Groger grinned and let out a loud sigh. "One day, my siblings and I went down to Mossy Lake for a swim. We met some friends there and planned to stay all day. It was a wonderful time." Groger looked away for a moment. "I took my eyes off the twins for just *seconds*. One moment they were splashing around, having a great time, and the next moment they were gone." Large tears filled Groger's eyes and trickled down his cheeks. Groger wiped his eyes and continued. "We searched everywhere. We swam all over the lake, searched in the nearby forest, and looked everywhere we thought they could possibly be. We found no trace.

After over an hour of searching, I decided to have another look in the lake. I dove in, swam toward the bottom, and there they were. Sage and Bo were curled up in each other's arms looking so peaceful."

Drake frowned. "They drowned? That's awful."

Groger's brows narrowed as he cocked his head. "What? They didn't drown. Sadcads can stay underwater for hours. They were just hiding from me."

Drake felt his mouth drop open.

Groger grinned a little. "Anyway, I gathered them in my arms and dragged them back to the surface, kicking and screaming. They were so mad at me for finding their hiding spot."

"Why were they hiding?"

"Because they were four, and were mischievous little snippets."

"I just don't get it. Why were you crying if your brothers were all right?"

"Because I lost my baby brothers for *over an hour.* After my sisters told my parents, they swore they'd never trust me again. My parents made me start working in the mines with them every day. After a year or so my dad finally had restored his trust in me, but *I* swore I'd never let myself be in charge again."

Drake nodded. "And that's why you want to let Sponke control things?"

"Yes. When I met Sponke, he talked so much, he seemed to have an answer for just about everything. He was headstrong and bossy, so I decided to let him lead me. Sponke is most happy when he is in charge. I'm fine with that because I don't *want* the responsibility. I look at Sponke as family now. I vowed to never drive him away."

"If he can't order you around you think that he'll leave you?"

"No, but Sponke can be very stubborn. I just like to leave it all up to him. It makes life much easier."

Drake looked at Groger. "But, Sponke really cares about you. I can't imagine him *ever* deserting you." Drake sat silent, staring at the ground for a few moments.

"Why so quiet?"

"I don't mean to get off topic, but there's something that's been bugging me."

"What is it?"

"Back at the field where Migisi and I landed, just before we found you, I had a really weird dream." Drake went on to tell Groger about the little white cottage, the moving trees, the strange voice, and finally Sponke's voice. "It's crazy, right? Just tell me it was nothing, and I'll forget about it."

"I wish I could tell you it was nothing, but I'd be lying. Is this the only dream you've had like it since you've been here?"

"No, I had one right before the foradore took me away from you and Sponke."

"What was that dream about?"

Drake scratched his head. "I think that one was a warning about Bleet. I dreamed about Migisi and shortly after, I found her."

"Strange."

"Should I be worried?"

Looking back at Drake, Groger said, "Dreams like that typically have a meaning, but I don't think this is anything you need to concern yourself with right now. If you have any other dreams like this, tell me right away, okay?"

Drake nodded and looked over at Sponke. Now the bug was sitting upon the riddle rock. He sat hunched over with his head rested in his hands.

"Maybe we should decide what it is that I need to see in this lake."

"That sounds like a good idea."

Drake tapped his chest. "I want to know what the Story Stone has to do with Bailey and Luke's disappearance, and are they together?"

Groger nodded. "I think we also need to ask why the Story Stone sent you to Kazoocal Field, and not directly to Bailey? And, where exactly *are* Bailey and Luke?"

Drake grinned. "Those are good, but we also need to know how I'm going to rescue them."

Just as Groger opened his mouth to speak, Sponke zoomed in next to him and began talking so fast Drake had to lean closer just to understand him.

"I have been mulling this entire thing over, and I feel that you are right. We really need to find out where your sister and Luke are. Once we find them, everything else will fall into place."

"I am agreeing with you, Sponkie," Groger said, back to his simple self again.

Drake chuckled and walked a short distance away from his friends. He listened for a while as they continued discussing the riddle, but soon grew tired. He strolled back over to the water. Drake glanced upward, squinting at the sun shining brightly in the cloudless sky. He drew in a deep breath then exhaled slowly while staring back at the water. A lone leaf fluttered down to the lake, sending ripples toward him. He marveled at the way the rippling water caught the reflections of the sun.

His foot fumbled with a small rock on the ground. Looking down at the stone, a thought crept over him. *What is the Story Stone anyway? Sponke has never really told me what it is or does.* Drake thought about the mysterious stone and questioned himself for not asking about it earlier. He presumed that all the strange things that were continually happening to him in Kropite had been enough distraction that he had not even *thought* to question the stone's purpose.

Drake kept mumbling to himself as he made his way over to Sponke and Groger. "Hey Sponke," he said. "Can I ask you something?"

"Ask away."

"What is the purpose of the Story Stone? What is it?"

Sponke cocked his head to one side. "Of course, I never really explained to you what this stone is or what it's capable of. Yes indeed, I'll tell you. Have a seat and listen up. Why didn't we discuss this earlier?"

"I don't know," Drake said with a chuckle. "We've been busy, I guess."

Drake took a seat on the ground. Sponke flew down closer to him. "The Story Stone is a mighty powerful object; however, it is *not* one of a kind. It is actually one of many. The stones lie on the bottom of this lake," he said, pointing to the water. "No one is sure how many stones lie at the bottom. All we know is that those who go in to find out never return."

Drake's eyes widened, but he remained quiet.

"Once in a great while, a Story Stone will appear on land. No one knows how or why. Luke seems to know where to find them, but even *he* is not sure why they emerge. The stones help Luke protect Kropite."

Drake's eyebrows narrowed. "The key!"

"I'm sorry, what?"

"The key! The stones are the secret key that helps Luke protect Kropite."

"Why yes, young Master. They are."

"But how does he use them?" Drake asked.

"The stones are viewing portals to the past and future. Luke uses them to see when trouble is coming: the story of the future, and why something might have happened: the story of the past. This is why we call them *Story* Stones. Knowing the story of the past and future enables Luke to keep watch over Kropite."

"I don't really understand how knowing about the past and future helps."

"If something bad should happen, then Luke is able to see into the past allowing him to find out who or what is responsible for causing it. Viewing the future is something he does to check up on Kropite to make sure nothing serious is headed our way," Sponke explained.

Drake thought about this for a moment. "I do remember seeing something that looked like a portal when I first arrived at Kazoocal Field." Drake stopped talking for a moment.

"What is it, Drake?"

"I know I must sound dense, but obviously the stone I found back home was a Story Stone, right?"

"Yes."

"How did it get to Cape Coast?"

"The stones are a mystery. No one controls them. It's as if they have minds of their own."

Drake tilted his head. "If a Story Stone only lets you view the past or future, how did it bring me here?"

"That's what doesn't make sense to Groger and me. The Stone brought you here, to present-day Kropite, and we have no idea how or why."

"How do you know *we* aren't in the past or the future right now?" Drake inquired.

"That doesn't matter. You traveled from your world to ours. The stones merely *show* Luke the past and future. You, however, traveled *through* it to Kropite. It's unheard of! We cannot figure out how you came to be here. There is something very *different* with your stone, and we are hoping that the lake will be able to make sense of all of this."

"Where's the stone now?" Drake asked with narrowed brows.

"We don't know that either. Maybe the lake will help us with that as well."

"This is unbelievable!" Drake sat quietly for several minutes, filtering through all he had just heard. "Do you think Luke knew about Bailey before she came?"

"Yes."

"He saw her through one of the lake's stones, didn't he?"

"Yes. Just before he left, he told me he was going to find Bailey—"

"And he never came back," Drake finished.

"No." Sponke looked sad.

Drake's eyes lit up as he pointed to Sponke. "When I came to Kazoocal Field at the beginning of all of this, you knew my name already, but you wouldn't tell me how. Did you see me through a stone?"

"No. Some things are unexplainable. They just happen and no one really knows why. *This* is one of those things," said Sponke. "After Luke disappeared, I flew to See-All-Lake in search of answers. The lake would not show me anything even though I *pleaded* with it repeatedly." Sponke folded his arms and pursed his lips. "Refusing to give up, I sat and stubbornly stared at the lake for hours. Finally, and I'm not sure why, an image appeared on the surface of the lake."

"An image of—"

"You. An image of you appeared right in front of me. You were standing alone in Kazoocal Field, looking quite *heroic* I must say. I remember just staring at you, wondering who you were. Then I heard your name, over and over. Your name was coming from so far away, yet I could hear it clearly. I wasn't sure what to do next, so I immediately flew to Kazoocal Field to wait."

"How long did you wait?" Drake asked, curious.

"I'm not sure. Remember time here is different. Besides, it really doesn't matter when you're expecting someone *great*."

Drake stared at his thigh and began fidgeting with a large tear in his shorts. "I want answers. I need to see if this lake will help me as well."

"Me too," Sponke said, speeding back to the rock.

"He is such an *impatient* little bug," Drake mumbled as he got to his feet. As Drake made his way over to his excited friend, a sudden booming off in the distance halted his steps.

CHAPTER 12

Collectors

"What's going on?" Drake asked, turning to face Groger. The giant swished his head this way and that, trying to determine what was making the sound.

"Migisi, was that you?" Drake called, glancing toward the mezork. Already on her feet sniffing the air, Migisi was on high alert. Her ears twitched back and forth. A low growl rumbled from her throat.

Drake stood on tiptoe, straining to see what could be making the drumming sounds. He spied a black cloud aiming straight for them.

"I see something coming. Look Groger, way over there."

Without a moment's hesitation, Groger grabbed Drake and pulled him to the ground. Shielding him with his body, just as he had done with the rock benders, Groger lay over him. A low droning, similar to a swarm of bees, filled the air.

"Sponke?" Drake yelled. Sponke did not answer.

"He'll be fine. There are plenty of hiding places for him!" Groger bellowed.

"What about Migisi?" He managed to pull himself out from under Groger's bulky body.

"Drake!" Groger yelled, trying to grab Drake's leg. He was much too fast for the giant. He looked in every direction but couldn't see his mezork.

"Migisi!" Drake roared.

Directly above him now, the black cloud descended upon Drake. He looked upward and noticed tiny, buzzing insects huddled tightly together. Acting as one large entity, the bug-cloud encompassed him, swarming and buzzing around his head. It swept back and knocked into him. Drake flipped backward into a pile of boulders. Feeling as though a car had just smashed into him, he groaned and slid to the ground. With pain shooting throughout his body, Drake managed to flip over onto his stomach and shield his head with his arms. An eruption of what felt like small sharp rocks pelted at his back and legs. He wanted to scream.

After what seemed like an eternity, the noise and pummeling ceased. The insects soared straight up, vanishing behind a cluster of billowing clouds. Drake rolled onto his back and wrapped his arms around his stomach. Pain soared through his back. Drake pushed himself to a sitting position then rolled up onto his knees. Groger was still slumped over.

"Groger? Are you okay?" Drake groaned.

Groger looked up. "Is it over?"

"I think so. What was that?"

"I think it was some type of advance team sent as a warning," Groger groaned.

"A warning for what?"

As if to answer his question, the air split with several mighty explosions.

"Take cover!" Groger yelled.

Still upon his knees, Drake's eyes shot upward toward the eruptions. One deafening burst after another filled the air. The din left Drake's world hollow and muted. He dropped his hands to the ground and pushed himself up with one heaving grunt. He gazed up.

"What's happening?" Drake shouted, covering his ears.

Through squinted eyes, Drake witnessed blazing bursts of light striking the earth. After each blast, a bear, posed on its hind feet, stood shrouded in smoke and ash. Each animal was black and at least seven foot tall. They wore blood-red cloaks with helmets to match. The bears shook the soot from their bodies and let out boisterous roars, then proceeded to advance toward Drake and Groger.

"Groger, what do we do?" Drake asked. Groger said not a word, but stood with his mouth gaping. "Groger!" Drake shouted. The giant turned toward him.

He pointed to the advancing bears. "Not now, Drake. Just do as they say. Don't rebel! Not now!"

Three of the bears surrounded Groger, pointing their sabers at his bulky body. None of the bears approached Drake.

"Groger?"

Out of the sky came a flaming mass of fire, landing just twenty feet in front of Drake. The explosion sent Drake stumbling backward. This fiery blast left behind a bear much larger than the rest. He shook the soot from his body.

This bear was different. His cloak was black, looking as smooth as velvet. He wore black leather boots embossed with intricate, scrolling designs in silver. A large blood-red helmet covered most of his face. Everything about him seemed gigantic. His paws were massive with razor-sharp claws jutting out from each finger. Strapped to his side was an immense saber, much larger than the ones the other bears brandished.

The beast walked directly up to Drake and removed his helmet. In a booming, deep voice, the bear asked, "Are you the one they call Drake?"

Drake puffed himself up. "Yes, sir."

"Then we have come to the right place." The bear scrutinized Drake while rubbing at his furry chin. "I must say, I am surprised you did not flee after my akua bug assault. Most run at the mere *sight* of them."

Drake glared at the bear. "I'm not from here."

"Be that as it may, it seems that you have upset one of my customers a *great* deal."

"One of your customers?"

"Yes. Please forgive me. I am Falco, chief of all Collectors. Surely you have heard of me?"

"I can't say that I have. Like I said, I'm not from here."

"That's odd. I have heard of you, but you have not heard of me." Falco cut his eyes at Drake. "My boy, I think it pertinent that you know there is a great *price* on your head."

"A price on my head?" Drake queried.

"It is my job to gather what needs to be collected. In this case: *you.* Do you know Mallainy of the Dragon Raiders?" Falco asked.

"Mallainy? I met her."

"Mallainy wants *you*, and someone called Migisi." Falco looked around. "She says you are a danger to Kropite. Usually, I don't want to know the *reason* for my collection, just the amount it is worth. However, Mallainy *insisted* that I know what to expect. She filled me in on a few details." The bear grinned. "I thanked her, bracing myself for a challenge. Now that I am here, I can't help but laugh. I feel in no way threatened by you or your friend, Migisi," Falco said, motioning over to Groger.

Drake considered his sadcad friend and chuckled. "That's not Migisi. That's Groger."

"Then who, may I ask, is Migisi?"

"Migisi is a mezork that I found in the Forest of Bleet. She's my friend."

"A mezork? Do you take me for a fool, boy? I can't possibly believe that you have befriended a mezork." Falco bellowed as he laughed.

Drake flinched at Falco's laugh, but stood tall, trying to appear unafraid. "I'm not sure what you heard, but I haven't done anything wrong. Mallainy and her goons came after us. Migisi and I were just flying along, trying to find my friends when her Dragon Raiders would not let us pass. I asked if we could be on our way—"

"Please, boy, stop your babbling. I don't care what happened. I just want my money. You mean nothing to me, but you certainly mean something to Mallainy, and I intend on bringing you to her." Falco's eyes narrowed. "I find it interesting that you spoke of *flying* along with the mezork. Can you fly, boy?"

Drake chuckled. "Me? Fly? No, I can't fly, but Migisi can. I was riding her."

Falco bent over laughing. "Please stop! You're killing me, boy. No one has ever ridden atop a mezork. If you expect me to believe such a tale then you are crazy."

Drake knew that talking to this stubborn bear was getting him nowhere. He threw his gaze to the heavens while yelling with all of his might, "Migisi! I need you!"

Everything grew silent. All of the Collectors peered into the sky. Falco never took his eyes off the boy. Drake looked into Falco's eyes.

As if responding like a dog would to her master, Migisi appeared from behind a dark cloud. While making her decent, she let out a roar that shook the ground and everyone standing upon it. Her screams oozed rage and hate.

Falco released Drake from his gaze. His eyes locked on the angry mezork before he grabbed Drake and sprinted for cover. Drake struggled, but could not escape Falco's grasp. Once safely hidden behind several huge trees, Falco pulled out a whistle. He blew into it but there was no sound. Drake glared at the bear then toward Migisi who was now pulling out of her earthbound dive. She hovered close to the ground and swung her head in both directions as if searching for something. The sky glazed over in darkness shrouded by another mezork. The creature churned the air with its outstretched, leathery wings, and hissed its challenge to anyone who would accept.

Drake studied the winged creature for a moment. Its body, coloring, and face all looked almost identical to Migisi. He scanned the mezork's nose, teeth and eyes. Drake squinted, taking in its cold, blue glare. His heart leapt unsteadily. Fire and hatred emitted from this cat-dragon's eyes. Concern filled his heart. Migisi permeated his thoughts causing Drake to choke on his strangled breaths.

Drake struggled against Falco's clutches. "Let me go! Please!" Drake screamed.

"Oh, no, boy. This will be something to watch. This is *my* mezork, if you will, and he is *very* powerful. Your friend will be no match for him," Falco gloated.

"Him?" Drake gritted his teeth and grumbled as he continued to pull against Falco's weight.

Spotting the male, Migisi shot for the sky, barreling directly for him. Rearing up, the male mezork exhaled his fire. Dodging his deadly breath, Migisi climbed higher into the sky then opened her wings to soar around him. Spinning to face her, he hissed more fire. Migisi glared at the male unblinkingly and surged onward. Drake closed his eyes.

"Why don't you look, boy? This will be a good show." Falco laughed.

"Let us go!" Drake said, stomping on Falco's paw. Falco bent over in pain. Drake made his escape. The leader yelled for his men to seize Drake. The Collectors instantly obeyed by grabbing Drake and forcing him to the ground.

He struggled under the weight of the bears, but was able to turn his head just enough to see his winged protector. Churning her wings, she held her gleaming body in the air. She screamed at the male. He screamed and hissed his own threats. They swiped their lethal claws, slashing at one another's massive bodies. After only seconds of brutal striking, the mezorks flew back a few paces, putting several feet between them. Continuing to growl and scream, they charged ahead. A sonorous thud filled the heavens as they collided. They wrapped their long legs around one other and tumbled toward the ground in a massive, shrieking ball of madness. Landing with a ground-shaking boom, the two separated from the impact.

The male mezork stumbled to his feet, shaking his head. Rolling back his jowls, he exposed his teeth. His eyes burned with wrath. He had no regard that a fellow mezork stood before him. He was determined to extinguish Migisi. As if in slow motion, she turned to glare at the male, then swung her head to meet Drake's eyes. Drake's tear-filled gaze spoke volumes to her. She raised her muzzle to the heavens and released a mournful cry.

Drake yelled with all his might, "Girl, go! Get out of here!"

Slinking low, the male prepared himself for his brutal pounce. Migisi spread her wings, rocketing back into the sky. The male stood for only a moment before he too launched his body into the air. His wings fought the wind, pulling him closer and closer to the female. Within inches of her, he stretched his neck and latched onto her tail. Migisi's body jolted to a stop. With her tail clutched in his teeth, he shook. He released her, sending Migisi sailing yards away. She thrashed her wings, pushing her body forward. Charging back into battle, Migisi rushed toward him. With shocking force, she smashed her head into his side. The male twisted in agony. Both mezorks hovered. As they whipped their wings, gusts of wind billowed toward the ground. They glared at each other, trying to guess the other's next move.

Migisi raised her head, breathing her fire upward. Drake closed his eyes but still could hear the commotion above. He knew she was warning the male to stop his assault. The male spit fire and Migisi adjusted her body so the fire skirted past, just singeing some of the fur on her belly. She hurled herself upward, climbing toward the clouds. The male accepted the chase, disappearing after her.

Falco cleared his throat and dragged Drake along. "Men, gather your weapons. We need to be going! Let's take both the boy *and* the giant. We can sell him to someone along the way, and deliver Drake to Mallainy."

As Falco pulled him, anger fueled Drake. "Stop, Falco! I'm *not going with you!*" He pushed his heels into the dirt to stop the bear from forcing him any farther.

"Do you think you are actually going to stop *me*, boy?"

"No, I don't think I can stop you, but Migisi can."

"Unless I've missed something, your Migisi is in a heated battle with my mezork. I don't see either one of them at the moment. I am certain he will destroy her in no time."

Drake tugged at Falco's hold. The bear held tight, laughing at Drake's wasted efforts. Drake bellowed at the top of his lungs, "Someone, help us!"

The fighting mezorks reappeared from the clouds in a heap of roaring mayhem. They slashed and bit at one another. Their growling cries filled the heavens. Drake looked at his friend while rage burned in his veins. His face turned scarlet as his muscles jerked.

"I won't let this happen. You won't take her from me!" Drake screamed. With one final wrench, Drake broke free of Falco's grasp and sprinted ahead. Drake flung his head back yelling, "Migisi! Fly away! Don't let him kill you!"

Migisi looked on the ground. Caught off guard, the male mezork crashed into her side. Migisi spiraled through the air. Holding her head high, she sent her roaring fire skyward. Her eyes then turned on the male. Like a mother tiger responding to her cub in peril, she unceasingly advanced on the male. A scornful, low growl bubbled inside her as she raised her hefty paw. With one swipe, she sent him twisting through the air. Not ready to end the fight just yet, she bulleted after him and latched onto one of his wings. With her jaws clamped tightly, she whipped her head. A chunk of winged-flesh hung in her mouth. The male's body twisted and fell straight to the ground. He stumbled a few yards. His hefty body skid across the dirt. Dust flew everywhere, blinding the onlookers. Once his body came to a halt, he staggered to his feet. With his head hung low, the male sulked into the nearby woods.

Drake pushed forward holding his hand above his head. "Migisi!" Migisi immediately descended toward the ground. Drake halted his run and remained rooted in place. The mezork continued her dive. She pulled up just in time to sweep low. Her belly skimmed the ground. As she passed by Drake, he grabbed hold of her fur and flung his leg over her back.

Groger grinned while staring wide-eyed at the boy. "Would ya be lookin' at that." He turned to glare at the gaping Collectors. "Now that is what yous be callin' amazin. That boy there is synced up with that flyin' kitten."

Migisi soared straight up. Drake flung his arms around the mezork, squeezing and silently vowing never to let go. He buried his face into her fur. "I knew you could do it. I just knew it."

Falco gazed upward in disbelief at Drake sitting atop the mezork. "I would have never in all my life believed it, had I not seen it with my own two eyes." The leader approached Groger. "Yell for the boy to come down."

Before Groger could respond, Sponke shot out of hiding. "Wait! Don't do it, Groger. Let Drake go."

"Sponkie? Where's you coming from?" Groger inquired.

"I was taking cover, as I instructed you two to do," Sponke scolded.

"Enough is enough. Call the boy down, or the bug's a goner!" Falco bellowed. He grabbed hold of Sponke and held him securely between his paws. Groger knew that with little effort the bear could crush his small friend.

Nodding his head, Groger yelled, "Drake, I need help!"

Upon hearing Groger's panicked voice, Drake searched the ground. "Migisi! My friend is in trouble. We have to help him."

Migisi reluctantly obeyed. She opened her wings and swiveled her body around in the sky. Drake continued to glare at the Collectors that surrounded his friend.

"It's okay, girl. I think we can handle them now. That male's nowhere to be seen. Just get me close enough so we can help Groger."

Migisi swung her head and aimed for the ground. Drake clung to her neck as she sliced through the air. With a bounding thump, her feet hit the ground, jolting Drake to a sitting position. Migisi lowered herself to let Drake slide from her back. A low growl gurgled from the mezork as she watched Drake approach the huge bear.

CHAPTER 13

Let Go of Your Fears

"Okay, Falco, Migisi is with me. She won't hesitate to scorch all of you." Drake tilted his head at his bug friend clutched between Falco's paws. "Sponke? Where did you come from?"

Falco released Sponke then made a deep bow before the advancing boy. Drake stopped and narrowed his brows. Sponke flew behind Groger.

"What's going on?" Drake asked.

Falco stood up. "I owe you my deepest apologies, sir Drake. I had no idea that anyone could *ride* upon a mezork. Now having seen it, it is a great honor to be in your presence."

Drake tilted his head. "I don't understand. Just a few minutes ago, you wanted to take me to Mallainy."

"You have to understand, my young friend. I had no idea *who* you were. Mallainy spoke of you as a great threat. When I discovered you were a mere child, I thought otherwise. But now, I see your dominance over this mezork." Falco clapped his paws together. "That is an *astounding* feat."

"Dominance? She's my friend."

Falco shook his head. "I just don't see how this is at all possible."

"Are you letting us go?"

Falco nodded.

"What about Mallainy?" Drake asked.

"She will get what is coming to her, if you will let me work for you."

"Work for me? What are you talking about?"

"If you will agree, I shall explain." Drake agreed to hear Falco's explanation. As the two began to walk away from the others, Migisi's growl grew in volume. She slowly rose to her feet while glaring at Falco. Drake glanced back at her. "It's okay, girl," Drake said while staring at Falco.

Falco smiled. "You can trust me. After seeing what I just saw, I'd be a *fool* to try anything. I can assure you, the boy is safe."

Drake smiled at the mezork and she lowered herself back to the ground, keeping a steady eye on her boy. They walked a few feet away and Falco took a seat on a rock. He motioned for Drake to do so as well. The large bear eyed Drake for several moments before beginning his explanation. "I have *heard* it is possible to tame a mezork, as I have *some*what done with the male that fought with your female."

A smile tugged at Drake's lips as he gazed at Migisi doctoring her wounds. While keeping a steady eye on Drake, she licked at her paws and swiped them over her ears and face.

"Your mezork had something to fight for."

"Me?"

"Yes. The male was only angry. He has nothing. She, however, was fighting *for you.*"

Drake stared at the ground, chewing at his lower lip. Placing his enormous hand on Drake's shoulder, Falco continued. "In my travels, I happened to meet up with a nearly starved male mezork. By feeding the beast, I found that he began trusting me, little by little." Falco pulled out his whistle. "I was never able to gain all of his trust, so I fashioned a whistle that could call the mezork when I needed him. He doesn't come to help me. The whistle infuriates him. Luckily, I know to vacate the premises," the bear said as he waved his paw through the air. "He attacks whatever *happens* to be attacking me. It works for now, I suppose," he said with a shrug. "Your mezork, however, is a whole different story. She would give her life for you. And for that, I am envious."

Drake glanced at Migisi again. He smiled, knowing Falco was right. "Mezorks have a history, Drake, and it is not a pleasant one. They did not start out the fierce killers they have now become. They were, so I've heard, rather gentle animals with a staggeringly lengthy lifespan. They lived peacefully together... until the Zotacks came along. The Zotack's killed them by the hundreds, hunted them for their wings and fur. As a result, the mezorks went into hiding. Over time, the mezorks have grown to hate anyone who even *remotely* resembles a Zotack."

"What does a Zotack look like?

"Like you. They are just the creatures that lived here in Kropite a long time ago. So, to see your mezork *protect* you like she does is unheard of. You must be something special. To tame a creature like that is unbelievable, so please forgive me for laughing off your claims at first."

"If mezorks were peaceful creatures that once lived together, why were Migisi and that male ready to kill each other?"

"These mezorks were battling because they have not been around other mezorks for some time now. They have become solitary animals and have trouble trusting even their own kind."

Drake nodded his head. "Are there a lot of mezorks still around?"

"No. There are very few left. The ones that still exist tend to keep to themselves. They live in Bleet Forest. Not many two-legged creatures would dare enter the dark woods, so they live a quiet life, all alone."

"That seems so sad. I wish there were a way to rescue them and let them know they are safe now."

"But is it safe for them? I really wouldn't call Kropite a *safe* place. Just recently, darkness has shrouded Kropite. I can't quite figure out why."

Drake knew why. Because of Luke's absence, Kropite was in danger. But, could he trust Falco? Drake rubbed at his forehead, pushing his hair out of his eyes. He stared at the bear then blurted out, "Falco, do you know Luke?"

"Yes! Who doesn't know Luke? He is a Helper, sent here to keep Kropite safe. Luke and I are old, old friends. We met in a similar situation as you and I just did. Someone sent my crew to capture the guardian, but we failed." Falco laughed. "I learned who he was the hard way." The Collector scratched his head and chuckled again. "Luke taught me a lesson or two. Luckily, we walked away friends."

Falco's brown eyes sparkled. His deep, jolly laugh shook his whole body. Drake let out a slow breath and with it, let down his guard. "The reason Kropite seems so dark lately is...because Luke is missing. Sponke says I'm the one who is supposed to save him."

Falco nodded. "I sensed something had changed. And, how else can you explain you and the mezork? You must be something *extraordinary* to be able to tame her as they did in legends."

Drake smirked. "Jude mentioned the legend to me while I was in Bleet. That's what gave me the idea to try and tame Migisi in the first place."

"A legend that, until now, no one has proven. Growing up, I always heard that mezorks are respected creatures. All living creatures, for that matter, need respect. Why is it some feel a need to harm the harmless?" Falco shook his head. "I don't expect an answer to this question. It's just something that I have always wondered."

"Don't you hunt creatures that *need collecting?*" Drake asked.

Falco laughed. "I guess you're right, but I rarely *kill* anything."

"But you collect things for others. What's to say they don't kill what you have brought them?"

"You are a smart boy. I've never really looked at my job the way you describe. Maybe I need a new line of work."

"All I know is, Migisi is my friend. We make a pretty good team. I don't really think I did anything special to tame her. I met her in the woods. After a stare-down, and getting up enough nerve, I just reached up and touched her. Next thing I knew, I was on her back and up in the clouds," Drake said swishing his hand skyward.

Falco leaned away from Drake and shook his head. "You, my boy, *are* something else. Why is it you have come to Kropite?"

Drake looked skeptical.

"It's okay. You can trust me, my boy. If *anything,* I am trustworthy. We are friends now. I promise I will *not* betray you."

Drake thought for only a moment. "Back home I found a stone. I took it home and, shortly after, my little sister went missing. I know now it was because of the stone. The same stone that brought my sister here also brought me here."

"Do you still have the stone?" Falco asked.

"No, that's the problem. I can't find it. I'm pretty much stranded here until I find my sister."

"What will you do once you find her?"

"That's kind of a problem as well, seeing as I don't have the Story Stone to take me home," Drake revealed.

Falco's eyes widened. He rose to his feet. "Did you say *Story Stone?*"

"Yeah. Why?"

"I have heard more than I can believe for one day. You have befriended a mezork and traveled from your world to mine by Story Stone. Those stones possess powers beyond *anything* I have ever known." Falco stared toward the lake. "I once came across one a while back. Just touching it *scorched* my paw," Falco said showing Drake his scar. "You say you actually moved the stone? You might want to listen to your little friend Sponke. He may be wiser then you give him credit." Falco stared into Drake's eyes. "I think you are underestimating yourself. You need to let go of your fears. You need to accept that you *do* have a purpose here."

Drake's mind drifted back to his dream. The voice in the cottage also told him to let go of his fears. "I understand that someone needs to help bring Luke back. Just because my little sister is missing, everyone assumes that I've volunteered to rescue him. Luke is the end-all-be-all protector of Kropite. How am I supposed to save him?" Drake said with raised hands. "I'm just a regular kid. But here I'm supposed to be some great hero. That's a *lot* of pressure."

Falco stood speechless for several seconds. Sitting back down beside Drake, Falco said, "You are so stubborn. But, I guess I was stubborn as well in my youth. I was supposed to become a great warrior among the Boabarb tribe. However, I decided to go into business for myself instead. My father was so disappointed in me when I told him about my plans."

"You started a business of becoming a Collector?"

"Ha! No, I didn't start out as a Collector. That just sort of happened. My business was selling handmade sabers," Falco said holding up his massive weapon.

Drake goggled at the weapon. "You made that?"

"I did. I found that I was good with my hands at an early age. It also didn't hurt that there was a demand for my sabers at one time. The warriors of my tribe all used them."

"What happened to your business?"

"My father was so ashamed he banished me from my tribe and village. I struck out on my own. The demand for my weapons seemed to diminish. Eventually, I met up with some friends and we formed this crew," Falco said, motioning to his men, who were now sitting and laughing with Sponke and Groger around a fire.

Drake smiled at Falco. "You still do sort of run your own business. Are there other Collectors around here?"

"We're all there are."

"Are you considered a bad guy or a good guy?"

Falco laughed. "It depends on how you look at it. Some of the people we collect are notorious criminals. However, not everyone we collect is a delinquent. Like you, for instance. We try not to ask too many questions because it makes it easier to live with what we do."

"That's crazy, but it sounds like kind of a cool job."

"I suppose."

Drake glanced out across the lake. "I have a question...do you know anything about this lake?"

"A little. Why?"

"Because it is supposed to give me the answers I'm looking for. But before it does, I have to answer a bunch of riddles."

The Collector pointed out across the water. "You know, from what I've heard this lake is all-knowing. I believe if you need answers, this is definitely the place to come."

Drake peered at the ground. "I need to start figuring out the answers to the riddles, so I can find my sister."

"Whatever the lake tells you is going to help you on your quest. You need to follow your instincts. Believe that everything will come out right in the end. I am sure the Story Stone will find its way back to you, because I think it has chosen you for a reason. Although it doesn't seem clear now, it will eventually." Falco raised his voice as he said, "I am a *firm* believer in destiny. There is a reason for everything, and you are a lucky boy." The bear tapped Drake on the head. "You have the ability to make a difference. Not many can say they have made a difference in the lives of so many, but you have the chance to help an entire world—a world worth saving in my eyes." He glanced around. "Kropite is a magnificent place, and if you can help restore order here, then by all means, you should stand tall and take on this challenge. I have seen and heard great things today. I have a good feeling about you, boy. If you should ever need me, you can find me here," Falco said, handing Drake a small piece of paper with a map scribbled on it.

"Is this your business card?" Drake laughed a little.

"You might say that. And don't worry about Mallainy. I'll take care of her, free of charge." This time, Falco laughed.

"Is that what you meant earlier about letting you work for me?"

"More or less. I would consider it a personal *honor* if I could say that I was able to help Drake the Great."

Tucking the small paper into his pocket, Drake held out his hand. Falco shook it, saying, "It was an honor to meet you. I want to bid you farewell and good luck."

Falco walked away, calling for his men to follow. Drake stood for a moment, watching Falco and his men explode back into the sky, headed for parts unknown.

Migisi's purring snapped Drake from his trance. He ran over to her and threw his arms around the mezork.

"You were awesome, Migisi! I owe my life to you, again. I know I'll never be able to repay you," he said as he rubbed under the mezork's chin. Migisi's purr grew to such a volume that Drake could feel the ground vibrating.

"Are you hurt anywhere?" Drake asked as he inspected her for injuries. Finding only minor cuts and scrapes, Drake snickered. "I am *so* proud of you. If what Falco said is true, I can't imagine you, or any other mezork, sitting in Bleet all alone. I wish I could help *all* of your kind," Drake said. Migisi let out a soft, kitten-like meow.

"You have to promise me that when I leave Kropite, you'll never return to Bleet. Groger and Sponke will take care of you, so you'll never have to be alone again." Pulling the mezork's ear close to his mouth, Drake whispered, "I love you, Migisi." Migisi answered with another pitiful meow, causing Drake to laugh.

He made his way over to Groger and Sponke. Sponke flew to Drake and began speaking. "Oh, Drake, you were so fantastic back there. I am so *proud* of you, my boy."

"I want to know where *you* were, Sponke. You just disappeared while Groger and I were left to fend for ourselves."

"I knew I would be able to hide a bit easier. If need be, I would be able to get help," Sponke stammered.

"Good plan." Drake said with a smirk. "Thank God for Migisi, or who knows what would have happened."

"Yeah, Sponkie. You really brave bug." Groger laughed.

"Okay, okay, enough of all of this. We need to get to work on the riddle," Sponke said.

CHAPTER 14

It Needs Your Help

Drake, Sponke, and Groger slowly approached the rock. "Okay, let's take this bit-by-bit," Drake said as he read the first part of the riddle aloud.

It is small and delicate, but huge in power.
You may touch it, but beware, it's as fragile as a flower.

Drake looked at this portion of the riddle and read it over to himself several times before saying, "It's small, which could be a lot of things, but it's also powerful. Could it be some kind of magical creature? Maybe something living in the lake, or someone

I have met since I've been here? It's fragile, which could mean it's small. I just don't know."

He thumped his head, then began pacing back and forth, stopping every now and again, shaking his finger and moving his lips as though he wanted to venture a guess. However, he would then resume pacing as if the thought was too ridiculous to say aloud. Sponke stared at Groger, who stood watching the boy walk back and forth in front of them.

"Delicate but powerful. What do I know that's delicate and powerful? I'm usually so good at riddles…unless it could be that obvious. Maybe I'm thinking too hard."

Suddenly, a smile filled Drake's face, but he said absolutely nothing. He pointed at Sponke and Groger. "Could it be? No way. No way." Drake shook his head.

"Drake? Do you have the answer?"

"What about the Story Stone! It's small and powerful, but…I wouldn't call it delicate. But, I mean, I never dropped it. Could it be the stone? Or does that seem too easy?"

"Go with it, Drake. Why *can't* it be something that obvious? Maybe it starts out easy. Maybe not everyone knows of the Story Stone. Consider yourself lucky to be able to answer this first part so easily," Sponke stated.

"But you said I had to offer the lake a gift. I don't have the Story Stone to offer to the lake."

"It doesn't matter, Drake. If the lake wants more, it won't show you anything. We won't know until you *try.*"

"What if something bad happens?"

"Don't be so paranoid." Sponke laughed. "Get down there and speak your answer."

Drake shuffled over to the lake's edge and looked down at the lapping water. He chewed at the inside of his cheek while contemplating what he would say. Sponke had told him if he answered the riddle incorrectly, he would only have to try again.

Drake took a deep breath and spoke to the lake. "Okay, I think the first answer is...the Story Stone!"

The lake began to glow and sparkle even more brilliantly than when they had first arrived. A huge spray of water gushed out, soaking Drake to the bone. He wiped at his eyes as he knelt down. The dirt was now muddy with lake water. His knees squished in the soft muck as he situated himself at the bank. Peering over the edge, his reflection stared back at him. His reflected image appeared confident and courageous. He sat back on his heels and shook his head. When he looked back into the lake, he saw Bailey. She was sitting on the floor, crossed-legged. She was talking to a boy. Drake strained his eyes to try and get a better glimpse of the stranger.

Is that Luke? Watching his sister laughing and talking with the boy gave Drake a sick feeling in the pit of his stomach. *Why does she look so happy? Why isn't she sad and missing us?* Drake focused on Bailey's mouth. He saw her lips form the word *Luke.*

It is Luke. Bailey and Luke are together. Drake gazed at the guardian sitting crossed legged directly in front of Bailey. He smiled at the boy's ability to make his sister laugh. Then he turned his gaze to Bailey. A rush of anger swept over him, as he knew she was out of reach. There she was, sitting so close yet so far away. Soon Bailey and Luke vanished under the water.

"Wait! I need more!" Drake yelled out. Just as he was about to touch the water, Groger grabbed him, pulling him back.

"Don't do that. Let's look back at the riddle," Sponke said as he helped coax the boy back to the rock. Drake told Sponke and Groger what he had seen.

"I knew it! I knew it! They *are* together. This is going to work. I can feel it," Sponke sang out.

Drake rolled his eyes and read the second part of the riddle.

It is smart and cunning, yet not at first glance.
It's not very intelligent 'til its inner-light is enhanced.

Everyone stared unblinkingly at the riddle rock until Drake broke the silence. "Inner light? What do they mean inner light? Is it about something that's not intelligent at first, but turns intelligent later? This time it has to be about *something* living, because it has intelligence. It's definitely not Migisi, because she is obviously smart. Maybe it's about Irick? No, I know him. Irick is just plain, old, simple Irick." Drake examined the riddle. He read it over and over. "It's got to be here. What are you saying?" Drake queried aloud. He resumed his pacing and continued to speak his thoughts.

"Whatever this is has an *inner* light that has to be *enhanced*. How do you enhance someone's inner light? Do you *show* it something that makes it intelligent? Is it intelligent all of the time and only shows it sometimes?" With Drake's last question a grin spread across the boy's face. *Groger. I always thought he was just some big, goofy giant, but now I know he's actually a smart guy,* he thought as he strolled toward the lake. Passing by the giant, Groger ripped a small, inconspicuous piece of his shirt and handed it to Drake. This action was so quick that Sponke was none the wiser.

"Has he figured this out, or has it stumped him?" Sponke asked Groger. Groger just donned his simple smile.

Drake knelt back down at the edge of the lake whispering, "My answer is a member of a rare breed of sadcad. One named Groger."

As Drake spoke these words, he tossed Groger's torn fabric into the lake as a gift. Just as before, pictures appeared on the surface. This time it was of Drake in the woods with Reigan. His arms prickled at the image of him and his friend shimmering in the water. To view a piece of home in Kropite was mind-blowing. He shook his head while he watched.

Drake saw himself talking with Reigan. Then it flashed forward to Reigan running away. Drake grinned at her hasty retreat.

Next, a blinding flash blasted in front of him. The lake revealed the explosion in the woods, followed by the stone lying among the smoldering leaves. He watched as his image lifted the stone and placed it into his pack. Then his room appeared. His muscles tensed as he watched Bailey lean over to lift *Luke of Kropite* from his rocking chair. Just as she laid her hand on the book, she vanished with a puff of smoke. Drake coughed as he sucked in air too quickly.

The next vision was of Bailey landing in the arms of an enormous, hideous creature. She screamed as she tried to claw her way free. Drake clenched his fists together as he watched. The monster forced his sister down a long corridor, but she was fighting like mad the whole way.

The water went blank for a few seconds then phrases splashed across the water's surface. *Imagination Stealers. Using their minds to create selfishly. Only you can save them.* Drake leaned forward, trying to will the lake to show him more. He stared unblinkingly at the surface, but nothing more appeared.

Drake ran back to Sponke and Groger telling them everything. Sponke scratched his head.

"I was right in saying you are the one who will save them, but we really didn't need the lake for that part," Sponke stated.

"I need to know why me? Let's look at the third part of the riddle," Drake said as he began to read.

Some don't believe, unless they can see
(Not a good idea unless you have the key).
You can see with your heart if only you try,
Open your mind and surely you'll spy.

"The key? What key? Is it an *actual* key? Could it be the Story Stone again?" Drake asked.

"I don't think it would be the same answer as the first part of this riddle. Drake, what about the stones Kreeper gave you? Could they be a key?" Sponke inquired, as he fluttered in front of Drake's face.

"Maybe." Drake reached into his pocket and pulled out one of the remaining three stones.

He placed the black stone next to the third portion of the riddle. A hush settled over the three as they watched intently.

"Should something be happening?" Drake asked.

"Don't know, Drakie," Groger said.

The rock began to jiggle. Its black coloring faded into sapphire blue. Drake leaned in closer, feeling heat rising from the tiny stone. A gentle hum surfaced as it vibrated against the riddle rock.

"I *think* something's happening," Sponke said.

"Me too," Drake said as he ran back to the lake. Standing over the blank water, Drake slouched. "That's not it. There has to be more. Maybe that's only *part* of it. What does the end of the phrase say again?"

"You can see with your heart if only you try. Open your mind and surely you'll spy!" Sponke read.

"See with your heart. How do you see with your heart? Is it courage? Is courage in your heart?"

"I don't know. Try," Sponke instructed.

Drake leaned over the lake whispering, "My answer is courage."

The lake remained dark and motionless. All was silent except the boy's drumming heartbeat in his ears. "Nothing's happening!" he shouted back.

"You should be trying something else, Drakie!" Groger bellowed.

Drake scratched his head. "Wait a minute. Maybe it has something to do with love. You can see love with your heart, right? Is it love?" he asked. Drake tapped on his head as he continued to speak his thoughts aloud. "Open your mind, Drake. What do I love? I love my family. I love Bailey. Could it be the love for my lost sister?" Drake labored as he looked back at Sponke.

"I don't know. *Try* it," Sponke encouraged as he threw Drake the stone.

He caught the stone, witnessing right away that it had lost its brilliant blue hue. It was as black as it had been when Kreeper first gave it to him.

"Okay, my answer is *love!*" Drake shouted as he tossed Kreeper's stone into the lake. He peered over the edge watching a shaky image immerge.

"I was right!" Drake shouted back. The first image that appeared in the lake was of Reigan. "Reigan?" Drake said, more confused than ever. "I don't love Reigan. No way, you're wrong!" he yelled. Irritation bubbled inside him, but he kept his gaze directed at the water. Reigan's image faded. Aerial views of Kropite replaced her. The views playing across the water reminded him of his sight upon Migisi's back. At the thought of Migisi, Drake looked up from the watery image, spotting her on the other side of the lake. He stood watching her while she playfully batted at a winged creature no larger than her paw. The poor thing tried desperately to take flight, but Migisi had no intentions of letting it go.

He looked back at the lake. A fuzzy image began to materialize. Drake knelt to the ground and leaned over for a closer look. The closer he tilted toward the water, the clearer the image became. He braced himself with his hands at the edge of the bank, watching a shimmery shadow skim across the grass. The shadow looked human, but entirely too short to be a man.

"A flying boy? Who's flying?" Drake smiled. "It must be Luke."

Migisi appeared next. She sat, a motionless statue. To see Migisi sitting so tall and erect made him burn with pride. He watched his stunning friend for several seconds when something off to the side caught his eye. Drake jerked his head to the left of Migisi's image. It was Luke's shadow again. The guardian soared over the lake.

Drake leaned in, closer than ever, staring into the water. His mouth dropped open as the mystery of who the flying boy really was became clear. The reflection mirroring back at Drake was not of Luke. The image he saw was his own.

He sat back on his heels. "This is crazy." Rising to his knees, Drake looked back into the water only to see Migisi and his image drift away. The now blank water rippled from a breath of wind sliding past. He waited, but nothing came.

"Is that all?"

The breeze drifted by again, ruffled his hair, and swept past his ear. This time it had a message. He tilted his head.

"*Believe,*" the voice whispered.

"What? Who's there?" He said as he looked back into the water.

The water's movement ceased and a town appeared. A factory with small houses stationed along its perimeter resided in the middle of the town. The setting seemed void of life, but Drake could hear children laughing. He wished the lake would show his image going into the town. However, the pictures disappeared yet again.

Drake jumped to his feet to report his findings to his friends. "This is getting hard. I think I am actually more confused now than ever before. Where is this going?" he asked.

"What have we learned so far?" Sponke asked.

Drake scratched his head. "We know that Bailey definitely traveled here by the Story Stone, and she is being held prisoner. We know that she and Luke are together. We know that, somehow, I can fly, and this takes me to a town with a huge factory in it. I'm guessing this is where Bailey is. Now, how do I find it?"

"There is one more part to the riddle. Let's see if we can learn more," Sponke suggested.

"All right, let me see," Drake said as he read the final portion printed on the rock.

It is all about imagination in the end,
Without this, you're truly not able to fend
Off the evil that lurks all around.
Believe in yourself, or you will surely drown.

"I really don't like that drowning part. This must have something to do with the lake, I guess. Can I go through the lake to get to the town?" His mind jumped from one thought to another. "No, I'm supposed to fly. Maybe the water from the lake will give me the ability to fly."

Sponke placed a hand onto Drake's shoulder. "I wouldn't touch the lake if I were you. This lake, although dazzling, is also dangerous. Touching it would be a mistake. It possesses powers that *no one* understands. We just can't take the chance."

Drake looked at him, then back at the riddle. "It says it's all about imagination. You have to have a pretty big imagination to believe in this place."

Sponke looked at Drake with narrowed eyes, but told him to continue.

"The evil portion is obvious. Whatever took Bailey has to be evil. So something needs to get *rid* of the evil. Could the answer be me? I mean, I saw myself flying. That would be awesome! I could definitely *imagine* myself doing that."

This time Groger spoke up. "Drake, I am thinking you are having it, little man."

"He's right! *You* are the last answer. Without you, none of this would have been possible. You have made it this far, and everything you have done has led us to the next step leading us closer to Bailey and Luke. This riddle was meant for you and *you alone,*" Sponke said.

"You really think all of this has to do with me? I'm supposed to save Kropite?" Drake said, staring at the ground. His face contorted as he battled with his own thoughts. "I just didn't think it was possible. It really is up to me." His face was neither happy nor sad.

Sponke smiled as he nodded his head vigorously. "Yes! Yes! Now you believe, so answer the last part of this riddle and we can save Bailey and Luke."

Drake walked over to the edge of the lake. He reached into his back pocket and pulled out his nylon wallet. Opening it, he retrieved a tattered drawing of a boy dressed as Superman. His thoughts wandered back to a dreary spring Saturday, two years ago, when his sister gave it to him.

With day after day of nothing but rain, Drake felt like a caged animal. He made up his mind to hang out with his friends regardless of the weather. Drake figured they could go to their secret hideout in the woods they had built the year before. It didn't matter what they did, as long as he could get outside.

As Drake headed for the door, he heard Bailey run up behind him. He turned around and yelled, "You are not coming with me today! I've been stuck in this house with you for *way* too long, and I'm going out with my friends. Go find something else to do on your own."

Bailey stood motionless for only a moment before tears slowly spilled from her eyes. Drake had been entirely too self-absorbed to care about his little sister's feelings and left anyway, slamming the door on his way out. Drake had not realized it, but he had hurt Bailey's feelings tremendously.

After Bailey had gathered herself, she ran out to look for him. She ran all around the house. Unfortunately, there was no sign of him anywhere. With chest heaving and tears cascading down her red cheeks, Bailey could barely catch her breath. She crumbled to the ground, infuriated and heartbroken by her brother's abandonment. When Bailey had these moments of extreme anger, she was often not able to think clearly. Her rage drove her straight into the woods, a place her mother had always forbidden her to go alone.

Bailey bolted into the woods, screaming her brother's name. She ran on and on. This area was not her usual playground, an unexplored territory for a six-year-old. Inevitably, she found herself lost. She yelled for help, but no one came to her rescue. Bailey walked a little while longer until she grew terribly cold and tired. The lost girl eventually found refuge in the nook of a massive tree trunk, concealed behind several bulky bushes. She slid down to the ground, huddling into a ball.

Several hours later, Drake returned home only to find a note attached to the door.

Drake, Bailey is missing! Gone to look for her. —Mom

Goosebumps immediately rose on his arms as he stared blankly at his mother's note. Drake held his hands up then began to back away from his door. Searching around, Drake took a moment to gather his mind.

"Where is she?" he asked aloud as he gazed toward the woods. Without another moment's hesitation, he went into the trees near his house. Drake sprinted through the thick brush. Several scraggly branches bounced up and scratched his face as he ripped through them. He was unfazed by any pain. Nothing was going to stop him.

Drake shouted his sister's name repeatedly while he explored everywhere he knew, and even some places that were unfamiliar. After about an hour of searching, an overwhelming desperation clouded his brain. His body was weak as thoughts of never finding Bailey again started to devour him. However, he pushed himself onward, because giving up on his little sister was not an option. Suddenly, he recalled that Bailey loved superheroes. He stopped one more time, yelling at the top of his lungs, "Bailey, it's Superman, and I've come to rescue you! But I need your help!"

By either fate or coincidence, Drake heard a rustling noise in the nearby bushes. He ran as fast as he could, and there lying in a ball was a dirty, wet, whimpering Bailey. She looked into his eyes. "Superman? You look more like my brother."

Drake grabbed her in his arms, hugging her tightly. He kept telling her how sorry he was and let her ride piggyback all the way home.

The next day, Bailey had tiptoed into Drake's room to deliver a drawing of *him* dressed as Superman. She had sketched him standing tall, on top of the world, with a long, red cape trailing out behind him. Just above the picture she had written, *Drake, my hero, my Superman*. Drake held that drawing as a prized possession.

Drake leaned over the lake once again yelling out his answer to the riddle, "My answer is me, Drake Hanson." After saying his name, he let the picture slip from his hand. Like a feather, it drifted downward, landing softly on the water. He stared at his drawing, watching the water leisurely engulf it. The lake consumed it, taking possession of his treasure. He stood for several minutes waiting for a reaction, but nothing happened.

Drake could not help but think he had answered this part of the riddle incorrectly. He turned to face Sponke and Groger. He shrugged his shoulders. "I don't think I am the answer after all, guys."

A smile sprawled across Sponke's face as he pointed toward the lake. "Are you sure about that?"

Drake turned back to the water only to witness it bubbling and foaming. Spray sloshed up, soaking Drake's legs. Then, like a whirlwind, images exploded past at a hectic rate. They were whirring by so fast that Drake was only able to make out a few. He saw his family and friends from home, his new Kropite friends, and he caught a glimpse of himself speed by. Drake wondered where all of this was leading. Next, he saw some sort of battle going on, but couldn't decipher exactly who was involved.

Drake continued to watch the images zoom past. He grew dizzier by the minute. What happened next caused him to think of an electrical blackout. Just as suddenly as the images had appeared, they disappeared, leaving everything pitch-black. Reminded of Bleet Forest, he began to panic. Drake yelled to Sponke and Groger, but his friends didn't answer. His hands shook. His whole body trembled.

"What have I done?"

Out of the darkness, an angelic voice rang out. "Do not be afraid, Drake."

The voice washed over him, caressing his fears into nothingness. A low light glowed from under the water. His trembling ceased. He gazed at the shimmering lake.

The elegant voice echoed around him. "I know this all seems like a dream, but I can assure you that it is very real. Kropite *does* exist, and it *needs your help.* Until this point, your journey through Kropite has been a perplexing one. I can sense your confusion and skepticism. However, after you hear my explanation, my hope is that your quest will make more sense. Please, open your mind and listen to what I have to tell you."

Drake nodded his head. "I'm listening." He gazed around him as a low light slowly consumed his body. Drake held his glowing hands in front of his face then looked back into the lake.

"When Bailey entered Kropite, secrets about a dangerous stranger were revealed. I have determined that this stranger, not a native of this world, has been stealing children and using their *imaginations.* I am perplexed as to the reason for this despicable act. Many children, along with Bailey, reside in a factory. From there, I am unclear as to what is happening. This is where Kropite looks to you and the Story Stone. You are our *only* hope."

"I don't understand how I'm supposed to help. I don't know any more than you do," Drake responded. He squinted. "Where does the Story Stone fit into all of this?"

"The Story Stone that found you belongs in this world, but somehow it has been tampered with. These stones are *powerful*. In the wrong hands, they can be quite destructive. The stranger has been able to use the stone to get the children he wants from *where* he wants, but now the stone seems to be fighting back. I have deduced that the Story Stone has brought your sister here only to lure *you* to Kropite. The stone has chosen you for a purpose, and I am uncertain as to the reasoning behind it. When you found the stone in the woods and moved it, it became apparent that you are someone very special. No one has ever been able to move the stones before," the voice explained.

Drake nodded. "Somehow, I knew I needed to bring the stone with me."

"Kropite is most fortunate that you did obtain the stone. However, I believe that if you had not taken it with you, it would have found you by some other means. I am *certain* that Bailey and Luke are in *grave* danger. Unless you truly accept your purpose here, truly and *wholly* accept it, they may be lost forever. Without Luke, this world is at risk of perishing. Evil will take over and quickly destroy all that is good. You must look deep inside yourself. Know that you can help save this world. But, it is important that you believe in yourself because you are capable of great things. I am *sorry* to put this burden on you, but please understand that if Kropite did not need you so *desperately* then we would not implore you for your help."

Drake stared wide-eyed. "But where do I find them?"

"I will leave a map for you to follow. It will lead you to Luke and your sister. Now, go and do what you were meant to do."

The voice faded away and sunlight lit the lake once again. Drake had to cover his eyes to block the glare from the water. Just as the voice had promised, a rolled up map lay at his feet. Drake knelt down and grabbed the map. Before getting up, he glanced in the lake once more. The water was still.

He ran back over to the rock to tell Sponke and Groger everything, as word for word as he could remember.

CHAPTER 15

A Determined Fellow

"**I** knew it. That's fantastic! What do we do next?" asked Sponke who buzzed around with excitement.

Drake's right eyebrow rose slightly and he smirked. "Flying practice." He glanced around to locate a nice, clear spot away from the lake, rocks, and trees. He located a safe area and smiled at his anxious friends. "Here goes nothing."

Drake took a few steps back and crouched toward the ground. Using only his leg muscles, Drake sprung as high as he could. He went up in the air about two feet before he fell back to the earth. "Okay. That didn't go as planned."

Drake tried his method of crouching a dozen more times without success. Migisi loped close to Drake and slumped to the ground. She nosed at his feet and meowed.

"I saw myself flying. I really did, guys," Drake said.

"Just keep trying," Sponke said. He leaned close to Groger. "I don't know about this. I've never seen anyone fly without wings. Except Luke, of course." Groger nodded with his eyes glued on Drake.

Drake crouched preparing to try again, when an idea suddenly came to him. He reached into his pocket and pulled out another one of Kreeper's stones. He held the stone tightly in his hand and closed his eyes. Notions of flying, saving Kropite, and finding Bailey consumed him. With the stone firmly concealed in his hand, he opened his eyes.

Drake squatted low for one last effort. He sat, for a moment, in his hunched position. "I can do this!"

With a grunt, Drake pushed off with all of his strength. Like a rocket, he shot straight up. Migisi tilted her head back and watched him soar upward. She swished her tail as she held her gaze onto Drake.

"I did it! Look guys, I did it!" His eyes rolled back when he saw how far away the ground was. He shook his head, trying to regain focus, but knew he might pass out at any moment. His body grew unsteady and abnormally heavy. Drake tried to remain airborne by flappng his arms.

Groger could see that his friend was in trouble. He ran underneath Drake with outstretched arms. Migisi rose to her feet, moving away from the frantic giant.

"I'll catch ya buddy. Don't you be worrying!" Groger yelled into the air.

Drake knew it was useless. He stopped fighting. As his body plummeted back to the ground, his only hope was that his giant friend would catch him. However, he crashed downward at such a speed Groger never stood a chance.

Drake landed on his rear, skid a couple of feet along the dirt, and stopped right in front of the mezork's beefy paws. She began licking him and nudging his body over with her nose. Groger stood several yards away, his arms still outstretched for his anticipated catch.

The giant ran up to him apologizing, but Drake was lost in his desire to fly. "Wow! That was...so cool. I've...I've got to try that again," he said between big breaths.

He suddenly realized that Kreeper's stone was no longer in his hand. Taking a deep breath, he got to his wobbly feet. Drake searched. Sweat beaded on his forehead as his hands began to shake.

Migisi tilted her head and issued a deep-throated growl. Forgetting about the stone, Drake glanced at the cat then smiled. "I'll be okay, girl. That wasn't so bad. Let's give it another go," Drake said as he crouched back to the ground. Knotted leg muscles twisted and jerked as he launched himself upward again. His body hurled straight up.

"I did it!" He screamed.

This time Drake tried to steady himself. He wanted to attempt hovering in mid-air. It worked for about thirty seconds. The next thing he knew, he was plunging toward the ground yet again. He was getting much better at crashing, though, as it seemed a little less painful the second time around.

"Third time's a charm," Drake said as he got to his feet. Instead of crouching low to the ground, he bent his knees slightly. He pushed with such force that he looked like a rocket blasting toward the clouds. Drake tried hovering again and it worked. Now floating in mid-air, he turned his body horizontally. As if swimming, Drake swished his arms and legs, trying to pull his body through the air. He moved along several feet before his body decided to rediscover gravity. Drake yelled as he fought to keep aloft, but soon found himself careening toward the ground headfirst. Migisi launched herself into the air and swooped under him just before he hit the ground. Drake stumbled over her back, but was able to grasp her fur tightly so to stop himself from tumbling off his rescuer.

"I could've used your help before, girl."

Migisi purred softly.

With each new attempt at flight, Drake managed to travel higher and higher. The sensation of moving through the air generated butterflies in his stomach. It was terrifying and exhilarating. After reassuring his overprotective mezork that he would be okay, he practiced his flying skills for the better part of an hour. He walked away from the day's self-taught lessons with only a few small cuts and bruises.

"A *determined* fellow," Sponke said with a proud look. "Master Drake, I think we need to take a look at the map to determine the best route for you to take. If all else fails, Migisi can get you where you need to go." Just as Sponke finished his last word, Migisi let out an impressively loud roar while jumping into flight. She headed into the air, vanishing within seconds. Drake stared at the now empty sky.

"Okay, maybe I'm wrong. Either way, if we wait too long, I fear we may be too late," Sponke said.

"Where's Migisi going?"

"Don't know. Are you even listening to me?" Sponke asked with raised hands.

"Yes!" retorted Drake.

Sponke smiled as he smoothed out the map. While they studied their directions, Groger wandered into the woods to see if he could rustle up something for dinner. He had not gone far when he encountered a pond full of creepods.

"Creepods! You are some *nasty* little buggers, but how tasty." He set about trapping a few dozen and carried them back to the lake. After making a small fire, and prepping the small creatures, Groger cooked his meal.

Drake quickly became confused with Sponke's map-reading lesson and decided he was done for the evening. He was quite amused that Sponke continued giving his lesson even as he walked away. Drake meandered over to Groger to see what he was doing.

"What's up, big guy?"

"Cooking some dinner."

"What's for dinn—oh, yuck. What *is* that?" Drake asked scrunching up his face.

Groger glanced toward Sponke who was still busy with his map. "These are a fine delicacy called creepods. Once they're cooked, you'll be begging for more."

"What's a creepod?"

"A creepod is a nasty, *vicious* little creature. Kind of like...a frog?"

"Frog? How do you know about frogs?" Drake asked.

"Luke told me. He knows many things."

"That must be how Jude knew about goats." Drake nodded.

"Goats?"

"Jude was trying to describe a zeekier to me. He compared it to a very large goat."

"Luckily, I have never had to encounter a zeekier. I've heard about them, though," Groger interjected.

Examining the creepods once again, Drake cringed. "They don't look like any frog I know."

"Oh, really? Maybe because these little buggers have very sharp teeth. Once one bites you, they all attack."

"A delicacy—I'll take your word for it," Drake said as he walked toward the lake.

Stomach rumbling, Drake slumped to the ground. His thoughts turned to what lay ahead. His eyes grew hazy. The flight exercises had proven exhausting. His body yearned for rest. Drake slumped over with a heavy head and fell into a deep sleep.

Drake finds himself walking through a dense fog so thick he may as well be in complete darkness. He slugs along, unsure of his direction. Laughter suddenly splits the air. Drake stops as the fog begins to melt away. His mouth drops open as he peers around.

In every direction, as far as the eye can see, children play and frolic through an open field. They laugh, sing, and run about. Drake smiles as he reaches to tap a small girl who is standing close to him. At Drake's touch, she turns around. Her sweet innocent smile diminishes and contorts into a look of pure terror. She shuffles backward away from him.

"Wait, I just wanted to talk."

The little girl shakes her head, belting an ear-piercing scream.

"What's wrong? I'm not going to hurt you. Please don't go," Drake pleads, but the girl runs away.

With all of the commotion, the other children take notice of Drake. They too look frightened.

"What's wrong with me? Why are you so afraid?" *He looks back and the field is empty. All of the children have vanished.* "Why is this happening? What did I do wrong?"

"You have done nothing, Drake," *an eerie voice whispers.*

"What?" *Drake turns to face a boy who appears to be about his age.* "Why aren't you afraid of me, too?"

"The others are not afraid of **you**. They are afraid of **him**." *The boy points to a shadowy image coming toward them. Drake backs away as the figure draws closer and closer.*

"Don't run, Drake. He will pass. He doesn't know you are here, so stay still."

Drake freezes. Just as the boy said, the shadow floats past them. Drake waits a few seconds before speaking again. "Who was that?"

The boy looks past Drake and shakes his head. "I can't tell you."

"Of course you can't tell me. No one seems to be able to tell me anything. Am I even still in Kropite, or have I traveled to some other world?"

"You are still in Kropite. This, however, is only a dream."

"A dream? I'm having another dream? Why am I having such strange dreams every time I fall asleep? I never dream at home."

The boy smiles. "You will always dream while sleeping in Kropite."

"Why?"

"Why is not important at this point in your quest. What **is** important is that your dreams can be very useful tools."

"How can they be useful if they don't make any sense?"

"This is where you are wrong. You must concentrate **very** hard. Focus on the important details. Your quest here in Kropite is a **puzzle** that you must solve. Your dreams are the missing pieces."

Drake tilts his head, trying to place the familiarity of the boy's way with words. He sounds much older than he looks. "So...you're not going to help me at all?"

The boy shakes his head and begins to walk away.

"Wait, who are you? What's your name? At least tell me that."

He turns his head so that his profile is backlit. "Sebastian. My name is Sebastian." *He grins then looks forward again.* "Drake?"

"What?"

"Tell him I'm here. Tell him I've always been here." *Sebastian moves ahead and vanishes into the field.*

"Wait, Sebastian! Who do I tell? What are you talking about?" *Drake yells, but Sebastian is gone.*

"Wake up, Drake," Sponke said, trying to rouse him from his slumber.

"What? What's wrong?"

"I have our heading."

"What?" Drake waves his hand at the bug. "No, let me sleep."

"Up! Up! Up boy, it's time to leave. Take a look at the map," Sponke says rustling the paper over Drake's ear. "See here, I've found the town...*Tons of Imagination, Inc.* This is where Luke and your sister are."

Drake yawned then blinked several times. "That's really what the town is called? That doesn't sound like the name of a town. It sounds more like a business." Drake straightened himself and rubbed the sleep from his eyes. He got to his feet. "*Tons of Imagination, Inc.* I've heard of that somewhere before. Let me think." He scratched his head. Groger and Sponke waited quietly for him. Drake repeated the name of the town over and over several times before it came to him. "I've got it!

That's who published *Luke of Kropite.* There was never an author's name on the book, just that company. I used to think that was odd because *every* book has an author." Drake shook his head. "I just figured several authors or a book company put it together. So that means...that means this *crazy* person that I have to go and fight is the person who published my favorite book." Drake scowled. "The lake told me he uses kids' imaginations for his own personal gain, but she wasn't sure why. He's actually sucked Luke's imagination and adventures *right* out of his head. That's how my book came to be. Don't you see?" Drake said kicking at the ground. "He's using thoughts and ideas right from children to fill the pages of the books he sells. And he has Bailey!" Drake stopped talking. He looked at his friends with narrowed eyes. His mouth drew together with determination. "I'm ready guys. Let's do this." Drake scanned the sky. "Migisi!" he screamed.

Migisi immediately emerged from what seemed like thin air and dove toward the ground. She landed with a thump and padded directly up to Drake. Sitting on her haunches, she gazed down at him and began to purr. The cat's sounds relaxed him and his anger slowly subsided. He placed his hand upon her leg, gently caressing it. Migisi's fur, softer and smoother than silk, reminded him of his dog's coat. Her purr was hypnotic, like a lullaby sung to the comforting rhythm of his favorite rocking chair. Drake let out a sigh. He stared at his furry friend for several moments, lost in her beauty.

Shaking his head, Drake took a few steps back. He stood and admired his new friends. He beamed with pride at his small army, readied for battle. United with a common purpose, they stood strong—ready to rescue Bailey and Luke. He knew that he could do anything with the help of his Kropite friends.

"We're ready. Where's the map?" he said, as though he were a general speaking to his soldiers.

"Right here. Take a look at this so you know where to go."

Drake studied the map with Sponke for several minutes. "I think we're good.

Drake moved back over to Migisi, stopping in front of her massive feet. Holding his head back, he gazed up at her. The mezork tucked her head to peer down at Drake. Their eyes met. Without a word between them, she lowered herself to the ground. She nosed at him then laid her head upon her paws. The cat-dragon continued to stare into Drake's eyes. Migisi's strong maternal instincts to nuzzle and protect him proved she regarded Drake as one of her own. He stroked her cheek and whispered into her ear.

"Migisi, I'm so glad I found you. None of this would be possible without you. I'm not sure what's gonna happen once we reach the town, but I do know that as long as you're on my side, I can do anything." She responded with a gentle growl.

Drake looked at Groger then jerked his head. "Go head, big guy."

Groger mounted Migisi, and Sponke flew up to perch in front of him. Drake looked into the sky. He shuddered at what he was about to do, but made himself focus. He stooped slightly then jumped with all his might. He shot directly into the sky. After rocketing about fifty feet off the ground, he steadied himself. Migisi followed suit, jumping into the air just behind him.

"This just might work," he said as he floated along.

Drake had not realized it, but upon his takeoff, the last of Kreeper's stones inched its way toward the opening of his pocket. As he continued to stable himself, the little stone slipped out falling into the water below with a splash.

Drake's only concern at this point was trying to remain in flight, so he took no notice of the churning, bubbling, and frothing water just below him. However, Sponke *did* notice. He tapped Groger on the shoulder. Groger nodded his head, having already spotted the strange activity taking place on the lake's surface.

Drake held his arms out horizontally, trying to balance himself in the air.

"Look guys. It's working," he said glancing back toward Migisi. Drake saw his friends staring at the water below. He looked down, as well.

The lake spouted its liquid upward, just missing his feet. He pulled himself higher and farther along to avoid the spray. Another huge geyser exploded into the air, but this time it sent an object rocketing skyward. Instinctively, Drake shot a hand forward to catch it. Something hard and fiery slammed into his hand. The sting burned his palm. Drake gazed at his clamped fist. He slowly loosened his fingers. His eyes widened as he stared at a treasure he thought he might never see again.

The Story Stone glowed and pulsed. "Where have you been?" Drake asked, forgetting about the pain. He turned it over and over. It felt warm. A steady hum emanated from the brilliant blue stone. After a second or two, Drake pushed it into his pocket. He looked down. The lake had become calm once more. Glancing around for his friends, he realized he had traveled some distance away from them. By the time Migisi caught up with him, he was off and flying again. Sponke and Groger sat speechless while Migisi flapped ferociously to follow Drake.

The pulsing stone emitted comforting warmth from inside his pocket. With the stone now in his possession, strength and confidence surged through him. He flew on. His body grew extremely light and agile, helping him to slice through the air when he held his arms outspread. As he brought his arms straight out in front of him, he resembled a bullet firing from the barrel of a gun. Glancing back, he saw Migisi flapping her wings for all she was worth just to keep up with *him.* He laughed.

"I'm flying!" he yelled for no one in particular to hear.

The travelers flew on and on with Drake referencing the map several times. Finally, he spotted the factory. It was colossal, with wide pipes on the roof billowing out gigantic clouds of dark smoke. He pointed in the direction of the factory, then motioned downward to the ground. Drake landed first with Migisi touching down next to him. Sponke was the first to speak.

"That was great flying, Master Drake. You really caught on fast."

"Thanks," Drake responded. His chest heaved as his heart beat heavy inside his chest. He flopped onto a nearby rock.

"I am not sure what was happening with the lake back there. It was almost as if it was upset we were leaving," Sponke said.

"I don't know. It was pretty weird though," Drake said, moving his hand over his pocket.

He flew up to pat Drake on the head. "I'm going to have a look around. I want to make sure we're alone and safe here." Sponke left to explore the surroundings. Once he had disappeared, Groger loped over.

"I don't suppose you have something to tell me?" Groger asked.

Drake's eyebrow rose. "I think the lake was right in saying the Story Stone wants me to help save Kropite."

"Why do you say that?"

Drake pulled out the exquisite pulsing stone. "I never could have flown like that without this." Groger's eyes widened. Boasting his huge Groger grin, he patted Drake on the back.

Drake half-heartedly returned Groger's smile, and the giant was quick to notice something was not right. "What's wrong, Drake?"

"Remember when you told me to tell you the next time I had one of those strange dreams?"

"Yes."

"I had another one right before we left the lake. This one was even weirder than the last one."

"I was afraid you might say that."

"Why? What does it all mean?"

"Let me hear about your dream, then maybe I can venture a guess."

As he retold his dream, every detail came flooding into his mind without one element forgotten. After he finished telling his story, Groger sat back and scratched his head. Hardly able to sit still, Drake began flicking his fingers and kicking at the dirt. Drake yearned for the great conclusion Groger was going to reach.

Eventually, the giant roused himself from his thoughts. He looked Drake straight in the eye whispering, "Very interesting." Then he got to his feet and walked away, leaving Drake sitting alone and deflated. "Groger! Wait! Where are you going?"

Groger held his hand up. Sitting back down, Drake shook his head and kicked at the dirt again.

"I don't get it. All that thinking for nothing. What is *very interesting* supposed mean?"

In no time at all, Groger came clomping back to where Drake sat stewing. "I think I have it!"

"Why did you have to leave just now?"

"You were making me nervous. I had to get away to think clearly."

Giving Groger his undivided attention, Drake waited to hear his deductions.

"In your first dream, you said that it seemed like a warning about Bleet."

"Yeah."

"You dreamed about Bleet and eventually you found yourself there, right?"

Drake nodded his head.

"In your second dream, you talked about a little cottage being picked up by massive trees, right?"

"Yeah."

"My guess is that the trees were the protectors of the house. That *might* equate to your being *Bailey's* protector. It could also mean that you are Kropite's protector as well. The voice instructed you to let go of your fears. I think you are well on your way to doing exactly that by learning how to fly, and accepting your responsibilities here. I guess this means you can see into the future a bit," Groger proclaimed.

"Sounds pretty good so far. What else?"

"The third dream is a little harder to interpret, but I *think* it is safe to conclude that the evil being who is kidnapping children is a man. The children were running and screaming, as they were obviously afraid of him. As for Sebastian…well, Luke had a younger brother named Sebastian. At least, he used to."

Drake's eyes widened. "The boy in my dream could be Luke's brother. But, you said used to. Where's his brother now?"

"I really don't know the whole story, but I do know that Luke's brother went missing right before he came to Kropite.

This is part of the reason Luke became a Helper. I guess he was hoping to find Sebastian one day, but he never did."

Drake glanced around. "Should we tell Sponke about my dreams?"

Groger shook his head. "Not now." The giant gazed ahead. "He has too much on his little mind as it is."

Drake nodded then yawned.

CHAPTER 16

Tons of Imagination, Inc.

Drake blinked several times, suddenly finding his eyelids heavy. His shoulders slumped as he tried to keep talking with Groger.

"You look exhausted. I think you should get some rest before we head into that town." Groger said pointing ahead.

"Why am I so tired? I haven't even been awake for that long."

Groger glanced around for Sponke. "Where has that bug flown off too?"

Drake released a huge yawn. "Don't know. He said something about going to look around."

Groger pointed back at Drake. "Flying has taken a lot out of you. Plus, you have quite a bit on your mind. I can't imagine the pressure you must be feeling."

"Oh, thanks for reminding me." Drake rolled his eyes.

"I'm sorry, but I speak the truth. You *are* the chosen one. If what we are about to do doesn't prove that to you, then I don't know what will. It won't be long before we find the maniac responsible for all of this. You need as much energy as possible. Get some *rest.*"

Drake shook his head while rubbing at his eyes. He just could not believe how tired he was. "I don't want to sleep again. I'm tired of the strange dreams."

"Your dreams mean something. Sebastian told you that. Maybe we can gather some more information from your dreams *before* we enter the factory."

Drake knew Groger was correct because his visions *were* turning out to be useful. Finally surrendering, he chose to rest. Drake walked clumsily over to Migisi and curled up next to her. The mezork's purr lulled him to sleep almost instantly.

At first, Drake finds himself in the town singlehandedly rescuing Bailey and any other child he can reach. He is the strongest person in Kropite. He is invincible.

As Drake slept, he tossed and turned. Migisi watched him nosing him every now and again.

His dream fades. It disappears altogether leaving him standing in a deep, dark abyss. Garbled images parade around him with broken voices emanating from all directions. In a snap, he finds himself in a room lit with bright lights and people talking all at once. Drake stares around him, wondering where he is, when a familiar face meets his eyes. Bailey sits huddled in the corner of the chaotic room. Hiding her face in her hands, she sobs hysterically. Strange people fill the room with no one even acknowledging his sister. She sits alone, crying. He reaches toward her, calling her name. There is so much noise and commotion with all the people crammed into the tiny room that she does not seem to hear him. He watches helplessly as Bailey continues sobbing.

After a while, a beautiful girl who looks to be about ten, shuffles into the room. Padding over to Bailey, she kneels beside her. The girl tucks her wavy, dirty blond locks behind her ears then lovingly strokes Bailey's hair. When Bailey glances at the girl, Drake can see tears streaming down his sister's face. Her hair is wet from her crying. Both Bailey and the girl are wearing, what appear to be, hospital gowns.

Why is she wearing that? Where are her clothes?

He tries desperately to remember what his sister had been wearing the day she went missing. He's frustrated that he can't remember at all.

Bailey moves her gaze across the room in Drake's direction. **Does she see me?** *She wipes her eyes, blinking several times. Bailey looks back at the girl, then at Drake again. A smile spreads across her face as she reaches out for her brother and calls his name. Drake returns her smile and moves toward his sister. He walks only a few steps when he smashes into an invisible barrier. Drake places his hands against the clear wall, pushing with all his strength. It remains unaffected by his efforts. He stands back helplessly watching Bailey. She calls to him repeatedly, but he cannot go to her.*

Her yelling stirs several adults in the room. They move as one toward Bailey, surrounding her, gathering her into their arms. Drake watches horrorstruck as they march her away, kicking and screaming. "Noooo! Let her go!" Drake yells pushing at the barrier. "Bring her back! Don't touch my sister!"

Realizing his efforts are futile, Drake stops pushing. He stands motionless as he watches the door. Out of breath and defeated, he hangs his head. After several moments, he glances back and is startled to see the girl who was comforting his sister just seconds ago, standing directly in front of him. Bringing her hand up slowly, the girl places it against the barrier. A bit puzzled, Drake holds his hand up so it covers hers. The clear obstacle stands between the two children, preventing them from touching. He has so many questions but does not even know where to begin. All he can do is shake his head as he bites his lower lip.

She gazes at Drake with piercing blue eyes and smiles. "My name is Ka-leel. Where is the stone, Drake?"

*Drake glances at his pocket then taps it. Ka-leel grins at him and nods her head. "Keep it safe, Drake. You have to stay strong and keep trying. We need your help because you are the only one who can save us. Please **come**," implores the girl.*

Ka-leel turns her sight to Drake's pocket then back to Drake. Looking into her eyes, Drake sees a shimmer of deep blue pass over her already bright eyes. The hue is a perfect match with his stone for several seconds, and then returns to her eyes' normal shade.

A lump rises in Drake's throat making it impossible for him to find his words. He tries speaking to the girl, but no voice materializes. Giving him a wink, she turns to leave. Drake beats on the glass. Finally, he is able to call to her, "Wait, don't leave. Please, don't leave!" Without hesitation, she vanishes through the door. Drake surveys the room and screams, "Bailey!"

His own screaming woke him from his nightmare. He was drenched in sweat and shivering all over. Migisi licked him while her purr filled his ears. Drake's heart rate slowed, his trembling vanished, and he could think clearly once again. He pushed himself to his feet using Migisi's nose as leverage.

"Thanks girl," he said patting his friend on the head.

Swiping his hand across his forehead, Drake wiped away the sweat then meandered over to his friends. He rubbed at his eyes then peered at Sponke. "When did you get back?"

"I returned while you were sleeping." Sponke's eyes narrowed. "You sure are a restless sleeper. You weren't dreaming by any chance where you?" Drake shook his head. "I mean, I don't often awake screaming." Sponke said gazing at the sweaty boy.

Drake turned to Groger. The giant smiled and cleared his throat. "What's ya thinkin bout, Drakie?

Drake gazed at the giant for a moment then blurted out, "I wanna go into the factory alone."

"No! You're going to need our help," replied Sponke.

Drake grunted and turned to face Migisi. Drawing close to her ear, he spoke softly. "Hang in the sky, but stay behind the cover of the trees, girl. I'll call you when I need you."

Migisi thrust herself to her feet and shook her giant head. A shudder ran through her back as she stretched her tight muscles. After a broad, toothy yawn, she grazed her tongue along one cheek then the other. Sitting upon the ground, the mezork stared down at Drake with glossy eyes. She seemed to understand the importance of Drake's mission. Concern welled in her gaze. It was as if she were trying to give him every bit of *her* strength just by looking at him. Her protection surrounded him like a security blanket. Drake could sense her worry.

"I'll be okay, Migisi. I promise."

Migisi lowered her head, gently butting him in the stomach. After catching his balance, he leaned forward and kissed her on the nose. She tossed her head to the sky, bellowing a sonorous roar filled with love, worry, and admiration for her boy. The mezork then snapped her wings open, startling Sponke. Drake laughed at the shaky bug. Migisi made her impressive leap into the air and disappeared into the clouds.

"Are you ready for this, Sponke?"

"I think the question is, are *you* ready for this?"

"I can do this. I *have* to do this."

"While I was scouting the area, I found the entrance to the town. It isn't far. It's just through that dense stand of trees ahead," Sponke explained.

They pushed their way through the woods, walking as quietly as possible.

"Keep quiet. I don't think anyone is out here, but I saw a couple of guards stationed at the entrance of the town," Sponke instructed.

The trees opened directly to the town. Drake, Sponke, and Groger made sure to keep cover behind the huge trunks and bushes lining the outskirts of the small forest.

"We have to devise a plan of attack," Drake whispered.

"I think it best we start out with Groger. He will divert the guard's attention," Sponke instructed.

"Are you okay with that, big guy?" Drake asked.

"I is great with that one. I have some tricksies up my sleeve."

"Sounds fine to me. If you can get me in there, I can do the rest." Drake smiled.

Sponke gave a little huff at Drake's cocky attitude. "My, my you sure do seem to have found your confidence, Master."

Drake glared at the bug through scrunched eyes. "What happens if this diversion of Groger's doesn't work?"

A big goofy grin spread across the giant's face. "Then I will be releasing my meeky bombs." Groger held out several small objects that looked to Drake like small hand-grenades. "If I can't be getting us in, these little beauties will be working." He went on to tell them the bombs would not harm anyone, but would create one heck of a commotion.

"Sounds cool. Can I see one of those?"

Sponke shook his head while wagging his finger. "No! Drake, pay attention. We need to play it smart, so only use the bombs if it is absolutely, positively necessary. We don't want to cause too much of a commotion, so remain calm and patient. I'm sure our first plan will work out *just fine.* The guards at the front entrance appear fairly brainless, so I don't think we are going to have much of a problem getting in."

Once the plan was set, Drake waited while Groger initiated the first diversion. The giant meandered clumsily up to the two guards posted outside the entrance of the town. Each guard stood at least six-feet-tall, covered head-to-toe in armor. Upon closer inspection, Drake saw they had razor-sharp fangs jutting upward from a ghastly under-bite. Greenish-brown drool oozed from the corners of their mouths. Their skin had a mustard yellow tinge, and a pimply rash covered most of their faces. Drake had to look away as his concern for Groger began to heighten.

Groger approached the hideous guards. "Hey yous two, I is a bit lost and in need of some help. Could you be pointing me in the direction of Zeefab?" The guards didn't seem very interested in Groger, so he cleared his throat and repeated, "Will you be excusing me, but I says I am a bit lost and in need of your helps."

One of the guards glared at Groger through slitted eyes. It began spluttering in a foreign language, spitting as it talked. "Yookoo tayanna!" The hideous guard made a strange noise deep inside his throat. He stepped back and hacked a vile, milky-green substance directly on Groger's shirt. Groger stared mortified as the substance oozed downward, as if alive.

Without warning, Sponke flew into action, executing the backup plan. He soared overhead dropping meeky bombs all over the ground. Bombs erupted left and right, one nearly hitting Groger. Smoke began to fill the air. The giant ran back and forth dodging the explosions yipping and yelping all the while. Sponke, finally pulling himself together, began to aim his attack at the intended targets. The hideous guards clumsily tromped around, trying to escape the mini-explosions. However, they were not as lucky as Groger. Several bombs exploded directly upon their heads. But, as the giant had promised earlier, they caused no injury. Just chaos.

The ruckus did the job, sending the panicked guards stumbling and tripping over each other as the mini-bombs discharged around them. They just could not seem to get out of each other's way.

Drake wanted to laugh, but he had to remind himself of the seriousness of the situation. *Get your stuff together*, he told himself. Amidst all of the mayhem and smoke, he decided to act. Drake carefully edged toward the entrance, easily slipping past the guards. Groger rolled on the ground laughing himself silly, with Sponke buzzing near his head trying to get him under control. By this time, the guards had run smack into each other knocking themselves out cold.

Groger got back to his feet glaring at Sponke. "What was happening to playing it cool?" Sponke shrugged his shoulders. The two entered the town, trying to keep up with Drake.

"Where did he go?" Sponke whispered while glancing around. "He is one fast boy!"

Groger clomped along trying to follow Sponke. "Lookie there Sponkie." Groger pointed toward the massive factory sprawled out before them. "Maybe he be finding a entrance inside already."

"I think you're right. Let's find our own way in."

Drake continued running while attempting to take cover behind things. He stealthily glided past a few houses. The lit windows began to pluck at his curiosity, so he decided to peek into the next home. He was surprised to see what looked like a normal family eating dinner. They appeared human in every way, except for their movements. Their motions were stiff and they wore fake smiles upon their faces.

Even with such an artificial scene, Drake could not help but think of home. He sat with his face pressed against the stranger's window, imagining he was home with his family. He thought of all the wonderful meals his mom cooked. Well, maybe not wonderful, but he enjoyed them anyway. He wanted so badly to be back home with Bailey eating one of his mom's concoctions.

He jolted himself out of his trance, pushing himself onward. Drake sidled past several more homes. He stared wide-eyed as the factory blossomed into view. Making his way to the side of the building, he hid behind three large, metal barrels. He moved one of them out of the way, uncovering a small basement window. Reaching down, he tried to open the window, but it would not budge.

"It doesn't look like it's locked. It must just be stuck. Maybe I can kick it a bit to shake it loose," Drake said as he lightly swung his foot. The window shattered. He knelt down, staring inside the dark basement. With only a moment's hesitation, Drake shimmied through the window, trying his best to avoid the sharp edges of the broken glass. As he pushed himself through, a shard of glass dug into his leg. He gritted his teeth at the bite of the jagged fragment on his skin, but he kept moving. Stumbling through the window, Drake landed flat on his back.

Once inside the building, Drake looked immediately at his leg to inspect his wound. He discovered a fading, bloodless scrape. He jumped to his feet, looking back at the broken window. Blood trickled down the glass. He looked at his leg then at the window again.

"How is this possible?" He felt the stone pulsing in his pocket. He pulled the warm, glowing gem out and held it in front of his face. "It's because of you." He held it tight. Drake was about to return it to his pocket but stopped. "Maybe my pocket isn't such a safe spot."

He knew that without the stone, his rescue mission was going to be impossible. While thinking about how to attach it to his body, an intense heat began to radiate from its surface. The stone became almost too hot to hold. He tossed it from hand to hand.

Smoke rose from the stone. Tugging on his shirttail, Drake wrapped it around the treasure. A strange humming came from within the illuminated rock. He put it up to his ear. It was now cooler. Releasing his shirt, Drake grasped the stone in his bare hand once again. He lowered the stone and stared at its bright light. It began to shrink. Within seconds, it was the size of a watch face. It rose out of his hand and began to spin around and around. The spinning moved so fast, it whistled. Within seconds, it dropped back into his still outstretched hand.

The stone popped, sizzled, and jumped on the top of his palm. With each pop, Drake jerked. The stone continued in this manner for several moments before lying still again. A last leap sent the stone jumping upward. It crashed down and clamped onto his wrist with a loud snap. An electrical shock soared up his arm and through his body, making his muscles and joints tighten.

"Whoa!" Drake exclaimed.

He gazed at his new Story Stone, set inside an intricately woven, black, leather strap. On either side of the stone were intertwining ropes forming a crisscross pattern that twisted its way around his wrist.

"Intense," Drake said.

The stone continued to glow and pulse just as it always did, but it was smaller now. Electricity continued to course through his veins, making the hairs on his arms stand on end. Glancing down Drake noticed that a dim glow encircled him. Drake held his hands up and turned them back and forth.

"I'm glowing again, just like I did back at the lake."

He stared at the pulsing stone nestled against his wrist. It grasped him with an unbreakable hold. It was now bound to him as a protector, a source of power, and a guide.

Drake tore his gaze away, knowing he needed to get moving. In his pursuit for an exit, he noticed several strange things being stored in the damp basement. There were shards of metal scattered around a huge open oven. Old suits of armor hung on the walls surrounded by helmets, swords and spears. Stacked in the corner were metal barrels identical to the ones he saw outside the window. He walked over to take a closer look at the label on one of the barrels. *Mezerol: use with caution. Overexposure can lead to permanent memory loss.* Drake shrugged and continued to look around.

To the left he was surprised to see several cages with live animals in them. He moved closer. Most of the cages were small, housing rabbits, guinea pigs, and mice. However, a larger cage imprisoned three kittens. Curled up in the corner of the huge cage, he spotted a tabby, jet-black Persian, and a white and black striped cat, that reminded him of a tiny Migisi.

The animals tugged at Drake's heartstrings. He looked back at the barrels, wondering if the animals were test dummies for some science experiment. After looking around to confirm he was alone, Drake opened the cages one by one and hoisted the animals out of the broken window. He smiled as they all scurried free.

"Back to work," Drake said to himself as he continued his search for a way out of the basement.

He spied a set of stairs toward the back of the room. He tiptoed up toward a closed door. Drake pressed his ear to the door. Hearing nothing, he ever-so-gently turned the handle.

It opened into a long, stark-white corridor lined with many other doors, reminding Drake of a hospital. He recognized the hall as the same one he had seen from the images in the lake. He walked to the nearest door and tugged on its handle. Finding it bolted, he moved on to check the others. Most of them wouldn't budge. The ones that did opened into vacant hospital rooms. Drake continued walking down the hall. His mind wandered to his friends. *I should have let Sponke and Groger come with me. This would have been a whole lot easier with their help. I wonder what they're doing?*

Unbeknownst to Drake, his friends had found a way into the factory as well and were searching for him. They wandered quietly down similar corridors.

"Where is that boy?"

"I don know Sponkie." Groger stared around him. "This place is being huge. It be smellin' funny too."

"Oh hush and keep looking." Sponke glanced around. "I think it might be better if we split up. This place is big. We'll never find him at the rate we're moving."

Groger clomped along checking door after door while Sponke buzzed on ahead.

By the time Drake had discovered his seventh hospital room, he decided to search inside. He pushed the thick, heavy door open and surveyed the room. Still holding the door, he stepped across the threshold. A waft of antiseptic filled his nostrils. He released the door. With a sucking noise, it swished closed. Moving to his right, he noticed several more metal barrels with *Mezerol* posted on the front of each. To his left, he observed various whirring and beeping machines. A railed bed resided in the center of the room, along with a table containing a tray full of strange instruments. His eyes fixed on six, blue, metal lockers situated in the back of the room. He scooted toward them

Drake threaded his finger around the metal latch of the first locker and tugged upward. The handle jiggled, shaking the entire door. After several attempts, he moved on. The next two rejected his efforts as well. However, he found the fourth locker slightly ajar.

As he reached to open the door, voices coming from the hallway startled him. He grabbed the locker door and jerked it all the way open. Relieved, he found it empty and just large enough for his body. Drake turned sideways and shimmied inside. Silently, he pulled the door closed behind him.

The lab door opened. Drake peeked through the slats on the front of the locker. Six people, all dressed in what looked like hospital uniforms, filed into the room. Two of the adults carried in a young girl, who was unconscious. The men walked over, gently placing her on the bed in the center of the room. It was the same girl from his dream earlier. He would never forget her face. *Ka-leel*, he remembered.

A tall woman moved toward Ka-leel and placed a mask over her mouth. Drake could see a tube running from the mask over to one of the Mezerol barrels. He remembered the sign on the barrels saying something about memory loss. Drake scrunched his face and thought of Bailey.

A burly, masked man approached Ka-leel next. Only his vivid green eyes were visible. Drake labeled him in his mind as an *evil* doctor. The man placed a helmet on her head and flipped a nearby switch. Drake could see wires that attached the helmet to a huge machine, which emitted beeping and clicking sounds. Ka-leel continued to lay peacefully on the table, seemingly unaffected by what was happening to her.

Drake's attention soon focused on an enormous television screen attached to the wall. Here he witnessed strange images flashing past as a movie played in triple fast-forward. He was unable to decipher a single clear picture on the screen. Drake's eyes traced a thick cable that ran from the bottom of the television straight back to the helmet. A second cable ran from the side of the screen to the whirring machines.

Drake's eyes shot back to the screen where the images continued to zoom past. After several minutes, the television screen went black. A red beam of light shot across the room to yet another machine. It had a small door on the front with a blue light flashing overhead. A short, stout woman strolled up to the container and opened its door. She removed a small metal case. This container looked slightly larger than a shoebox. She lifted its lid. Drake blinked a few times, as he strained to see what was inside. It contained a single book. The woman grasped the book, giving a thumbs up to the people standing around the child. She carefully cradled the book. "Another *masterpiece* ready for copy."

Drake got a horribly sick feeling in the pit of his stomach. He suddenly never wanted to see *Luke of Kropite* again. Drake ground his teeth and watched as the woman, still clutching the book, exited the room. Shifting his attention to Ka-leel lying on the bed, anger bubbled inside of him. He yearned to get Bailey out of this demonic place.

A slender woman strolled over to Ka-leel. She gingerly removed the helmet and mask, and then carefully pulled her up into a sitting position. The lady stroked Ka-leel's hair until she opened her eyes. Ka-leel looked around the room. She reached out to a man in front of her who handed her a teddy bear. She grasped the stuffed bear close and smiled at the strangers. The woman helped her off the bed. She held her hand and they walked toward the lab door. As she opened the door to lead the young girl out, Ka-leel looked back at Drake's locker. Overhead lighting sliced across Ka-leel's face causing her eyes to sparkle. Then she winked.

Does she see me? Does she know I'm in here?

Drake waited for the adults to clear the room before he emerged from his hiding place. He shuddered at all he had just witnessed. Running for the door, he jerked it open and bulleted back into the corridor.

After checking about twenty or more doors, he slowed his pace, feeling a bit dejected. *I'll be happy if I never see another door again*, he thought to himself as he walked past several more without even inspecting them. He slouched and grumbled just under his breath, "This seems hopeless."

Looking ahead, he noticed a strange light coming from underneath one of the doors. As he moved closer, the light grew brighter and brighter. He could not help but reach for the handle. He wanted so badly to see what was behind it. With great care, he turned the knob.

CHAPTER 17

The Power of the Stone

Drake, expecting to walk into another white room, frowned in confusion. His feet brushed through thick grass. "What?" Drake asked, looking around at the unforeseen setting. He stood, staring wide-eyed at an exquisite garden. It was an *outside* world located *inside* the building. He could see the walls lining the perimeter of the room, but no ceiling above him. *What is this?*

Stretched before him, a rainbow of flowers and shrubs carpeted the garden floor. Fragrant roses, lavender, and lilacs invaded his nostrils. A kaleidoscope of butterflies fluttered about the garden as children ran freely on the grass, playing games and laughing.

Brightly colored benches occupied by children lined the edge of a sublime pond in the center of this retreat. Dainty lily pads floated like islands on the pond's surface where croaking frogs playfully leaped. It was like a paradise.

To his left, Drake spied lop-eared bunnies hopping about, while others ate right out of the children's hands. It was a child's dream world. Light, wispy, music played all around him, adding to the tranquility of the setting. The music caused him to yawn. He contemplated lying down for a rest, but something kept him from giving in. Drake shook his head.

He deeply wanted to run and play with the others so he too could be worry-free and just enjoy being alive, to ditch his burdens. For a few moments, Drake forgot why he had come to the factory in the first place. The garden was hypnotic.

"This isn't real. I have to get it *together*," he said. He scurried over to a row of bushes to take cover and think. He twisted along, hiding behind the shrubs as he went. Drake peeked out every now and again to scan as many children as he could. It was hard to distinguish one from another, as they all wore their long beige nightgowns. *Bailey, where are you? Please be here*, he thought as he searched.

Several times he was *sure* he spotted Bailey. Little girls with long, dirty-blond hair flowing down their backs made him catch his breath. But after moving to get a better look, Drake's heart would sink. He stood in his shrubbery grumbling to himself. He hit his thigh with his fist, then kicked at a hanging branch. Drake peered at the ground, unsure of what to do next when a familiar giggle sounded in front of him. He looked up, and there she was! Drake gazed at his content sister. Her happiness caused Drake to frown. She didn't look sad, but looked almost over*joyed* to be there.

Bailey was talking to a boy who looked about seventeen. His mind wandered back to his book. Drake grinned. *Luke.* The guardian had the exact same hair color as his, but wore it a bit longer. He was roughly the same height and build as Drake, with uncannily similar facial features. Drake stared at Bailey and Luke for several minutes becoming absorbed in the board game they were playing. A slight breeze swept across her face, blowing some loose strands of hair over to the side. Seeing his sister sent his mind reeling once again with memories.

The day they brought her home from the hospital changed Drake's life forever. She screamed and cried all the time, sending Drake running for the sanctuary of his room where he would bury his head into his pillow. She was little and helpless, taking every moment of his parents' attention. He felt as though his parents had forgotten about him. He remembered, at five-years-old, thinking, *I need Mom and Dad, too. Why won't they play with me anymore?*

Drake had begun acting out in the hopes of getting his parents' attention, but this only resulted in time-outs. One day, he screamed at his mom that he hated Bailey, and wished she would go back to wherever it was she came from. Then he stomped away, pouting and slammed his door. After about an hour, he emerged from his room and crept down the hall. All was quiet, so he tiptoed. He peeked into her room, seeing Bailey in her crib fast asleep. He slipped inside, over to the bed. Drake gripped the crib bars and pushed his face against them to stare at his sleeping sister.

He had remained by her side for several minutes thinking, *Why are you here? Life was just fine before you came.* As he stepped back to leave, his hand caught in between the bars of the crib, twisting his skinny wrist. Without thinking, he grunted loudly, waking Bailey from her sleep. Instead of screaming at the top of her lungs, as she always did, she turned her head and looked right into Drake's eyes. She gurgled, then the biggest grin spread across her face.

Bailey was smiling for the first time, and it was at Drake. He forgot about the pain in his wrist as he leaned against the bars. With her brown eyes glued to her big brother, she made cooing noises, waving her arms around in excitement. Bailey never stopped smiling at him, and from then on, he had proudly accepted the job of big brother.

Drake had to jolt himself out of his memory to get his mind back on the mission. *I have to get Bailey's attention*, he thought as he stepped partially out of the bushes. He was not sure what he was going to do, but she was *his* sister and he was not leaving without her. Drake cupped his hands around his mouth. "Pssst, Bailey. Over here." Bailey turned her head at the mention of her name and met Drake's eyes. He motioned for her to come to him.

Bailey looked apprehensive, but got to her feet. She slowly walked toward Drake. She did not look like herself. Dark circles under her eyes reflected her exhaustion. As she approached him, Drake took her hand and smiled.

"I didn't think I'd ever find you. Are you okay? Are you hurt?" Drake asked, scanning his sister. Bailey shook her head. Drake looked around then back to Bailey. "I don't think any-one saw me. We have to leave *now*." Drake gave her hand a squeeze.

Bailey squinted her eyes. "Why?"

"Because it's time to go home."

"I am home."

"No, you're not. What are you talking about?"

Bailey tilted her head to the side. "Who are you?"

Drake felt as though someone had just punched him in the stomach. "Who am I? I'm—" Drake stopped talking. "Mezerol." He stared at his sister. "It's Drake, your big brother."

Bailey shook her head.

"I can't believe this is happening." Drake stared blankly at his sister.

After several moments, Luke approached them. "Bailey, are you okay?" he asked. He had the same weary look and dark circles.

"Don't they let you guys sleep around here?" Drake asked.

Luke shrugged his shoulders.

"Look, I really can't explain everything right here and now, but you guys, both of you, need to come with me."

"Do I know you?" Luke asked.

"No, but I know you. I'm here to help you."

Luke stood in mute for a moment. "I cannot explain it, but I sense that you *are* here to help us. I don't feel that I belong here, but I cannot remember where it is that I *do* belong." Luke looked around him. "My presence here seems wrong, yet I am unable to escape. The only thing that feels right is staying close to Bailey." He glanced down at her. "I feel a kind of connection with her."

Even though he looked only seventeen, Drake knew Luke was so much older. It was obvious in listening to him speak that he was an adult.

"My only hope is that you have brought help with you. This place is swarming with ghastly guards who answer to a superior beast."

Drake began to fidget as he glanced around. "I do have help, but I'm not real sure where they are right now. I think if—"

Suddenly, loud explosions burst all around them and smoke filled the air. *Groger's meeky bombs.*

Drake felt a torrent of power dart through his body. He seized Bailey and slung her over his left shoulder. Grabbing onto Luke with his free hand, he pulled him along, too. Drake rushed to the door, flung it open, and sprinted down the long corridor.

He could not remember which way led back to the basement, so he made a guess, twisting the first available door handle. The door opened into a strange, empty room with two doors on each of the four walls. He stopped for a moment, placing Bailey back to the ground and trying to catch his breath. Bailey screamed and Luke pulled away from him. Drake instinctively raised his hand and gently moved it over Bailey's eyes. Her body slumped unconscious. He grabbed her just before she hit the floor.

It must be the power of the stone.

He pulled Bailey over his shoulder as Luke stared at him, horrified. Without thinking, he ran his hand over Luke's eyes, and he too slumped to the ground. "Now what am I going to do?"

Six of the eight doors opened to reveal the hideous guards Drake had seen at the entrance of the town. The guards emitted an ear-piercing wail. He held onto Bailey, who was still slumped on his shoulder, grabbed Luke by the shirt, and jumped. He flew straight up, nearly hitting his head on the high ceiling.

Hovering above, he watched as chaos unfolded below. As he jumped, the guards had simultaneously charged toward him. They smashed into one another, leaving a pile of monster-debris below. Drake struggled to hold onto Luke, but his limp, heavy body was proving too much for his fingers. Just as the guardian slipped out of his grasp, Groger barged through one of the closed doors, catching Luke before he hit the floor. The giant kept running, clutching Luke like a football. He headed straight through an open door on the opposite wall, as though he were running for the game-wining touchdown.

Drake stared mystified at Groger's sudden appearance and disappearance, but figured he had better follow. He floated back to the ground and landed next to the pile of guards. Some of the monsters lay unconscious, while others rolled, moaning in pain. Not wanting to waste another minute, Drake fled through the door following Groger. Sprinting down yet another corridor, Drake spotted his burly friend ahead. The giant appeared to know where he was going.

They ran until Groger stopped at a door. He smiled at Drake, grabbed the handle, and yanked it open. This door gave way to *another* garden. Drake looked around the vacant park. The last garden had been full of children and animals, but this room was desolate.

"Where are we?"

"I don't know," said Groger, "but Sponke does. He told me to wait here for him."

"How do you know where *here* is?"

"I don't, but *he* does," Groger said pointing upward. Drake looked skyward spotting Sponke diving toward the ground.

"Yes!" Drake yelled.

Sponke flew straight down yelling, "You did it! I knew you could!" He hurried over to Luke lying in Groger's arms. Sponke held his ear to Luke's chest.

"He's alive, isn't he?"

"Yup, boss. Drakie saved him."

"Only with the help of your meeky bombs. You should have seen it, Sponke. Groger came sailing—" Drake stopped mid-sentence as everything lapsed into complete darkness. Not a breath stirred. "How did the lights go out?" Drake questioned, remembering the room lacked a ceiling. "Sponke, Groger, are you here?" He waited in the ominous silence. He heard small groaning noises. After a few moments, the light returned. Drake squinted at the sudden brightness. He moved forward calling for his friends.

"Drake...don't come any closer," Sponke spluttered from the ground. The bug lay dazed and groaning rubbing his aching head.

"What's going on?" Drake asked as his vision adjusted to the bright lights. Five grotesque guards shoved their spears at Groger. They chanted at the giant in an undecipherable language while jabbing at his bulky body.

Drake latched onto Bailey's legs as they dangled over his chest. He jumped for the sky. Tossing his head upward he screamed, "Migisi, I need you!"

A massive wind invaded through the room. The flowers tussled in the wind while dirt whipped through the air. The guards froze in their spots, gazing skyward. She emerged from the clouds like a great storm, flapping her wings with enough force to hold her body hovering in mid-air. Her eyes scanned below while a deep, turbulent growl rumbled from her belly. She spotted Drake several yards below and she made her dive. Soaring past him, the mezork charged toward the ground. Her body struck the surface, sending a ripple through the dirt. Everyone rocked unsteadily as if an earthquake were taking place. She flung back her head, breathing her awesome fire into the sky. The flames billowed out, lighting the whole room as if everything were set on fire.

The guards stared paralyzed, unable to move from their stance, until the big cat shot her gaze directly at them. She pulled back her jowls and hissed a ferocious scream. The guards trembled, screeched unnatural sounds, and abandoned their spears and captives. A flurry of monsters rushed through the door heading back into the factory.

Drake floated to the ground, running over to fling his arms around Migisi. She nuzzled him while issuing her soft, grumbling purr.

"We need to hurry, Master Drake. Those guards might be sending for reinforcements, and we can't wait around for it."

"You're right," Drake said carefully slinging Bailey over Migisi's back. Groger did the same with Luke. After hoisting himself up, Groger settled in just behind Luke and Bailey. Sponke flew up and perched on Groger's shoulder while Drake drew close to Migisi's ear.

"I need you to take my sister back to See-All-Lake. Guard her. I'll be along soon."

The creature gazed disapprovingly into Drake's eyes and refused to budge.

"I have to do this, Migisi. You're going to have to trust me."

She snorted and jerked her head toward the sky.

"Go on, girl. I won't be long."

Sponke looked confused. He was just about to ask Drake what he had said, when Migisi spread her wings and shot for the clouds. Drake heard Sponke and Groger yelling his name, but their voices grew fainter and fainter as they melted into the sky.

Drake turned to walk through the door that led into the corridor. Unsure of why he was heading back down the long hallway, he continued. He kept moving until he found an open door. It led him back into the same room where he escaped his attackers moments ago. He stood and looked around wondering why he had returned to this room.

"Why didn't I go with Migisi?" he whispered to himself.

A door on the opposite end of the room opened revealing a huge, beastly man. With his gaze trained on Drake, he slithered into the room. Though he did not slither as a snake would, Drake's first impression was of a scaly reptile.

The man was at least six feet tall and extremely overweight. He had trouble walking, so he used a cane to keep himself upright. Drake felt confident that, if nothing else, he could definitely outrun him. A large, bald, bulbous head, sat upon the man's shoulders. Clouds of smoke encircled his skull as he puffed on the stub of a cigar. He wore a white suit and wire-rimmed glasses that squeezed into the flesh on either side of his face. His bushy white eyebrows joined in a huge unibrow. The man's nose pointed up slightly, like a pig, and he made grunting noises that resembled a sow as he moved. He introduced himself with a deep, booming voice.

"Hello, young Drake. My name is Koozog. I've been waiting for you." He snorted. "You took quite a while to get here. I've been growing rather impatient." He smiled as he shifted his weight. "I think you'll like it here."

Drake could barely stand the stink radiating off the man, and he spoke between gasps of breath. "Like it…here? I don't plan on…staying."

"Oh Drake, you have no choice. Your friends are gone. There is no one left to rescue *you*. Besides, you were the one I wanted all along. I took Bailey in the *hope* you would come rescue her. Congratulations, you succeeded! I am a bit perplexed though as to why you chose to save the boy. Why did you take Luke from me?"

Drake glared at Koozog through slitted eyes. Rage boiled inside of him, but he chose to say nothing. Koozog shrugged.

"I'm glad to have had them as my subjects, as they have proved *very* useful. I was able to use quite a *bit* of their imaginations. However, they are *nothing* in comparison to what lies inside you." Koozog burst into maniacal laughter.

Drake shuttered, but stood strong and brave. "How do you know who I am?"

"You underestimate me, boy." Koozog smirked. "The powers that flow through my veins are beyond your understanding. I know everything about you and your *Cape Coast.*" Koozog tapped at his head and said, "You're a very smart boy. I've been watching you for quite a while." He leaned closer and lowered his voice. "I think you and I could take over this simple little world, and turn it into a money-making machine." Koozog straightened up and smiled while sweeping one arm in the air. "I like it here, and I plan to stay for quite a while. This is a good place to lure in my subjects. After all, Kropite brought you to me, and you will be my best subject yet." The vile man snorted then rubbed his chin. "Your little friends could be of some benefit to me as well—Groger and Sponke I think you call them. I also like your pet—Migisi, is it? Yes, she will be a prize."

"Enough!" Drake interrupted. He scowled at Koozog. With every word the vile man had uttered, Drake's face had grown hotter and hotter. He felt the heat building up behind his eyes just as it had in Bleet. Closing them as tightly as he could, Drake was able to calm himself, suppressing his anger.

He opened his eyes. "Koozog, there is *no* way I would *ever* join with you. You are a foul, *disgusting* thing. What you do here is *sick*, and I plan to stop you. If you touch my friends, it will be the *last* thing you ever do."

Koozog threw back his head again, laughing at Drake. The stinking man's laughter thundered around them. Drake cut his eyes at him. "I need to know one thing, Koozog."

Koozog responded, baring his hideous, yellow teeth. "What, boy?"

"I want to know how you are using the Story Stone."

Koozog laughed. "If I gave away all my secrets, how would I be able to accomplish anything? I am the only one who knows the secrets of how to travel through the Story Stone," he growled.

Drake glared back at Koozog. "If *you* are the only one who knows the secrets of traveling by stone, then how am *I* able to do it?"

Koozog looked puzzled. "*My* stone brought you here, idiot. You don't know the secret."

Drake smirked and thought, **Your** *stone? I think* **your** *stone is on* **my** *wrist. Who's the idiot now?* Drake tilted his head asking, "Have *you* actually traveled by Story Stone?"

Koozog glared at Drake. "I don't have to answer your questions, boy."

The two stood for a moment glaring at one another. Not knowing what Drake might be up to, Koozog summoned his guards. About twenty-five of Koozog's henchmen flooded through the doors.

"Don't let that boy leave my factory!" Koozog bellowed.

As they came at Drake, a blinding flash surrounded him, knocking down over half of the drooling monsters. Drake tilted his head astonished by what had just occurred. Smiling, he glanced at his wrist. The stone produced an intense blue glow. The other guards withdrew, but Koozog relentlessly ordered them to capture Drake. The mindless drones pressed on. Two succeeded in grabbing Drake's arms. He found that he could *easily* throw them off. He swung his arms, sending the guards flying across the room to smash headfirst into the wall.

During the scuffle, one of the guards latched onto the boy's right arm and sank its razor sharp teeth into Drake's flesh. Drake bellowed in pain as he thrust his left fist into the head of the monster. The guard released his arm and fell to the ground. Grabbing his wound and holding it tightly, he dodged the last few guards. Drake moved so quickly the guards looked as though they were moving in slow motion. Koozog's lower jaw gaped as if frozen.

Drake faced the remaining henchmen. They advanced toward him, growling and gnashing their sloppy, drooling jaws. Drake jumped, kicking his legs like a windmill, knocking most of them off their feet. He looked at the bite in his arm and was only a little surprised that it was already healing.

Beginning to feel superhuman, Drake desired more. As several other guards came at him, he discovered he could fend them off with ease. Drake threw a number of them against the wall, hurled others into the air, and kicked some into unconsciousness right at Koozog's feet. The few remaining guards seemed hesitant to approach Drake, making the boy a little *too* sure of himself. Looking at the chaos he caused, Drake strutted around and laughed.

While he was busy relishing in his own glory, Koozog caught him off-guard. Like a stealth predator, he slipped in behind Drake. He used his cane to reach around Drake's neck, strangling him close and trapping him. Drake fought, struggling for breath, but soon realized Koozog was much stronger than he had anticipated.

"You see, Drake, fighting is useless. I am *much* more powerful than you are. You're a mere boy. I am a *god!*" Koozog bellowed.

"You are not…a god. You are a…monster who…*can't win*," Drake sputtered between gasps.

Koozog held Drake in his trap, laughing at his feeble attempts of escape. The Story Stone began to pulse as Drake continued to struggle against the monster's weight. Out of the corner of his eye, he saw his stone. He could feel with each pulse a new energy inside him. With strength unknown to him, he pushed at Koozog's hold and slipped out from under his cane. Koozog stared at Drake in bewilderment.

Stepping backward and rubbing his neck, Drake said, "You actually think of yourself as a *god?*"

"Of course. The definition of a god is a person who possesses superior qualities that others see as god-like. The people of this town worship me."

"The people of this town are *not real.* You're crazy if you think anyone normal would think of *you* as a god. You are foul and evil and you *will fall.*" As Drake spoke, he reached down to collect a discarded spear lying on the ground. He twirled it in front of him. Koozog gaped at Drake's ability to handle the weapon.

"You are not worthy of calling yourself a god," said Drake. "Your victims are children, *helpless children.* You have chosen victims who are unable to fight back, and that makes you a coward!"

He swung his spear low to the ground, hitting Koozog in the ankles. His legs buckled under him, sending him clattering to the floor. Drake grabbed Koozog's cane and broke it over his knee. "Unfortunately for you, I am a *child* that *fights back.*"

Drake threw the cane pieces at the now gasping man, and raised his arm high in the air yelling, "I have the power of the Story Stone, not you! You *will* be defeated. If not today, then another day. That I *promise.*" A powerful explosion erupted from the stone, causing Drake to fly backward and smash against the wall. Everything crumbled around him.

Koozog's face turned ruby red. The monster slammed his fist onto the ground, sending sparks everywhere. An enormous crack opened in the ground. The crack headed toward Drake like a bolt of lightning.

Jumping to his feet, Drake ran to the opposite end of the room. Koozog yelled for more guards. Drake crouched, ready to make his escape. The ceiling was solid. Drake groaned. He protectively wrapped his arms around his head and sprung up with such force that he burst through the roof, soaring up and out of the factory. *That wasn't so bad.* Drake raised his arms above his head, spiraling skyward, and disappeared into the clouds beyond.

Koozog shook his fists at the sky. "I will find you, Drake. You *cannot* win!" Several more guards burst in and stared around in confusion at the disorder that filled the room. They helped Koozog to his feet and out the door. He grumbled on his way out saying, "There *will* be another time, Drake Hanson. Next time it won't be so *easy* for you."

CHAPTER 18

Evil is On the Rise

A warm cloak of comfort surrounded Drake as he thought of Bailey being safe with his friends. Now worry free, it was time to have a little fun with his newfound power. Glancing at the stone he said, "Let's see what you can *really* do." He looked up and flew straight for the sun. Raising his arms above his head, he soared in and out of clouds, spiraling along at breakneck speed. The wind cut across his body as if he were a knife slicing through soft cheese. The air was crisp and cool sweeping across his face and into his mouth. Even after the struggle he had just experienced, his anger flowed out of his body, caught the wind, and soared away into the clouds.

Drake grinned as he captured a subtle scent skimming across the sky. Honeysuckle. Drake drank in the sweet scent, letting it fill his insides with calmness.

"I could stay up here forever," Drake said as he rubbed his head. "Where am I supposed to go anyway?"

Drake shook his head as he hovered high in the air. Gazing down, he didn't recognize what was below him. He pulled the map out of his pocket. He tried to decipher where he might be. "The lake. I need to get back to the lake," Drake remembered.

The boy peered below him, scrutinizing his surroundings. A small creek lined with trees and large rocks skirted along to his right. A cluster of oddly warped trees lay directly below him, and a deserted field lay to his left. He glanced at his map, locating all three landmarks. Pinpointing his general location, Drake concluded he still had a few miles until he reached his friends.

Carefully folding the map, he returned it to his pocket. Drake took a deep breath, trying to catch the honey smell that dangled in the atmosphere just moments ago, but it had vanished. He tilted his head up, opened his arms, and pushed his body high into the sky. Drake sped along. He shot in and out of the fog, feeling as though he had been flying all of his life. The sensation was indescribable. He knew it would be easy for him to become accustomed to his new life in Kropite.

The thought of never going home interrupted his fantasy. Picturing his mother, father, and Bailey at home without him was unbearable. His body sagged with exhaustion. He thought he might drop from the sky at any moment. Drake blamed the weakness on the after-effects of his fight with Koozog.

As he flew on, he felt fatigue consuming him, making the world spin. It was as though he were an airplane running out of fuel, and falling to the ground seemed inescapable. Before he could decide where he should land, a blast from behind sent him plummeting to the ground. His head and back smacked against the dirt. He sat up with a groan and held his aching head. Pain soared throughout his back.

"Why can't I see anything?" he moaned. With painful effort, he held his hand directly in front of his face. "I'm blind!" Drake struggled to his feet. He forgot his pain as his fear of blindness overwhelmed him.

"What's going on? Is anyone there?" Drake screamed.

No one answered him. However, he could sense the presence of someone, or something, close by. He reached to the ground to find something with which to defend himself. He gripped a long stick. He spun the staff in front of him and above him. *All right, focus, and concentrate on any noise you can hear.*

A low growling circled him. Keeping as deathly quiet as possible, he held his stance and listened intently. Feeling hot breath, he knew whatever circled him was closing in fast. Drake squatted low, swishing his stick close to the ground. Loud grunts followed his swings. Drake forced himself to stand, despite the aches. *No pain. Forget about the pain.* Spinning slowly, Drake swung his stick several more times, resulting in more grumbling and moaning from his attacker, or attackers. He sensed more than one. The creatures continued to advance on him. Drake was able to fend off quite a few, but as agile and quick as he was with his staff, he was still not quick enough. Two creatures closed in fast and overtook him.

Throwing him to the ground face first, the assailants kicked and jabbed him. Managing to roll over on his back, Drake pumped his legs into the air, launching his body back into a standing position. The pain from his fall subsided. A renewed energy pushed through his veins. Still unable to see, Drake realized he no longer had possession of his weapon. Three more creatures jumped him from behind and pulled him to the ground. A steady trickle of slime dripped onto his face as one of his captors spoke above him in a gurgled voice.

"Youuu are Drake, yesss?"

"I might be, why?"

"Why have you sssaved the one they call Luuuke? We thought we were freee of his good deedsss, and now you have brought him back. Thisss is *not* a good thing," the creature said, continuing to dribble slime all over Drake.

"You need to let me go and stop spitting all over me. Who are you?" Drake inquired.

The creature snorted. "I am Woknok. Jopper isss on your left leg, and Reezer on yourrr right. The rest of my army standsss in a circle around you, so I wouldn't move ifff I were you. We are pockaroos. You will come with usss."

Drake struggled to free himself, managing to get one arm loose. With his free hand, he swung his fist, succeeding in knocking all three of the creatures off him. The moment Drake rose up, five more pockaroos jumped him, forcing him to the ground once again.

"I'm at a huge disadvantage here. I can't see a thing!" Drake held his hands in the air. "Maybe we could talk things over. I'm willing to work something out," Drake argued.

"You mussst send Luuuke back to Koozog."

"Koozog? You work for Koozog?" As he spoke, his vision began to return. It was blurry, and faded in and out, but it was better than being blind.

"I work for no one but myssself. Koozog was merely a way to keep Luuuke out of my hair, but youuu had to go and ressscue him. Maybe by imprisoning you, Luke will come to meee," Woknok said.

Drake blinked several times. Everything was still terribly blurry.

"You won't have to wait long, you know. My friends will be coming to find me soon. I told them I would be right behind them, and I know that I'm late. I wouldn't doubt if they were already on their way," Drake told Woknok.

"Do you take me for a fool?"

"Kinda," Drake retorted.

Woknok began jumping around, violently swinging his arms and squealing. Drake's vision was becoming better with each passing minute. He was now able to view much of his captors. They wore hooded, black cloaks and their hairy paws dangled out of the yawning sleeves. Each creature boasted a smashed face with a tiny, pink nose sunken in just above the mouth. They reminded Drake of unsightly teddy bears, no taller than his knee.

You should be ashamed of yourself. You can take these guys. Get up and fight.

Before he could get to his feet, Woknok ordered his men to shoot him. Instantly, Drake fell back, unable to move a muscle.

"What did you do?" Drake asked through gritted teeth.

"Not to worry. The effectsss are temporary. We need to be able to mooove you without a fight, and thisss is the easiest way," Woknok insisted.

"My friends will be here any minute!"

Woknok held up what looked to Drake like a pocket watch. The object swung back and forth on a long chain.

"What's that?"

"*This?* This is my insurance that your friendsss will not discover your absenccce until I am good and ready for them. My brother invented this little beauty. It isss a Motion Sssaver."

"What does it do?"

"It setsss things in slooow motion. Your friends, wherrrever they are, are none the wiiiser of your absssence. To them, you are only a sssmidgen late. By the time they realize you aaare missing, it will be *too* late. They will come looking for you. I will caaapture Luke and return himmm to Koooozog. Then I will get rrrid of your friends." Woknok grew silent for a moment. His furry eyebrows rose as he drew close to Drake's face. "Evilll is on the rrrise. Kropite will fall. I can feeeel it in my bonesss."

Drake scrunched his face as Woknok's mildewed breath wafted up his nose. "What do you mean?" Drake asked.

"You are no longer a threat, ssso I will enlighten you. Kropite was once a very darrrk place. Before *heee* came." Woknok snarled. "Thisss world should not exissst. It should have perished long ago. Weee were sent here to make *sure* Kropite fell."

"We?" Drake continued to question, knowing it was irritating the furry beast.

"Me and the othersss. I'm not going to tell you whooo, but be sure that there are *farrr* worssse than usss. Should my mennn and I fail, the others will come."

The pockaroos loaded Drake's paralyzed body onto a cart they seemed to have constructed for this purpose.

"I'm sure you're a reasonable guy. Can't we make a deal or something?"

Woknok laughed and shook his head. Drake strained and gritted his teeth while trying desperately to look at his wrist. Finally able to view his stone, Drake frowned as a feeling of dread washed over him. The Story Stone, still attached to his arm, was black.

Woknok ordered his men to move the cart. The pockaroos scrambled about, assembling themselves around Drake. The small creatures pushed with heavy groans. It was a struggle, but in the end they were able to move along at a moderate pace.

Drake gazed at the sky, speaking his thoughts aloud. "It's like I'm a *magnet* for trouble. One bad thing after another, and I'm always right in the *middle* of it. No friends to get you out of this one, Drake. Now what?" Drake tried to turn his head as best he could. "I sure wish I could call Irick or Falco to help me."

"Master Drake, if you really think you can escape this predicament then by all means, try," a mysterious voice encouraged.

"What? Who said that?" Drake asked, trying to turn his head to see who was talking to him.

"I wouldn't try to move just yet, as the effects of that shot will last for a while," the voice instructed. It wasn't coming from inside his head, but he couldn't locate the source of the voice.

"Can you help me?"

"Yes, but I won't." The voice sounded relaxed.

"Why not?"

"Because you have to get out of this *yourself*. You need to prove to yourself that you can do this. Come on, Drake, you have been in *far* worse predicaments than this."

"You're right," said Drake, "but I always had some kind of help. My friends, or the stone, have always been there in the past. Now I'm alone." Drake found himself whispering.

"What about Bleet? You were alone there. You did just fine," the voice said as it slowly faded away.

"Bleet? How do you know about Bleet?"

There was no response. Drake knew the voice was right. He was alone in Bleet, with the exception of Jude, but *he* had done all the work. His confidence slowly resurfaced. He knew he had to regain the ability to move before he could act. He lay on the cart, waiting.

Eventually, the pockaroos stopped pushing. They had arrived at the entrance to a vast cave.

"Let me guess. There's a huge monster in there that is going to come out and eat me, right?" Drake asked, his voice dripping with sarcasm.

"Not toooday. We are going to hide you here for a whiiile then, when the time is right, we maaay feed you to our pettt," Woknok retorted.

"Whoa. I was only kidding. Do you really have a pet that's going to *eat* me?"

Woknok smirked. He shouted for his men to untie Drake and dump him into a hole to the left of the cave entrance.

Falling at least fifteen feet, Drake landed with a thud at the bottom of a huge hole. A thick layer of straw cushioned his fall. He lay there as the paralysis slowly subsided. Drake first bent his arms then his legs. He labored to his feet, attempting to scale the side of the cavity. He slid back to the floor.

A slight gleam caught his eye. He stared down at his stone. It was glowing once again. "Maybe I can just fly out," he said as he jumped. Upon reaching the top of the hole, he smashed into an obstruction that sent him careening back to the ground at full force.

"Do you really think I would put you in an *open* hole?" Woknok yelled down at him. Woknok tapped on an invisible shield blocking him from escaping his prison. Drake sat down and shook his head.

"Perfect," he uttered.

Drake tried to listen to what was happening above. He heard creatures yelling back and forth to each other. He heard the sounds of construction.

"Maybe if I figure out how to float up to the top of this hole, I could see what they're building." He got to his feet, concentrating on making his body as light as he could. At first, nothing happened. After several attempts, he found he could hover just above the ground.

"*Focus*, Drake," he said as he concentrated with all of his might. Slowly, his body lifted further and further off the ground. Drake floated like a feather to the top of the hole. Pressing his face to the invisible obstacle, he was able to see some activity, but could not decipher what it was.

After several moments of listening, a dark figure hovered just above his hole, startling him. The creature wore a hooded cloak to conceal its body.

"You're not going to get away with this!" Drake yelled.

The figure floated close to him and partially removed its hood. A ghastly face stared back at Drake. As grotesque as the creature appeared, it was beautiful to Drake.

"Kreeper?" Drake nearly shouted.

Kreeper held a gnarled finger to his lips.

Drake whispered now. "It was *you* talking to me while I was on that cart, wasn't it?"

Kreeper nodded his head.

"How did you know these guys were gonna ambush me?"

"I know a lot of things. That's not important right now. We need to get you *out* of there," Kreeper whispered.

"If you can get rid of that barrier, I think that I can do the rest."

Kreeper ran his gnarled hand over the barricade, chanting something just under his breath. As intently as Drake listened, he could not make out anything that the kreeton was saying. Whatever he recited seemed to be working though, as the obstruction took on a gray hue, wobbling up and down in a warped manner. In no time, it disappeared, leaving Drake free to fly out of his cage. Landing next to Kreeper, he held out his hand to him. Kreeper shook it and commanded Drake to leave.

"I will, just as soon as I put a stop to Woknok's plan," he said, kneeling down to gather as many rocks as he could. Drake stuffed the stones into his pockets.

"You are asking for trouble, Drake. I think you might want to listen to me."

"But Woknok wants to recapture Luke! Then this whole mess starts over again. I've saved Luke once. I don't want to have to do it again," Drake practically yelled. "Kreeper?" The kreeton had vanished almost as if in thin air. "Where'd he go?"

Woknok heard Drake ranting. He ordered his men to grab him. Drake did not wait around. He jumped off the ground shooting into the sky. Glancing down, he saw a large cage on wheels.

"That wouldn't hold Luke," Drake said with a chuckle.

He reached into his pocket and proceeded to hurl his rock raid upon the pockaroos. Drake pulled out rock after rock, chucking them at the wretched creatures. Hopping about over the ground, the small beings desperately tried to dodge the assault.

The pockaroos found cover behind some nearby trees. Within seconds, the small creatures popped back into view brandishing bows and arrows. Shielding themselves with the large trunks, they took aim at Drake, shooting sharp, poison-filled darts in his direction.

Without missing a beat, Drake easily reached out and caught every single arrow shot his way. The stone pulsated in its brilliant blue hue. Woknok was unsure of how to retaliate. A dim light encircled Drake, making him glow. Drake looked down at his body and smiled. "I'm glowing again."

The pockaroos scurried about in terror. Drake threw a few of their own arrows at them. He purposely missed his targets, not wanting to cause too much harm. Drake smirked as he watched the creatures jumping and yelping as the arrows whizzed past them.

Out of the corner of his eye, Drake saw Woknok trying to escape. He saved the last two darts for him. Aiming them both at Woknok, Drake threw them, watching as they glided toward the fleeing creature. The arrows never made contact with Woknok's body, but they did stab through his cloak, pinning him to the ground.

"Perfect shot!" Drake yelled as he descended toward the squealing Pockaroo.

"Who's feeling helpless now? All of his men gone and the fearless leader left to deal with Drake, a *mere boy*."

"Pleassse don't huuurt meee! I am sooo sssorry! I will do aaanything. Juuust don't huuurt meee," Woknok pleaded.

Feeling ashamed of his bullying, Drake stopped his taunting. He pulled the arrows from Woknok's coat. The creature jumped to his feet and tried again to retreat. Drake grabbed him by the wrist.

"I'm not going to hurt you, but you have to promise me you will leave Luke alone, and *stop* dealing with Koozog. If you can promise me this, then I'll let you go unharmed," Drake said pulling Woknok toward him. "I'm serious, Woknok. I'll be watching you."

"Okaaay! I promissse to leave Master Luuuke alooone."

"And?" Drake encouraged.

"And ssstop dealing with Koooozoggg. He is verrry powerfulll and at one time, I thought the mooost powerful creature in Krooopite. But now, I am unsuuure."

"That isn't important. What is important is that you gather your men and *leave*. Don't stand in Luke's way, because if you do, I'll come for you."

Just before releasing him, Drake reached into Woknok's coat and pulled out the Motion Saver. "I'll take this."

Obeying Drake, Woknok ran and called for his hiding army to retreat. Drake smiled as the pockaroos gathered their things and tried to evacuate as fast as they could.

"I *guess* that went well," Drake said to himself, walking away from the frantic creatures.

Drake surveyed the area, unsure of which way he should travel. He walked aimlessly for a while, feeling the impact of all that he had endured. His only desire was to get back to the lake to rest. As he walked on, he encountered a small, wooded area. It was dark and somewhat foreboding, but he was too tired to be cautious. Without much thought, he headed into the woods.

Hooting and high-pitched shrills exploded around him. Drake continued walking. Several small flying creatures divebombed him, but with a quick swipe of his hand, he sent them smashing into the nearby trees.

"It looks as though someone has come to grips with his powers," a voice from behind Drake declared. The boy spun around finding himself face-to-face with Kreeper.

"Kreeper! I thought you left because you were mad at me."

"Mad at you? No, I knew you could handle yourself. I was a bit agitated, as I am used to everyone following my orders. Somehow I knew you had your own agenda, and *I* certainly was not going to stand in *your* way."

"Kreeper, I don't have any more strength to fight. I'm so tired. If I were to stop walking and lie down right now, I might never get up," Drake said followed by a heavy sigh. "There are so many evil creatures running amok in Kropite that Luke is really gonna have his work cut out for him." Drake shook his head. "It's unbelievable how one person is able to control *all* of this. I'm glad that, once I leave, it won't be my responsibility anymore. Luke can keep this job." He leaned in and whispered, "I wouldn't do it for all the money in the world."

"From what I know of Luke, he doesn't think of it as a *job.* He takes pleasure in knowing that he has the ability to keep Kropite safe. I'm sorry you feel that we have burdened you," Kreeper said in a saddened voice.

"I'm sorry. I don't really know what I'm saying. So much has happened to me. I'm just so incredibly tired. Please, don't be offended."

The two continued without words for a while until a thought occurred to Drake. "Hey, Kreeper, I thought you had to stay in the darkness of the woods. How come you were able to come out into the daylight back there?"

"I'm not particularly a fan of daylight, true, but I knew you were in trouble and needed help," Kreeper said.

"Doesn't the sunlight hurt you?"

"No. Kreetons used to live with others in the sun." Kreeper sounded wistful.

"What happened?"

"We wanted to escape the persecution of others. Most do not find my kind to be...visually appealing. Over time, we grew tired of having to hide because of how we looked. We were harassed on a daily basis because of our appearance. Eventually, we took refuge in the dark forest. Bleet has become our safe haven, as most are afraid to enter it. Over time, we have adapted to living in the dark and gained the ability to create our *own* light," Kreeper explained.

Drake stopped walking and hung his head in shame. He too had judged the kreetons based on how they looked. He reflected back to when he had met the creatures in Bleet. They terrified him because of their appearance.

"That's awful, Kreeper. I'm sorry this had to happen to you and your people. I know where I come from people judge others in pretty much the same way. It's a horrible thing to do, and so wrong."

"No need to be sorry. I think it is safe to say *we* are friends, and have broken through a barrier I could have never imagined possible. I just may try to break out a bit more and see if I can make friends with others." Kreeper grinned. "Maybe."

"I think that would be a good idea, because you're a really great guy. Anyone who can't see that isn't *worthy* of your friendship."

As they walked, silence developed and grew.

"What is it, Master Drake?" Kreeper inquired.

"Nothing really. I just wish that somehow I could take a piece of Kropite home with me. I know I'll never be able to talk about this place when I get back home, because no one will believe me."

"Why wouldn't they believe you?"

"In my world, places like Kropite only exist in books, or dreams. In fact, when I first came to Kropite, I thought it was all a dream." Drake bit at the inside of his cheek. "Sometimes, I *still* feel as if I'm dreaming. There are only humans, like me, where I live. We have animals and stuff, but they can't talk to us. And the only things that fly are insects, birds and machines."

"That's sad. It doesn't sound like a very nice place to be."

Drake scrunched his face. "Why is that?"

"Because everyone seems…skeptical in your world. Maybe with a little imagination, your people would be able to open their minds to a world such as Kropite. Just because they have never experienced the creatures of this world doesn't mean they don't *exist*." Kreeper placed a hand on Drake's shoulder. "You are a *fine* young boy. I would like to think that someone would believe you. Jude spoke to me about your *strange* relationship with your mother and father. Surely they would support you?"

"My parents do support imagination. They encourage it. My mom is always saying children grow up too fast. She thinks they lose their imaginations too early. But I just don't think they would honestly *believe* me if I told them about Kropite." Drake's head drooped. "My mom would probably tell me to write about it, because it would make a great story."

"Interesting. I believe I have heard that you are eager to return home anyway, so why would you want to possess a reminder of *this* world?"

"I do want to go home, but my time here has been…I can't put it into words. Even though it's been pretty stressful, and dangerous at times, I wouldn't change it." Smiling, Drake got a far off look in his eyes. "I mean, how many kids can say they helped save an *entire* world?"

"I'm not sure. How many?"

Drake laughed softly. "None that I know of. Being in Kropite is one thing, but I've made *so* many friends here. I am going to miss all of you *so much*."

"And we will miss you."

Drake stopped again, his hands over his grumbling stomach. "Hey Kreeper, do you think there is anything to eat around here? I feel like I haven't eaten in weeks."

Pulling his hands from his cloak, Kreeper started to swirl them around in a circular motion. "What is it that you desire, Drake?"

"Oh, wow, I would *love* a huge cheeseburger."

"First you must picture this *cheeseburger* in your head, as I have no idea what it is," Kreeper said, continuing to swirl his hands. Drake thought about a massive burger piled high with cheese, lettuce, tomato, mayonnaise and ketchup.

Kreeper stopped swirling his hands and clapped them together. "Hold out your hands, Drake," he said as he revealed the biggest burger Drake had ever laid eyes on. He carefully placed it into the boy's open palms, offering an endearing smile.

"Yes!" Drake yelled as he commenced stuffing his face.

Once he had consumed the entire burger, he wiped his mouth with his shirt and thanked Kreeper again.

"I guess I better get back to the lake. I need to make sure Bailey's okay."

"Yes. That is very important."

"Maybe you could come back with me, Kreeper?"

"No. My place for now is in Bleet, with my people. But, I have a suspicion that we will cross paths again, young Master," Kreeper said. "I feel that there is something that *connects* you to Kropite. I just can't put my finger on what it is."

"I'm not sure about that Kreeper, but thank you for all your time and help," Drake said as he reached out to shake Kreeper's hand again.

"Good luck. And thank you for opening my eyes to endless possibilities," the kreeton said as he turned to leave.

Drake smiled, and the two headed in opposite directions. He walked on a bit farther before taking out Woknok's Motion Saver.

"We don't need you any longer," he said as he threw it on the ground and stomped it into tiny pieces. With this, he felt a sudden jolt, which he suspected was motion catching up to itself. Jumping forcefully, Drake shot into the sky heading back to the lake.

During his return flight, he referenced the lake's map, making sure he was aiming in the right direction. He saw that he was not far from his destination and continued onward.

CHAPTER 19

You Are the One

Migisi met Drake in the air. He smiled, patted her on the head, and promised to fly with her another time. As the two descended to the ground, Sponke darted over to Drake, talking as he approached.

"Drake, now I want you to be calm. No need to overreact."

"Overreact about what?"

"It's Bailey. She, well…she doesn't have her memory back," Sponke said hesitantly.

"I already know she doesn't remember me. We'll figure it out. At least I know she's safe."

Sponke looked around, avoiding eye contact with Drake. "Luke got his memory back right away."

"You think something more serious is wrong with Bailey?"

"Come see for yourself," Sponke said.

Drake slowly approached Bailey, who was sitting next to Luke on the ground. She was trembling and clutching Luke's leg. The guardian sat with his arm around her, trying to comfort her. Drake took a seat in front of them and held out his hand for Luke to shake. Bailey kept her head down.

Luke shook Drake's hand and nodded. "The famous Drake. I am eternally grateful to you for saving my life."

Drake smiled at him. "I need to thank *you* for watching over my sister."

Luke nodded. Drake lowered his head slowly to meet Bailey's eyes. She followed his gaze until they were on eye level.

"Hi, Bailey. How's it going?"

Bailey just shrugged her shoulders and whimpered. "Fine."

Drake was not sure what to do next. He finally held out his hand and asked her if she would take a walk with him. She reluctantly agreed after a small push from Luke. Drake took her hand and walked her over to the lake. He spoke to her in a soft voice, but she reacted to him as if he were a complete stranger.

"Bay, do you remember anything? Anything at all?"

"What am I *supposed* to remember?"

"Our house, our parents, our dog Jessie?"

"Our parents? Jessie? I...don't know."

Drake was at a loss. After several moments, he noticed the stone on his wrist was pulsing and changing from blue, to yellow, to red. The last time he saw the stone change colors like this was when he found it in the woods. He asked Bailey to sit, and sat next to her. He placed his hand on her forehead. It was warm, feverish. "Do you feel okay?"

Bailey nodded her head.

A tingling sensation pulsed down his arm and into his hand. He held it firmly against his sister's head, not sure of what was happening. In a matter of seconds, the tingling in his hand became much more intense. Electricity radiated from him into Bailey. All of their shared memories and thoughts erupted inside Bailey's head. They stayed this way for several long moments. Beginning to feel weak with exhaustion, he pulled his hand away from his sister. She fainted. Drake caught her before she hit the dirt.

In his periphery, Drake saw Sponke and Groger move in his direction, only to be stopped by Luke. The guardian's apparent confidence in Drake supported him, though Drake did not feel as confident as Luke did. It was as if his body was overriding his brain and acting on its own. He glanced at his stone—still pulsing—then back at his unconscious sister.

He sat next to Bailey, and gently placed her head on his lap. Bailey's hair lay across her face. Her mouth twitched and her eyelids fluttered like she was dreaming.

"I sure hope this works," Drake said aloud. She slept on and on. Drake's legs fell asleep.

Finally, she began to stir. Her eyes slowly opened. Bailey blinked a couple of times before reaching up to touch Drake's face. She whispered, "Drake, is that you?"

A huge grin spread across his face. "Yeah Bay, I'm here."

She jumped up and wrapped her skinny arms around his neck. Drake returned her hug. "You feeling okay?"

"I feel okay. Except, I have a little headache," she said, pulling away and rubbing her temple.

Drake breathed a sigh of relief and looked toward his anxious friends. He gave them thumbs up then motioned for them to come closer. Sponke was the first to arrive.

"Bailey, this is Sponke."

Sponke was too excited to speak. He flapped around and mumbled incomprehensibly.

"Okay." Drake laughed. "Maybe you two can talk later. This big guy is my friend, Groger," Drake said patting the giant on the arm.

Groger beamed, completely taken with Bailey's adorable smile. Bailey got to her feet and greeted him with a big hug. Groger grinned from ear to ear as he nestled her close, holding her like a baby, or a doll.

Drake smiled and chuckled. "This is Migisi," Drake said motioning for the mezork to come forward. Migisi pushed her way past the others. Bailey took one look at the mezork and hid behind her brother. "You don't need to be afraid of her. I know she looks fierce, but she's a gentle creature. She's saved my life more times than I can count."

Trusting Drake completely, Bailey slowly reached her hand out to the cat-dragon. The mezork sniffed Bailey's hand, and welcomed her with an enormous tongue. She giggled and wiped her hand on her nightgown.

Bailey glanced at Luke as if he were a stranger. Luke's body slumped as he held out his hand. She shook it and told him she was glad to meet him. Bailey looked back at Drake with narrowed eyes.

"I'll explain later," Drake reassured her.

Groger began to build a huge fire pit. As he placed the logs in the middle, Migisi ignited a roaring blaze. The comforting warmth and glow of the flames wrapped around the friends while Groger provided everyone one with a bit of his merlump.

"Do you ever run out of this stuff?" Drake asked.

Groger chuckled as he placed some of his snack on the ground for Migisi. She nosed at it for a moment, and then leisurely took it into her mouth. Throwing back her head, she forced the dough down her throat in one gulp then licked her lips. Drake leaned against the mezork with Bailey nestled close to him. Sponke's wings settled into a calm hum as he perched on Groger's shoulder, the giant leaned against a large round rock, and Luke sprawled upon the ground, bracing his head with his folded arms.

The fire filled the air with pops and crackles. Sponke hopped down from Groger's shoulder and approached Drake.

"Drake...why did you stay at the factory? We expected you to follow us, but you did not."

Drake put his hands behind his head, and began to tell his story. "After you guys left on Migisi, I went back into the factory. I got into a bit of a scuffle with Koozog."

"Koozog?" asked Sponke. Luke remained quiet.

"He's a crazy guy, but I held my own okay." Drake described his fight with Koozog. His dialogue interrupted only by gasps.

"You're very lucky to have escaped," Luke finally said.

"I know I am. He thinks he's a god. When he said that, I knew he was nuts."

"What happened next?" Bailey asked.

"When I tried to leave, to come here, pockaroos ambushed me. Their leader was mad that I had helped rescue Luke. He'd come up with a plan to get rid of me and recapture Luke." Drake stopped and looked at the guardian. "Dude, you really have your work cut out for you, because Kropite is *crawling* with scum right now."

Luke shook his head saying, "I know…I know."

Sponke cleared his throat loudly. "So, how did you escape the pockaroos?"

"Kreeper helped me," Drake stated matter-of-factly.

"Kreeper came out of Bleet?" Sponke nearly yelled, flying into the air suddenly.

"Yeah. He said he thought I'd need help." Drake shrugged. "Anyway, I escaped with his help. Then, after talking to Kreeper for a while, I made it here."

"You be waiting a minute…you came following shortly after we reached this lake," Groger chimed in, squinting at Drake.

"Oh! Woknok, the pockaroos' leader, had a device that slowed your all's motions, so none of you would know that I had been gone that long. But don't worry, I took it and smashed it."

"Oh? Too bad. That might have come in handy," Sponke said.

Groger and Sponke asked a few more questions about details, until everyone began to yawn. Each of the friends slowly drifted to sleep where they sat.

Drake was the last to succumb to the drowsiness that hung in the air. He shimmied close to the ground and nestled next to the mezork's paw. His eyes grew heavy, his body felt weak. With one last look around, he settled in for what he thought would be a restful night's sleep.

Drake flies over a place that looks like Kropite except it's darker. Everything looks sad. Kropite's brilliant sun is no longer visible. There's a slight mist falling from the clouds. Frowning, he flies on, eventually spotting Kazoocal Field. His friends are standing in the middle of the field and his heart starts to beat hard against his chest. He heads in their direction. On the ground, he approaches Sponke and Groger. Drake stops abruptly when he sees they are both sobbing. They look at him with wet eyes and wave goodbye.

"Wait! Can we talk?" Both Sponke and Groger shake their heads and walk away.

Drake stares after them until he hears a thud behind him. Migisi gracefully folds her wings to her sides and lowers herself to the ground. Drake runs to her.

"Migisi, Sponke and Groger are acting weird."

Migisi begins to speak to him in an eloquent voice. "Oh Drake. My **sweet** *Drake, don't you understand?"*

Drake steps back. He chokes on air as he gasps. "You can talk?"

"Yes. I can talk to you in your dreams."

"I'm dreaming again? I thought that was all over."

Migisi shakes her head and gazes at the boy with glistening eyes.

"Why are Sponke and Groger crying? Why do you sound so sad?"

"We are very sad because you are leaving us. All of Kropite is unhappy, in case you have not noticed. Look around you. The sun is hiding. The skies weep for you. You mean so much to all of us that **already** *we are mourning your departure." Migisi lowers her head. "I know it is important that you return home, but you must know...my heart is broken" The large cat peers back at Drake. "You have filled me with joy. You have given me purpose. Finding you has made me whole again.* **You** *are responsible for rescuing me from the darkness of Bleet." Migisi nudges him in the stomach. "I feel powerful when you are with me. I don't know how I will make it here alone."*

"Migisi...I'm going to miss you so much. I would have never made it this far without you."

"You underestimate yourself, but thank you. We have been a tremendous team. It will be very hard to let you go."

Drake stares at the ground and bites his lip, hard.

"Drake, look at me." He raises his eyes to meet Migisi's. "I want you to know how much my name means to me. I will respond to it with pride, cherishing it **always.**" Drake continues to bite at his lower lip, causing small drops of blood to appear. He tries to hide his sorrow.

The beautiful flying feline smiles, as much as any cat can. "Don't be sad, Drake. I want you to be happy."

"But I am **un**happy. I don't want to leave you. What will you do? Where will you go?"

"I will be right here, waiting for your return. When you do come back to me, we will fly together and soar high into the clouds. You will always be in my heart, Drake. Please promise me you will **never** forget."

Migisi gently rubs her cheek against Drake causing him to stumble backward. Her purr echoes deep inside his chest. He reaches up to rub her muzzle, and she closes her eyes, relishing in her boy's touch.

"Migisi, leaving you is the hardest thing I will ever do. If I **could** stay…I would. I just don't belong here."

Migisi opens her eyes. "You are the one. The one that has helped restore order in my world. You have brought back Kropite's guardian so we may live in peace. One day, you will learn your purpose. When you do, I will be waiting for you."

"My purpose? I don't understand."

"You will one day, my Drake."

Migisi turns her head to look out into the field. Drake turns to see Bailey running toward them with arms outstretched.

"Bailey!" Drake yells as he scoops her up into his arms. She embraces him, sobbing.

"What's wrong, Bay?" he asks, but she is crying too hard to speak. He glances back toward Migisi, he is startled to see she is gone, "Migisi! Where did you go, girl?" There is no answer, no sign of his mezork any-where. He feels his heart break. He gently places Bailey on the ground and lowers himself to her level. "Why are you crying?"

She wipes at her eyes. "I want to stay here."

"We can't. What about Mom and Dad?"

Bailey stared in the distance.

"Bay, what's wrong?" Drake asks as she starts to walk away from him. "Where are you going?"

She continues to walk away without answering her brother. Drake tries to move in an attempt to follow her, but finds his feet stuck to the ground.

"Wait! What's going on? Bailey, come back!"

The sky's gray hue turns to black, and a great wind whips all around. Off in the distance, Drake can make out a large shadowy figure coming toward him. He tries to pry his feet loose, to turn and run, but can't. He stands helpless as the shadow approaches. The figure stops several feet in front of him and glares.

"Koozog!"

*"Thanks to you, my grand plans have been set back. You have not stopped me altogether, but you have caused me **quite** a bit of trouble. However, we will meet another time, Drake. When we do, you will not escape. The stone you possess is mine. I **will** take it back. Once I obtain that Story Stone, **I** will hold all of the power!"*

"You can't have my stone." Drake quit struggling and faced the monster.

"We shall see about that," Koozog whispers. "You have no idea what you have started, boy." Koozog's shadowy image vanishes in a puff of black smoke.

Drake glances around, trying to find someone to help him, when he discovers he can move again. The sky brightens, removing Drake's fear and sadness. All his friends appear around him. No one is crying. Everyone is speaking to him at once.

CHAPTER 20

My Place is Here

Jolted awake, Drake sat up and glanced around. It was still
dark. Breathing a heavy sigh, he flopped to the ground and
quickly drifted back to sleep. Sponke kept waking up just to
make sure everyone was still safe. Groger and Bailey slept like
babies. Luke was never one for sleeping, so he sat upon a large
boulder keeping a nightly vigil over his friends.

Morning came too quickly. Moans and groans welcomed the
sun. "When I get home, I'm gonna stay in bed for a week,"
Drake mumbled.

"I'm hungry," said Bailey. "What do you eat here?"

Drake looked at Groger. The giant happily held up a finger. "Oh, goody, I'll be back."

Despite Drake's trepidation, he was very hungry, and waited. "Maybe this one meal will be okay."

Groger meandered into the woods nearby and reappeared with something Drake did not dare question. He watched with concerned eyes as Groger prepared the meal.

"Eat up, everyone!" Groger bellowed once his breakfast was complete.

Drake and Bailey nibbled on their share with scrunched faces.

"It kinda tastes like mom's pulled pork," Bailey said while stuffing a whole handful into her mouth.

Drake chuckled and agreed with her. "Not bad, Groger. This wouldn't be the creepods you tried to make me eat earlier would it?"

"No sirree. This here is a creature we be calling cooffa. Easy to catch and cook." Groger grinned at Drake. "I'll be getting ya to try my creepods one day." Drake smiled and nodded at the giant.

Sponke quickly finished his meal and began flapping about in front of Drake and Bailey. "We need to get you two back to Kazoocal Field. I think the best way to do this is by traveling on Migisi," Sponke said, always the planner.

"I think you guys can travel on Migisi. Luke and I will fly, if that's okay with you, Luke?" Luke nodded. "Besides," said Drake, "I'll never be able to fly again after I leave here, so I want to get in as much air time as possible."

Bailey mouth fell open. "You can fly?"

"Yup."

Bailey stared at the ground, then looked up to him again with a smile. "You really *are* Superman."

He took a moment to enjoy the feeling he got when his sister referred to him as Superman. Drake bent down to help Bailey onto Migisi's back. She wrapped her arms around her brother's neck. He hugged her back. "I'm gonna get you home. I promise."

"I know you will, Drakie." She said, grabbing onto Migisi's fur. Groger climbed on, settling in behind her. He put his arms around her to keep her from falling. Sponke flew up and perched on Groger's shoulder with a forced smile. Drake could see the sadness behind his façade.

Drake made his way over to Migisi's head and asked her to keep Bailey safe. The bulky, banded feline responded by licking his face. He wrapped his arms around her, as best he could, whispering, "Take them to Kazoocal Field. I'll be right behind you."

Migisi spread her leathery wings and jumped into the sky. A gust of wind whipped from her launch, knocking Drake backward. He laughed. Getting back to his feet, Drake watched as they ascended higher and higher.

Drake turned toward Luke. Unsure of what to say to the guardian, Drake ran his hand through his hair and smiled. They stood silent for several seconds before Drake wandered over to the lake. Peering across the glistening water, Drake's expression wilted.

"I can't imagine never being here again," Drake said so Luke could hear him. He glanced at the riddle rock then back to the lake.

Luke moved next to him and placed his hand on Drake's shoulder. "I cannot even begin to express my gratitude toward you. You have done some astonishing things here. Things I could only dream of doing. Seeing you with Groger and Sponke, and the mezork you call Migisi..."

"It means *eagle.* She reminds me of one. A creature full of majesty and grace."

Luke nodded. "Do you know why you were able to tame your mezork?"

"No."

"She sensed in you what *all* of us have sensed. You're kind-hearted, determined, and courageous. When you touched her, she could *feel* what kind of a person you are. Your touch was gentle, so she knew you were kind. You stood strong and unflinching, so she knew you were determined and brave. She was also able to feel your desperation to find Bailey. Migisi *knew* you needed her," Luke explained.

"She could tell all of this by my touch?" Drake asked.

Luke turned, staring at Drake as if he were looking right through him. A warm, sincere smile bloomed on his face. "Yes. And she needed you every bit as much as you needed her."

"How do you know all of this?"

"Migisi told me. She told me that without you she would have died in Bleet, alone."

"That's a difference between you and me. I can talk to Migisi, but she can't talk to me, not in a way I can understand," Drake said. Something kept him from telling Luke that he could talk to her in his dreams.

Luke nodded. "With more time here in Kropite, I think that would change."

"Maybe...but I can't stay here."

The guardian looked out across the lake, and said, "Bailey?"

"I need to get her home."

"I remember when I first arrived at Koozog's place, before he tried to steal my mind. I was scared. I've never been scared in my life. Much of what happened after that is fuzzy, but one thing I remember vividly is your sister. I was drawn to her, and I can't explain why. When I came to the factory, she was sitting all alone. She was crying. I knelt down, and she looked at me and smiled. I can't explain it, but it was as though she recognized me. From then on, we sought each other, trying to make our stay at Koozog's somehow more bearable. I think that perhaps she saw a bit of you in me. This is what comforted her," Luke explained.

"Why can you remember Koozog's factory, but Bailey can't?" Drake asked.

"Bailey is a *true* child from your world. I am grown, and not human. It is best that Bailey not remember her stay at the factory."

"But she doesn't remember *you.*"

"You can tell her about me...when *you* think she is ready."

Drake kicked a rock back and forth between his feet.

"What's on your mind, Drake?"

"I have something I need to tell you."

"What is it?" Luke looked at Drake with old eyes.

"I had a dream right before I got to the factory. A boy, a boy I've never met, talked to me."

Luke looked at Drake, waiting for him to continue.

Drake took a deep breath. "His name was Sebastian."

Luke's eyes grew wider. "What did you say his name was?" Luke asked.

"Sebastian," Drake repeated, a bit louder this time.

Luke shook his head. "It can't be. No...it can't be!"

Drake placed his hand on Luke's shoulder, suddenly feeling like the adult. "I think it was your brother. He looked about my age, and reminded me of you."

"What did he say?"

"He told me my dreams here in Kropite are important. He said I needed them to help me solve the puzzle. Then he just walked away."

"That sounds like Sebastian, showing up out of the blue and talking nonsense." Luke scratched his head. "I can barely remember when he first vanished."

"Do you mind my asking what happened?"

"I really cannot tell you exactly when he disappeared. I don't really remember. We were very young and very irresponsible. We did foolish things. We never thought about our actions."

"I can understand that." Drake nodded.

Luke laughed. "We were nearly inseparable, often causing quite a bit of trouble. Our parents were always threatening to send us away to a place that could teach us some responsibility." Luke chuckled again. "We would just laugh off these threats, carrying on in our mischievous ways. We had a wonderful time… until the fateful day of Sebastian's disappearance.

I remember it was a quiet day in Zebenon. We had decided to wreak a little playful havoc on the elderly leaders. We had taken flight early that morning to sneak up on one particular leader named Zogrosen." Luke scrunched his face. "He was a hateful man who took pride in forcing children to grow up too fast. He would pay visits to orphanages near and far, collecting children to bring back to Zebenon. He would brainwash them into becoming little adults who could do his bidding. They were completely under his control.

On this particular day, Sebastian and I decided to break into his place to free all of his unwilling followers. Our plan was working until Zogrosen burst in." Luke swished his hand through the air. "He was a bit of a magic man who had some powerful tricks up his sleeve. I barely escaped. Sebastian never made it out." Luke gazed out across the lake. "I returned to Zogrosen's place every day searching for my brother, but I was never able to enter the leader's home again. He had put some kind of spell on it. At one point I thought my parents had something to do with Sebastian's disappearance, as they wouldn't help me get him, so I disowned them."

"What happened then?"

"Eventually, Zogrosen left. No one heard from him again."

"Do you think Sebastian is still alive? I mean, since he came to me in my dream and all?"

"I don't know."

Drake's eyes widened as he stared at Luke. "Are you going to try and find him?"

"I left Zebenon a long time ago. I have a job to do here. I am guardian of Kropite. It is my job to keep *this* world safe." Luke met Drake's gaze. "If I stumble on Sebastian again, I will be over*joyed*. He is my only brother, but he has to come to me. I cannot afford to leave and search now."

Drake's eyes lit up as he remembered something from his dream. "Wait! I just remembered. Sebastian had a message for you! He wanted me to tell you that he's here! He said he's always been here!" Drake stared at Luke waiting for him to say something about his brother, but Luke just stared at the ground. "What would have happened if I had given up on Bailey?"

"What do you mean?"

"I mean, I could *never* do that. She can be pest at times, but she's family. If you don't have family, what *do* you have?"

"I understand what you are saying, but things are *different* here."

Drake rolled his eyes. "I've heard that before. All I'm saying is, you shouldn't give up on Sebastian. If he's alive, you *need* to find him."

"We'll see."

Drake shrugged his shoulders and began kicking at the rocks again.

"You have more on your mind, Drake?"

"Can I ask you about one more thing?"

"Anything."

"Woknok said Kropite is *meant* to fall. Is that true?"

"I think if left unattended any place is subject to fall, yes?"

"I guess." Drake shrugged.

"Don't worry. I will make sure Kropite remains safe."

"Are you going to be able to do it on your own?"

"Yes. I have always done it alone. You know that." Drake looked at Luke skeptically. "Your book, *Luke of Kropite*. I believe you have already read about many of my adventures." Luke laughed lightly.

"How do you know about my book?"

"Sponke filled me in while we were waiting for you to return to the lake," Luke said as he looked at Drake, once more the adult.

"Sponke told me he knows about my world because of you. Have you really been to my world?"

"Drake, I know I am leaving you with many unanswered questions, but you are going to have to trust me when I say this is *best* for you...at present. One day everything will make sense to you, but for now I must go. I thank you once again for all you have done for me, and for Kropite."

Drake felt his heart jump. "Aren't you coming with me? At least back to Kazoocal Field?"

"No. My place is here. I have a lot of work to do." Luke gazed across the lake standing silent for a moment. "Will you tell your sister something for me?"

"Of course."

"When you think she is ready, please tell her I would have been very alone at Koozog's without her."

"I'll tell her."

Luke turned to look at Drake and chuckled.

"What?"

"I am simply astounded that you are here and have been able to do all that you have."

"What do you mean?" Drake asked, knowing he wouldn't get an answer.

"One day I will explain, but now is not the time."

"I've heard that one before, too," Drake mumbled as he started to walk away. He stopped and turned his head to say goodbye, but the guardian was already gone. He looked into the sky in hopes of seeing him again, but he had vanished.

The air was cool, sending a slight chill through Drake. A steady breeze blew off the water. He walked back a few paces and stumbled over a large rock. He tumbled to the ground and smiled. "Real graceful, Drake." Not ready to get up just yet, he sat where he fell. He looked upward. Kropite's sky reminded Drake of home. He pushed himself to his feet, thinking about his sister waiting for him in Kazoocal Field.

He looked at the lake for a long moment before turning away.

CHAPTER 21

Heroes Always Come Back

Just as Drake was about to leave, another breeze floated off the water. It blew stronger now, whispering something as it skirted past his ear. He turned his head from side to side, trying to hear. He thought he might be imagining it until he heard it again.

"Come, Drake. Come to me."

"What? Who said that?" Drake asked, turning to look around him.

The whispering commanded him once again. It seemed to be coming from the lake. He moved toward the water and knelt beside it. Disregarding Sponke's directions, Drake reached out and dipped his hand into the water. A strange coolness glided up his arm and rapidly spread through his whole body. The lake was pulling him in. He was unable to stop it.

Rather than fight it, Drake eased into the water. He sucked in his breath as the cold liquid soaked through his clothes, chilling his skin. He pressed onward. As he had expected, the lake was shallow near the shore. His feet touched a solid sandy bottom, making his forward momentum easy. He continued walking toward the center of the lake. He felt the water around his waist, his chest, his neck. He couldn't stop himself from going farther.

"What's happening? Why can't I stop?"

Once the water was over his head, the lake floor disappeared completely, sending him sinking to the lake's depths. Nothing obstructed his view, making it easy to see everything around him. As large as the lake was, he could not believe how barren it seemed. There were no fish, no floating objects, just water as far as he could see.

Drake sank to the bottom quickly, as though he had lead in his shoes. He held out his arms to steady himself and was surprised to find he did not float upward.

Shuffling his feet along the bottom of the lake, the floor felt unstable and rocky. He looked down and saw thousands of stones resembling the one on his wrist. The only difference was that these brilliant stones were much larger. They were all glowing and emitting colorful, radiant light. A rainbow of smooth rocks spread beneath his feet. He looked at his wrist, witnessing his own stone glowing as well.

Taking in his surroundings for several minutes, a thought occurred to him. *I'm not breathing.* It was not that he was holding his breath and needed to come up for air, he just didn't feel the need to breathe.

He remembered Sponke telling him that people had tried to find the Story Stones at the bottom of See-All-Lake but had never returned.

Am I going to die here? Maybe I'm already dead, and that's why I'm not breathing, he thought to himself, but he no longer cared.

The glowing stones before him sparkled. Their light sliced through the water, sending sheets of color cascading all around. All of his cares and worries melted away. Everything was perfect at the bottom of the lake. He reached down and picked up a random stone. It felt warm in his hands. He touched the stone to the one on his wrist, creating small arcing sparks. As he tried to pull the stones apart, the sparks became more intense. His stone pulled the other stone in like a magnet. As the two stones touched again, a flash of light exploded underwater. A huge bubble encased him.

Faint images appeared on the walls of his bubble. They scrolled around him, making him dizzy at first. He focused on one image and followed it around, which helped ease the vertigo. It was like watching television on a merry-go-round. Images of unfamiliar children flashed before him, followed by pictures of the labs at the factory. He saw Koozog and his repugnant guards running away from something, but he could not make out what was chasing them.

The walls of the watery cave went blank for several seconds. Then a face Drake didn't recognize appeared in front of him. It was the face of a beautiful woman, smiling at him. She hovered above the lake floor, suspended. Only her long, white, flowing gown and glistening, turquoise hair gracefully moved with the water around her body. Her long locks skimmed across her face and drew attention to her stone-blue eyes that seemed to pierce Drake.

"Drake. My name is Madori. We have spoken before." Drake remembered the unforgettable, angelic voice of the lake. The melodious tone had rung out to him from the water as he was solving the final portion of the riddle.

"I am not sure where to begin," said Madori, "I know you have experienced a great deal while here in Kropite. Your experiences have brought you close to death, yet you persevered. Your determination is astounding, and something I have *never,* in my long life, witnessed. Kropite bestowed a heavy burden upon you, but you were able to face and conquer that challenge." Madori waved her arm through the water and pointed at Drake. "Because of you, our world is safe once again." She gazed down at his arm. "The stone on your wrist is yours, as it has chosen you. You are forever Kropite's hero."

"What about Luke?"

"Luke has one job to do, to keep our world free of evil. You have a different task. Together, the two of you would be unstoppable."

"I can't stay here!" Drake yelled, panic welling up inside.

"No. You *could* stay here, but you choose not to, and that is perfectly acceptable. I know this will not be the last time we see you. When we need you again, you will come back to us. *You are Kropite's hero,* whether you want to be or not. It is your destiny, and we welcome you."

Drake looked away and shook his head. "Destiny?"

Madori nodded. "Yes, Drake."

"I'm afraid I don't understand."

"You do not need to understand it, just accept it."

Drake gazed back at her with questioning eyes.

The lake-lady's brilliant smile glowed. "Through you, we have learned the evil that presently exists in Kropite is a monster named Koozog. He is dangerous, and his use of children for gain is ghastly. My conjecture is he lacks imagination himself and has resorted to stealing it."

"How was Koozog able to create a book using Luke? He *isn't* a child," Drake interjected.

"Koozog was able to use Luke's thoughts and memories because, though Luke is not human nor a child, Koozog thought he was using Luke's imagination when he created your book. In reality, he was using actual events from Luke's life. Koozog never found out the truth, and the result was Luke's life was spared."

"If *Luke of Kropite* was an account of Luke's life, then how come I never read about Sponke, Groger, Irick, you, or anyone else I've met here? None of you were in the story."

"That is hard to explain. If I were to venture a guess, I would say that the book included only the events you needed to know for that particular story. You had to discover the rest while here in Kropite."

"I'm not sure if that makes any sense." Drake sat quietly for a moment then gazed back at the beautiful woman. "There's something else I wonder, Madori."

"What is it?" Madori's voice glided over his eardrums like silk.

"If Luke went missing after Bailey came to Kropite, how is it I was able to read *Luke of Kropite* in the first place? I mean, the book had to have been made *after* Luke became one of Koozog's prisoners, but I read the book way before that," Drake finished.

"Time works differently here than it does in your world, Drake. The two timelines do not always coincide. It is difficult to explain. Maybe one day we will learn more about this but for now, my knowledge is limited."

"I guess that makes sense," Drake said, shrugging his shoulders. "What about Bailey? Will she be okay after what Koozog did?"

"Children's imaginations are always a part of them, and cannot be completely removed. Children have an endless supply of imagination. However, the others, the ones still in Koozog's possession, are in grave danger. I do not think he plans to return them to their families. Eventually, their parents will notice their absence. If parents become aware of their missing children, it will create pandemonium in your world, and others. It will be far worse than here."

"What about Ka-leel?" Drake asked, suddenly remembering the girl.

"Ka-leel?"

"She's this girl who talked to me in my dream. Her eyes were *so* blue." Drake glanced at the Story Stone on his wrist.

"I'm sorry, Drake. I do not know of her."

A scowl tugged at Drake's lips. "How do we stop him? How do we stop Koozog?"

"Luke will train in hopes of destroying Koozog. He will try to rescue the remaining children and return them to their homes."

"That's gonna be hard. He'll need help. Can you give him his own Story Stone?"

Madori smiled. "I live in, and control, the lake, but not what lies in it. The stones control themselves. I can only give Luke guidance."

Drake looked down at his wrist. "I can give my stone to Luke."

"No, you cannot. This stone has chosen you and you alone," said Madori. "You will need it, not only to return home, but also to return to Kropite one day."

Drake smiled at Madori's stubbornness. She was so adamant he would be returning. There was no way he could convince her otherwise. Staring back at his stone, a thought occurred to him.

"Madori, there's something else I need to know."

"What is it, Drake?"

"Why is it every time I fall asleep here I have strange dreams? Groger thinks they're premonitions."

"Groger is very wise. Your dreams are proof of your connection to Kropite. Through your dreams, you were able to find Koozog uncovering his evil plan. Your dreams have also helped you to believe in yourself, proving you can persevere." She shook her head. "Not just anyone has the capability of dreaming here in Kropite. The individuals who do dream possess abilities beyond most.

This is a lot for you to absorb. In time, you will accept your responsibilities. A hero does not come along every day, but when one does we cherish and respect him." She tilted her head. "I respect your decision to leave us, as I *know* you will be back. Heroes always come back." Madori held up her hand and smiled. Her sparkling eyes and beautiful grin filled his heart with a warmth he had never felt before. His skin grew hot and prickly as a smile tugged at his mouth. Madori's flowing hair lapped across her face and her image slowly faded away.

Drake grasped the stone firmly in his hand. Using every ounce of strength left in him, he wrenched it from the stone on his wrist. The stones separated with a muffled ripping sound. At their severance, the bubble imploded on Drake. A massive deluge of water poured in on him, nearly crushing him. It felt as though he were caught in a gigantic wave, causing him to tumble over and over, leaving him guessing which way was up. He couldn't see anything, and the need for oxygen was overwhelming. There was no need to breathe before, but now his lungs begged for just one gulp of air.

His stone forced his arm vertical, pulling him upward. Once he broke the water's surface, the stone pulled his body out of the lake. He hovered above the water, gasping for air.

An odd sense of calmness surrounded him as he glided back to land. Being on land again cleared his head. An image of Bailey and his friends waiting for him in Kazoocal Field appeared in his mind.

He yelled at the lake, "It's time for me to go. I have to get my sister back home, where she and I are safe. I know you can hear me, Madori! Kropite has its protector back. I know he will be able to fix everything. I've had an awesome adventure. I even like the thought of being Kropite's hero." Drake stared at the ground. "But without the stone, I'm not sure any of this would have been possible." Looking back at the lake, Drake yelled, "Why am I a hero here anyway? I wish someone would explain that one to me." The lake remained calm and unaffected by his speech. *So much for that.*

He gazed upward and leapt as high as he could. Drake tried to fly, but his feet never got far off the ground. "What's going on?" he asked as he glanced at his wrist. The stone was gone!

"Great," he said, turning to look at the lake. "Now you've taken the stone from me? How am I going to get back to my friends?" He picked up a nearby rock and hurled it into the water. The lake remained unresponsive. "Fine. I'll find my own way," he said, stomping off.

"This is unbelievable. There has to be a way for me to get back to Kazoocal Field." He pushed the anger out of his head. "Maybe...maybe I can still fly. The stone might still be with me somehow. Madori said the stone *chose* me. Maybe its power is always with..." Drake trailed off. He stopped doubting himself. Determined to get back to his sister and friends, he jumped. With a strong belief he still possessed the power of the stone, he shot like a rocket into the heavens.

He felt his heart surge with joy. Unsure of his direction, he hoped he would be able to find Kazoocal Field on his own. As he flew over Kropite, it was as though he was reliving his journey, for down below him were all of the places he had traveled. The vastness of the Forest of Bleet was still unnerving. Thoughts of the terrifying forest played though his mind. A scowl covered his face as an ache filled his stomach. He reached up to push his hair out of his eyes. Forcing the darkness from his memory, he stared ahead as he zoomed over fields, creeks, lakes, and mountains. Mt. Creesious came into view. Drake cringed at the thought of its monstrous inhabitant lying lifeless and bleeding upon the cold, hard floor of its home. He studied his hands, then his chest. He shivered at the zatherosod's blue blood still evident on his shirt.

He looked back up and saw his destination. Seeing his friends gathered together among the tall grasses of Kazoocal Field caused the boy's tension to disappear completely. He aimed for the ground at such a high speed it startled Sponke. Thinking Drake might crash, Sponke flew behind Groger with his arms outstretched to protect him. The giant chortled. Drake pulled up just in time, landing with grace. Drake glanced at his sister and nodded with a smile. She waved at him.

Migisi pawed at the grass, let out a low droning growl, and lowered herself to the ground. Drake moved slowly toward his winged-friend and placed his hand under her chin. He ran his fingers upward along her cheek, skimmed her ear and rubbed the top of her head. An overwhelming sadness filled him. Knowing he would be leaving the mezork behind was almost too much for him to bear. He chewed at his lower lip. Groger, Sponke, and Bailey stepped back a few paces to give him space.

With wet eyes, Drake turned to look at his friends. Groger's bottom lip shot out as he rubbed at his own eyes. Holding onto Migisi's ears, Drake drew close to her face, speaking in a choked whisper.

"Migisi, I will *always* remember you. I hate that I have to leave you, but your life is here in Kropite. Stay close to Luke, and keep my friends safe, okay?" Migisi purred as he spoke to her. "I know you can understand me. Thank you for talking to me in my dreams. I promise never to forget about you. Ever!" Migisi closed her eyes and rubbed her face across Drake's stomach.

Drake hesitantly stepped away. He knew it would be impossible to leave Migisi if he kept talking. Walking backward a few steps, he turned, nearly running into Groger.

He gazed into the giant's eyes. "Groger, I don't have the stone. It's gone."

Groger smiled and put his arm around Drake. He guided him away from the others. Sponke and Bailey watched the two walk away.

Sponke cocked his head. "Where are you two going?" Groger raised a hand in the air, but never looked at the bug. Sponke let out a huff.

"What's wrong with Drake? Why is he so sad?" Bailey asked with a frown.

Turning away from Groger and Drake, Sponke hovered in front of Bailey. "He will be fine. Drake is strong and he wants to get you home.

"I know he does," Bailey said peering at the ground.

"Don't you want to go home?" Sponke asked.

"I guess so. I think this place is so cool though." Bailey gazed at Migisi. "I hope we get to come back." Bailey walked over to the mezork and began to rub her cheek. Migisi issued her sedative purr but never took her eyes off her boy. Sponke hovered close while continuing to watch Groger and Drake.

Groger leaned close to him. "You must quit being so stubborn. You need to reach *way* down inside and pull up what you truly already know."

"What are you talking about?"

"The stone, Drake! The stone brought you to Kropite. It has helped you along the way, but the true ability lies *within you.* The stone was a guide that gave you the ability, and aided you in finding your confidence. Once you believed in yourself, you were able to save Bailey, Luke, and all of Kropite."

"You mean to tell me that, even without the stone, I had this power all along?"

"Yes, my friend. You just had to believe in yourself. From the first day you set foot in Kropite, you always had the ability to do great things. All you lacked was self-confidence. Because of that it was a long, treacherous journey. Once you started believing the stone was the source of all your greatness, you let go of your doubts and became the hero we all *knew* you were."

Drake shook his head saying, "I don't get it. You say all I had to do was believe in myself? That sounds like something my mom would say."

"Then she is a very smart lady," Groger stated.

"It sounds kinda hokey to me," Drake mumbled.

"Hokey it may sound, but I speak the *truth.* Belief in oneself is an *amazing* thing. If you truly believe in yourself, you can accomplish almost anything."

"The stone must have *some* powers." Drake was stubbornly refusing to believe that it was all *him.*

"Don't get me wrong, Drake. The Story Stone is a mighty powerful object, and because of it, you have returned to Kropite."

"*Returned* to Kropite? What do you mean? I've never been to Kropite before now."

"I'm sorry. I didn't mean to say return. I meant to say, because of the stone you *came* to Kropite."

Drake tilted his head in confusion. Groger began to fidget. "Don't mind me. I'm just overwhelmed that you're leaving us."

"Will we be able to leave Kropite without the stone?"

"I don't know about that," Groger said as he pulled Drake's stone out of his pocket. Careful not to touch the stone itself, Groger strapped the glowing treasure back onto Drake's wrist.

"But...how? How did *you* get it?" Drake asked. Groger gave him a wink then walked back over to join the others. Drake stared wide-eyed at the retreating giant.

Sponke soared directly up to Groger. "What were you two discussing over there?"

"Oh, Sponkie. Yous full of curiosities. I talkin' to him to cheer him up. He's a mighty sad boy." Groger ginned. "Let him sit a spell. We need to be givin' him a bit of space."

Sponke looked over at Drake and puffed out his lip.

Drake plopped to the ground and tried to digest everything Groger had just said. Not caring how foolish he looked, he talked aloud to himself, and to the Story Stone.

"He says you're nothing but a...a good luck charm. How can that be? When I put you on my wrist back at the factory, I felt so much *power* rush through me. Could that have all been in my imagination?" Drake shook his head. "I've heard of the mind playing tricks on you...but this is *crazy.*"

The stone pulsed gently. Its colors were so vibrant Drake had to squint. It changed from brilliant blue to diamond white. It was hypnotic. He couldn't look away. A strange energy grew inside of him, making the hairs on his arm stand on end. A prickly sensation moved from his toes up to his head. He reached down to touch the ground, just to make sure he was not floating. His body felt so light.

"I guess I did do it. I mean, I began flying without the stone back at the lake. I was able to fly here without the stone. Maybe I did kick Koozog's butt at the factory on my own." He couldn't help but grin. "A regular kid back home, but a superhero in Kropite. If nothing else, it sounds cool. One day, I'll find out why this is all happening." Drake chuckled to himself as he got back to his feet. "I wish I knew more about this whole *destiny* thing that Madori spoke of. I'd also like to know why *I* was chosen. No one seems to have a straight answer for that one."

After a few moments, he walked back over to his friends. So many things were running through in his mind. He felt more confused than ever. Groger grabbed Drake, taking him clear off his feet. The giant squeezed him in such a tight hug that Drake gasped for air.

Sponke made Groger release him. With tear-filled eyes, Sponke said, "Drake, you are a unique young man, and we are *honored* to have traveled with you. Kropite owes you a debt of gratitude. I want you to take this, to remember *us* and our journey." Sponke handed Drake a small leather pouch. He went to open the worn pouch, but Sponke stopped him. "Wait until you get home. When you start to miss us, open it and you will understand the meaning behind my gift."

Drake nodded and smiled back at Sponke. "I'll never forget you guys."

Unable to contain himself any longer, Sponke erupted into a tear-filled tantrum. Drake slowly backed away and took hold of Bailey's hand. She broke into an uncontrollable fit of crying as well and jerked her hand out of Drake's. She ran and jumped into Groger's arms. Groger held her for a few moments and told her he loved her, and that she needed to keep an eye on Drake for him. She agreed and ran back to grasp her brother's hand once again. They stood together for several seconds, taking in as much of Kropite as they could.

Drake looked off into the distance and saw Luke riding a creature he had not had the opportunity to meet yet. He held up his hand and waved goodbye. Surprisingly, Luke saw him and returned his wave. Drake smiled and looked down at Bailey.

"Are you ready to go home?"

Bailey's answer was a hesitant nod.

Drake gazed at Migisi one last time as a single tear ran down his cheek and over his chin. He reached to wipe it away then held up his left arm. Touching the stone to his lips, he closed his eyes as tightly as he could, and told Bailey to do the same. Drake thought with all his might, *Take us home!*

A blinding light exploded around Bailey and Drake. In seconds, they were gone.

Groger and Sponke wept in each other's arms. Migisi roared so loudly it shook the ground, then took off for the clouds.

All was back to normal in Kropite.

CHAPTER 22

Human After All

Drake and Bailey knew what to expect on their journey home, as they had already experienced the stone's winding portal once before. Within seconds, they erupted out of the book and landed on Drake's bedroom floor with a thud. Drake heard a whirring-hum, reminding him of Sponke's wings. He looked toward his rocker only to see *Luke of Kropite* vanish.

"That was awesome!"

At the sound of Drake's voice, Jessie barreled into his room. Startled with excitement, she ran in circles, barking and licking Drake's face.

"Jessie, wait girl," Drake said looking to see if Bailey was okay. Bailey was laughing with tears in her eyes. Her laughter was contagious, and Drake began to laugh as well. Both Bailey and Drake rolled around, causing such a ruckus that Jessie leapt in the air yipping at them both.

Drake's parents were the next to bustle into the room with worried looks upon their faces. "What are you two *doing* up here?" Their father asked.

Drake and Bailey tried their best to stop laughing but couldn't.

"Is everything okay?" their mom asked.

"We're...we're fine!" Drake said as best he could.

Drake's dad chuckled. "I think we're just being paranoid. They're playing, not arguing."

"Well, clean up for dinner. You both are filthy. Drake, is that blue *paint* all over your shirt?" their mom asked as she leaned over for a closer look.

"What? Oh. Yeah...it's paint." His laughter ceased.

"Well, *please* clean up" she said as she turned to leave. Their mother spun back around. "What are you wearing, Bailey."

Bailey glanced down at the beige hospital gown that still clung to her body. She shook her head unsure of what to say.

Drake thought quickly. "Ummmm, Bay isn't that something your friend, Addy left here?"

"Yeah, mom. Remember when Addy went in to get her tonsils removed last year?"

"Yes."

"This is hers. We were playing dress up the other day and she left it here."

Their mom pointed at both of them, smiled, and left the room. They erupted into a fit of laughter once again.

"They didn't even know we were gone," Drake said, finally calming down.

"That's crazy," Bailey responded.

Drake glared at his sister. "You can't tell *anyone* about this. This has to be *our secret*. I mean it."

Bailey nodded. "No one would believe us anyway."

After cleaning up, they raced down the stairs. "Real food!" Drake yelled.

As they ate, Drake's mom beamed proudly thinking she had cooked a stupendous meal. She jumped from the table to refill both children's portions and encouraged them to eat as much as they liked. Drake winked at Bailey and continued to shovel food into his mouth.

After he'd eaten three platefuls, Drake yawned and excused himself from the table. "I'm going to bed."

"Are you feeling okay," his mother asked.

Drake nodded. "I'm just tired,"

Bailey yawned. "Me too."

Their parents shrugged and watched their children head off to bed before nine o'clock.

As Drake and Bailey reached the top of the stairs, they said goodnight and headed to their rooms. Upon entering his bedroom, Drake reached back and shoved his door shut. The black enveloped him, and he quickly switched on his lamp. Having experienced the deepest kind of darkness in Bleet, he wasn't keen to be in the absolute dark again. Drake rummaged around his room to find his old nightlight and plugged it into the outlet. When he switched off his lamp, its low glow cut through the dark.

"A little extra light won't hurt," he whispered aloud.

Drake stumbled over to his bed and collapsed into the soft warmth of his blankets. Turning onto his back, he burrowed into his pillow and folded his hands behind his head. His eyelids sagged while his body yearned for a restful night's sleep. Melting into his mattress, Drake could not help but relish in the comfort of his own bed. His mind drifted back to the hard ground he had slept on in Kropite.

It had only been a couple of hours since returning home from his adventure, but a deep pain worked its way inside him, wrapping around his heart and squeezing tightly. Migisi's face pervaded his thoughts. He found himself missing her more than he could have ever thought possible. Her image appeared with such clarity that Drake longed to reach out and caress her cheek. The rumble of her purr echoed in his head, touching every nerve in his body. He envisioned her piercing blue eyes as they bore into his heart.

Even though she was much larger and stronger than he was, Drake felt in a strange way as though he were *her* protector. He would give his life for her without a second thought, and this frightened him. The thought of her alone in Bleet caused his stomach to ache.

"She won't go back there—" he whispered in the darkness of his room. "Will she? No…She'll stay with Groger, Sponke and Luke."

Turning onto his side, he clutched his midsection and tried to force her image out of his mind. But her soft growl, along with the sound of her wings beating against the wind, resonated in his memory. Of all of his experiences in Kropite, finding Migisi had affected him the most. Her absence was like having a limb chopped off. He knew they should be together, but she was nowhere near him.

Drake stared around his room and looked at all of his belongings. Everything was so *normal.* His warm bed, his television perched on his dresser, even his faithful dog lying at the foot of his bed felt normal.

Kropite, on the other hand, was not normal. It was a realm that existed somewhere beyond his world. He pictured his mezork flying through the clouds. For a split second, he questioned whether she had been real—a creature unlike anything that existed on Earth. A lump rose up in his throat, making it hard for him to swallow. Sorrow pricked at his heart. How could he ever question whether Migisi was real? She was as real and genuine as anything he had ever experienced. He glanced at the Story Stone, still bound to his wrist, wishing there was some way it could take away his sadness.

Drake thought he might never be able to fall asleep, but eventually his weariness overcame his sadness. His eyes grew heavy as his mind drifted into nothingness. Within minutes, he fell into a deep, dreamless slumber.

After a restful night's sleep, he woke up the next day at 9 a.m. "Finally, a night without dreams. It's good to be home," he said to himself. He got up, stretched, and decided to spend the day with his friends. He wanted to see them, hoping to assemble some normalcy back into his life. Before leaving his room, he reached for the top drawer of his dresser where he had left the pouch Sponke had given him. Then he stopped himself. *Not now...I'll wait.* He closed his dresser drawer. Drake already missed his Kropite friends, especially Migisi, but it was too soon. Drake wanted to try to *forget*—at least for a little while—to ease his own pain.

As he headed for the door, he noticed Bailey's lucky ring still lying on the floor next to his chair. He picked up the ring to examine it. He flipped it off his thumb as you would a coin, caught it, and headed out of his room. He peeked into Bailey's room. She was near her bed playing superhero with her stuffed animals. Drake went inside.

"I found your ring and thought you might want it back." As he handed it to her, she grinned and placed it on her finger.

"Thanks, Drakie."

"No problem."

Just as Drake tuned to leave, Bailey whispered, "Drake?"

"Yeah?"

"I don't want to talk about it right *now*, but...will you tell me more about Kropite soon?"

"Sure. I'm gonna hang out with the guys today. Maybe we can talk about it tomorrow?"

"Okay. I *really* want to know more about Migisi, and that boy. What was his name?"

Drake turned to stare at his sister. "His name is Luke."

Bailey smiled, then looked at her stuffed animals. "He seemed nice."

"He is nice. You'd really like him," Drake said as he walked out of her room.

Practically springing down the stairs, he headed for the kitchen. There he found his mother singing as she placed a plate of pancakes, lathered in pumpkin butter, in front of Drake's spot at the table. He smiled, licked his lips, and gobbled an entire stack.

"My, my, we're hungry this morning."

"You know I love your pancakes," Drake responded quickly.

"Oh, do you?"

"Of course, Mom." He rolled his eyes and she laughed. "Is it okay if I hang out with the guys today?"

"Yes, but be home for lunch."

He agreed. As he was leaving the kitchen, he stopped and surprised his mother with a huge hug. The sentiment caught her off guard, but she hugged him back. "Are you okay, sweetie?"

"Can't a guy give his mom a hug?"

"Of course! Anytime."

Drake headed for the door. He had missed his parents terribly, but they had no idea he had even been gone. He decided he had better be a bit less obvious with the rest of his day.

As he headed down his driveway, he was surprised to see Reigan and her friend Mackenzie nearby. Any other time he would have thought up some clever way to ditch them, but not today. After spending time in Kropite, Drake had learned the real value of friendship. His Kropite friends had helped him find Bailey, and opened his mind. Drake knew he had turned his back on Reigan one too many times, and he wasn't going to do it anymore. His friends would just have to accept her, because she was important to him.

"Hey guys, whatcha up to?" Drake asked with a smile.

Reigan narrowed her eyes and said, "Nothing much. What about you?"

"Not a whole lot. I was gonna find the guys, and maybe hang out at the beach. Do you want to come?"

Both girls stared blankly at Drake. Drake chuckled and repeated his question. Reigan grabbed onto Mackenzie's arm, causing her to jump. Mackenzie glared at Drake. "What are you up to?"

Drake chuckled again. "*Nothing.* I just wanted to know if you guys wanted to come to the beach with us."

Mackenzie huffed and declared that she wanted no part of it. Knowing Drake would be hanging out with her brother, Collin, was enough for her.

"Well…I want to come with you," Reigan said peering first at Drake then at her friend. "Mackenzie, I'll catch up with you later."

"Go right ahead! See if I care." Mackenzie sulked away, leaving Drake smiling and shaking his head.

"I can understand not wanting to hang out with your brother or sister. I'm always trying to lose mine…I mean, trying to get Bailey to play somewhere else," Drake corrected himself, as he did not intend to *lose* his sister again.

Reigan shrugged. "No way. You're *so* lucky. I would love to have a little sister, especially one as sweet as Bailey."

As Reigan and Drake walked, it was obvious Reigan felt awkward. The natural easiness between the two of them had long since faded. Feeling bad for the way he had acted toward her, he stopped and gently grabbed her arm. "Hey, I just wanted to say I'm sorry for the way I've acted toward you. I know I've been a real jerk, and there's absolutely *no* excuse for it."

Reigan's eyes widened and her mouth fell open just a little. "Why are you apologizing now?"

He let go of her arm and looked down at his feet. "I feel bad for ditching you, and ignoring you whenever the guys have been around. I just wanted you to know…I'm not gonna do it anymore. We've been friends since almost before I can remember. That *means* something. Just because you're a girl doesn't mean we can't hang out."

Reigan smiled her mesmerizing smile, then reached out and gave Drake a forceful shove. He was unable to catch his balance and tumbled to the ground.

"What was that for?" he questioned, trying to smile.

Reigan held out her hand to help him up. "That was for all the mean things you've done to me over the last three years.

Now, we're even." She held out her hand as a gesture of friend-ship. Drake shook it and smiled.

"Friends?" Drake asked.

"Friends," Reigan responded.

"Good. I've missed talking to you."

"You've missed talking to me? We just talked yester—" Reigan's eyes widened as a sudden thought occurred to her. "Drake, the woods! Do you remember when we were in the woods yesterday?"

"Yeah. What about it?"

"That *noise* I heard. It was so creepy. I wonder what it was."

"Oh, the noise in the woods—" Drake said trying to come up with a logical explanation. "It was nothing. When you went running off, I decided to stay and check it out."

"You stayed? Are you *crazy?*"

"No, I'm not *crazy*. It was only a couple of squirrels ripping through the woods, chasing each other around. It was pretty funny to see you running away like you did though."

"Oh, funny. It was only a couple squirrels? I would have sworn it was something else."

"Well, it wasn't."

Reigan stared at Drake for several moments and finally asked, "Have you been upset about something lately?"

"No. Why?"

"When we were younger, I remember, whenever you used to get upset or were about to cry, you would always bite your lip. I can see you obviously still do that," Reigan said reaching out to point at Drake's mouth.

"I don't do that anymore," Drake lied, covering his lips with his hand. He knew he'd gnawed at his lip several times while in Kropite. It was either that or cry, and heroes don't cry.

Wanting to change the subject, Drake blurted out, "I'll race you to the beach."

"Oh, you're on!" Reigan said, bolting.

Drake stalled for only a second before he took off in a full sprint. "You are such a cheater!"

Reigan laughed, keeping ahead of him for a short time before he passed her. They didn't make the beach before they ran into Shane, Collin, and Zack. Reigan and Drake ended their race, but continued laughing and trying to catch their breath.

"That was not…a fair race…but I still…beat you," Drake said between gasps.

Shane began to make funny faces and mock them.

"Cut it out, Shane!" Drake said, becoming stern.

"Yeah, *Shane*," Zack agreed shoving him to the ground.

Shane got back to his feet grumbling. "I was only kidding. Chill out."

Collin asked, "So, Drake, where ya been?"

Drake stepped back a few paces. "Nowhere…why?"

"Chill, dude. I was just wondering because you're late," Collin replied, lifting one eyebrow.

Drake realized he *was* late. During summer vacation, they always woke early so they wouldn't miss an ounce of daylight. Drake breathed out a heavy breath then explained he had been up late the night before and slept in. Collin slapped him on the back.

They all moved toward the beach, and Collin began to fidget while mumbling under his breath. He glared at Reigan through narrowed eyes. "Hey Reigan, where's Mack?"

"Oh, she had something else to do."

"Well, don't *you* have something else to do, too?"

Drake broke in quickly. "Reigan's cool. I asked her to hang out with us today."

Zack scrunched his mouth, scratched his head, and then smiled. "That's cool."

"Yeah, man. Fine with me," Shane followed, quickly.

Once they reached the beach, Zack, Shane, and Reigan ran toward the water. Drake and Collin trailed behind continuing to walk toward the beach.

"So...what's up with the bracelet? Does that mean you and Reigan are going out?"

Drake glanced at his arm. He had forgotten he still had the Story Stone on. He stopped and abruptly grabbed Collin's shoulder. "What's your problem, man? She's my friend and has been for a *long* time. We grew up together. I've known her a lot longer than I've known *you.*"

Collin's face slumped as he ran his hand over his stubby hair. "I'm sorry. It's just not *normal* to have girls hanging out with us. But if it means that much to you...then it's okay with me."

"Thanks. I'm just tired of ignoring her *just* so you guys won't make fun of me. She's nice. I think you'd like her a lot if you just gave her a chance."

Collin shrugged his shoulders. "She's pretty cute."

Drake laughed as he slapped his friend on the back. "I'll race you," Drake yelled as he bolted toward the water. Collin sprinted to catch up.

No one bothered to change into swimsuits. They simply careened into the bay, fully clothed. Drake was proud to see that the guys were willing to accept Reigan for him. Seeing her splashing around with his friends reminded him of the image of Reigan's face shimmering in the lake. He shook the vision out of his head right away. Drake knew he wasn't ready for that now.

The kids played in the water for several hours. Drake was glad to be home with his friends, where life seemed simple and normal.

The sun shone brightly, and the bay was crisp and clear. Reigan became a member of the crew, fitting in as though she had always been there, without even trying. They treated her as one of them, not thinking twice before dunking her, or letting her climb onto their shoulders for a game of chicken fight. At times, Drake stood back just to take it in. He felt great to be alive and to know he could just be a kid again. Today, no one's life was dependent on *him*.

He glanced into the sky, suddenly remembering what it felt like to fly. However, there was no urge to fly on *this* day. He was content just being a thirteen-year-old boy. He smiled, chuckling to himself at the notion of jumping up and taking flight in front of his friends. He laughed as he imagined their reactions.

The sun floated high in the sky. Drake asked Shane what time it was. Shane told him it was almost twelve o'clock.

"Oh, man! I told my mom I'd be home for lunch."

"Since when do you go home for lunch in the summer?" Collin asked. Drake shrugged and told him he just had to, but he would be back afterward.

While heading for land, a sharp pain shot through his left foot. Assuming that he had stepped on a piece of glass, Drake wondered whether he would see a wound this time. Again, his thoughts drifted back to Kropite where he always seemed to heal within minutes, if not seconds. Hobbling the rest of the way up to the beach, he sat in the sand examining his cut. Blood oozed out of a deep gash in the arch of his foot.

"I'm human after all," he said under his breath.

Shane saw Drake sitting on the sand and yelled, "Are you okay, man?"

Drake waved and limped up the beach. Stopping halfway, he glanced back to watch everyone splashing and jumping about in the water. *Home sweet home.*

Taking one last look, he turned and headed for his house.

Reigan only stayed for a few minutes after Drake left. She gazed up the beach saying, "Well guys, I'd better be going home, too."

Looking glum from all of the desertion, the boys told her they would see her around. They watched as she walked up the beach. Zack, Shane, and Collin were unsure of what to make of Drake and Reigan's sudden departure. Eventually, Shane said, "She's pretty cool. For a girl."

The others agreed.

Reigan ambled up the beach, caught up in her curiosity at Drake's sudden change of heart toward her. Wanting to know more about it, she decided to follow him. It did not take long for her to spot him, as he was not moving very fast with his limp. Nervous and not knowing what to say to him, she decided that she would wait until after he ate lunch to talk.

As Drake limped home, he glanced down at his stone every now and again. "Here I thought all of my abilities were because of you," he said. "Why am I a hero only in Kropite and not here? That would be too weird: *Drake, the Superhero Guy,*" he chuckled to himself. He continued his wobbly trek home, trying not to put too much pressure on his cut foot.

285

His efforts to walk fast were unsuccessful as his foot began to throb more and more. Hopping on one foot, he fared no better. He lost his balance several times falling to the ground. Pushing himself back up to his feet, he stood for a moment trying to catch his breath.

"Okay, maybe I *do* miss the healing powers I had in Kropite," Drake admitted with a chuckle. Beginning to limp once again, he started to dread how far he still had to go before reaching home. "At this rate, I ought to be home by 1:30."

He looked down at the stone again. It went from a brilliant blue to an unusual shade of dark red. The color reminded him of a garnet.

"That's odd," Drake said aloud. A buzzing began to emanate from the stone and suddenly he felt lightheaded. He reached up to rub his head, only to find his muscles locked, forcing him to the ground. Drake lay paralyzed while visions flashed through his mind. The first image was of a raging fire, but he was unable to decipher where it was taking place. The fire blazed, burning everything in its path. It seemed so real he felt as though he could reach out and touch it.

"Where is this?" he asked. The flames disappeared, replaced by a serene lake. It was See-All-Lake. "I'm seeing Kropite. I shouldn't be seeing Kropite. Could something be wrong?" The peaceful lake quickly disappeared, turning into a churning, bubbling body of water.

The image of the lake vanished, superseded with a vision of Migisi flying fiercely, as if she were in a rush. Flashes of crying children reeled through his mind, and then the fire reappeared. This time, Drake guessed that the fire had to be blazing through Kazoocal Field.

"Why am I seeing all of this? What do I do?" Drake asked. His hands began to shake at the thought of his friends in peril.

Shaking his head, he tried to gather himself, "Okay, everything is fine. I'm at home, and everything is *fine*." Trying to get back to his feet, another vision sprung before his eyes. This time he saw Koozog, howling his full-bodied laugh. The sound was grotesque. His last vision included Sebastian standing next to Koozog, but not by choice. It looked as though Sebastian was a prisoner.

"Koozog? Sebastian and Koozog? That sounds so familiar. Luke said Sebastian went missing a long time ago. Is he with Koozog? Wait a minute…Koo-zog. It can't be. Is Koozog… What did Luke call him?"

He desperately tried to remember the name Luke had given the elderly leader, when it finally came to him.

"Zogrosen! That's it!" he yelled. His paralysis vanished, enabling him to stand once again. "I need to get a message to Luke, but how?" he asked himself.

Forgetting about his injury, Drake ran the rest of the way home. Bailey greeted him at the door.

"Drake! Drake! Aunt Jenny sent us a present!" She was practically squealing at him. Aunt Jenny was their mother's best friend.

"Okay, I'll check it out in a minute."

Drake entered his house spotting that his mother had lunch waiting on the table. Instead of heading for his meal, he dashed up the stairs. He barged into his room, slammed the door, and locked it behind him. Tearing open his dresser drawer, he grabbed Sponke's leather pouch. Sponke's words came flooding back to him. *Open this when you really miss us.*

Ripping open the pouch, Drake stared at two black stones. They looked exactly like the ones Kreeper had given him in Bleet. Drake dumped the stones onto his bed, relieved to find a note. It read:

Dear Drake,

*I obtained these two stones from a good friend sometime back. I believe you are familiar with how to use them. I hope, at some point, you will miss us. If you ever get the inkling to know how we are doing, you can use the stones as a spyglass. Use them wisely, for they will show you a **great** deal.*

Your comrade,
Sponke

Drake picked one of the stones off his bed and grasped it tightly. "Okay stone, I need to see my friends in Kropite," he said aloud as Sponke, Groger, and Migisi entered his mind.

Everything grew dark. He sat waiting, terrified of what he might see based on the visions of chaos he had earlier. Slowly, an image began to form before his eyes. It was hard to decipher at first, but he quickly realized it was Sponke. He was flying around, aimlessly and alone.

"Where's Groger?" Drake asked with his brows knitted together.

As if answering his question, Groger appeared. He sat atop a large rock near See-All-Lake. The giant looked forlorn. Drake began to feel horrible. Groger looked up. Drake could see fresh tears in his eyes as he looked out over the lake.

"Sponke is flying around alone. Groger is alone. Why aren't they together?" Drake asked.

The stone responded by showing Sponke again, only this time Drake saw that a chain bound his body. He followed the chain back to a tree holding Sponke captive.

"Who chained Sponke? Is he a prisoner?" Drake inquired.

Instead of answering this question, the stone revealed Migisi. She was soaring through the sky, an enraged look on her face. Flying alongside her was Luke, with the same look on his face. The next image was of Koozog laughing.

"That's it! I've seen enough!" Drake said as he placed the second black stone in his pocket. He headed for his bedroom door. He flung it open and darted back downstairs.

Bailey was sitting on the bottom step, waiting for him.

"What's up, Bay?" he asked.

"I'm waiting for *you,* dummy. Mom says I can't open Aunt Jenny's gift until you come down."

"Oh. Okay, let's check it out."

Bailey led him to the table. There were two parcels. Bailey ran over tearing her present open right away. She beamed at the new book clutched in her hand.

"I got a new book," Bailey sang out.

"There's a note attached," their mother said.

Dear Sweet Bailey,

*I saw this book, and I really thought the little girl on the cover looked **just** like you. She shares your name as well. I checked with my kids, and they said it was a good one, so I **had** to buy it. I hope you like it!*

Love,
Aunt Jenny

Drake snatched the book and held it out of her reach. "Wait a minute, Bay! I just want to *see* it. I'll give it right back."

She finally agreed. Drake brought his arm down to view the book's cover.

Aunt Jenny was right. The little girl on the cover looked exactly like Bailey. Next to her stood a girl who bore a remarkable resemblance to Ka-leel. The book was titled *Bailey's Dream World.* He quickly scanned the cover for the author, and scrolled across the bottom was *Tons of Imagination, Inc.* Drake stood still, completely incapable of words. His thoughts went back to Ka-leel. There she was on the cover of this book next to his sister. *Why didn't I try to find her? I could have saved her, too.*

Bailey grabbed the book from Drake, which shook him from his trance. He glared at Bailey, ripping the book right out of her hands. He grabbed the package Aunt Jenny had sent for him. With both gifts clutched securely in his hands, he dashed for the door. He could hear Bailey squealing as he ran into the woods.

No longer affected by his injured foot, he ran as fast as he could, deeper and deeper, into the shelter of the trees. Drake couldn't get the image of the little girl, and all the other children Koozog was imprisoning, out of his mind. He stopped running, and stood with his chest heaving. Slowly, he brought Bailey's book close to his face and examined it again.

"What does this mean?" Drake said aloud. He decided to have a look at his gift. He saw it too had a note attached. Ripping open the note, he read:

Dear Drake,
I saw this book, and thought it looked exciting. It's created by the same company as Bailey's book. This company really puts out

*some **fantastic** stories, and they seem to be all the rage with the kids in my area. The books are so full of imagination, just like you and Bailey. Ah, to be a kid again. I hope you enjoy it.*

Love,
Aunt Jenny

Slashing at the paper that bound his package, he searched frantically for some other clue. He was unable to think straight. He nearly screamed as he observed the illustrations on the cover of his book. Sketched to perfection were Groger, Migisi, and Sponke. They were all fighting what looked to be an impossible battle. The title was *A War to the End*. He read the title over and over, trying to make sense of it all.

"Whose imagination did Koozog steal to write this one? Is this title meant for me? Does he *really* want a *war?*"

Drake no longer felt as lighthearted as he had back at the beach. An ache crawled into his stomach. Numbness gripped his body, leaving him guessing whether he could stand on his own. Drake grabbed hold of a nearby tree and peered at the stone attached to his wrist. It was pulsing again. Like a heartbeat, it hummed with a *new* energy. Dim then bright. Dim then bright. He watched it pulse. Drake swallowed hard, making a gulping sound. He pushed himself off the tree keeping his eyes glued to his stone.

Without even thinking, he jerked his arm up toward the sky. A brisk wind swooshed up, leaves swirled wildly around him, and a mighty explosion erupted from Drake's Story Stone.

THE END

About the Author

Tammie F. Pumphrey is the author of Drake's Story Stone, the first novel in the four-part fantasy series for young adult readers.

Though born in California, Tammie spent a good bit of her early childhood living in various places overseas, as her father was in the US Army. However, her family moved back to the states when she was ten and she has been living in Maryland ever since.

Mrs. Pumphrey earned a bachelor's degree in elementary education from the University of Maryland at College Park and a master's degree in library science from the College of Notre Dame in Baltimore, Maryland. She has taught at an elementary school in Annapolis, MD for the last fourteen years.

It may seem surprising that a multi-colored rocking chair could be the inspiration behind a novel, but it was. While pregnant with her first child, she painted this chair much like a robe of many colors. She hoped it would become a thinking chair where all manner of child-like fantasy could unravel. Like a dream, she was swept away into a whole new world. Thoughts of a young boy and his fantastic adventures played in her head as though on a movie screen. Pumphrey rushed to put on paper what was racing through her mind. This was her first real step toward realizing her true creative passion.

Tammie currently works, writes and lives in Maryland with her loving husband, beautiful daughters and amusing cat.

Acknowledgements

To my wonderful husband Brian—words will never express my gratitude. You have been my springboard, first editor, biggest fan, and best friend. I would have never gotten this far without your encouragement and support. There is no doubt, you are the best!

To Madison and Rori, my beautiful daughters—you have Mommy's deepest appreciation for always encouraging me *to believe in myself*. My girls are amazing!

Extra special thanks go to Marie Pickett for her *labor of love* editing sessions. You have helped me hone my writing skills and unlock the true writer within.

To Steve and Marybeth Pumphrey—thank you for your support, countless hours in design aid, brainstorming, and believing in Drake enough to encouraging me to take the *big leap.*

To Mom and Dad Pumphrey—thank you for your encouragement, late night readings, countless newspaper articles about publishing, and always believing in me.

To my mom, brothers, family, and friends—thank you for being my fan club, support team, and cheering section.

To all my students, past and present—thank you *all* for being an imaginative and inspirational force in my life as well as my sounding board. Your overwhelming response to Drake's story has further fueled my passion for writing.

Thank you to everyone at CreateSpace.

DRAKE'S
STORY
STONE

Visit Drake's website
www.drakesstorystone.com

Keep up with Drake on Facebook

Made in the USA
Charleston, SC
03 June 2012